WARD OF THE FBI

SCHOOL OF NECESSARY MAGIC RAINE CAMPBELL™
BOOK ONE

JUDITH BERENS   MARTHA CARR   MICHAEL ANDERLE

DISRUPTIVE IMAGINATION

WARD OF THE FBI TEAM

Thanks to the JIT Readers

Keith Verret
Misty Roa
Daniel Weigert
Angel LaVey
Nicole Emens
Kelly O'Donnell
Paul Westman
Sarah Weir
Larry Omans
Micky Cocker

If we've missed anyone, please let us know!

CHAPTER ONE

Mara Berens stood in the circular driveway of the School of Necessary Magic. A cool breeze finally broke the heat of a Virginia summer and stirred her senses. She felt the magic open without a need to turn and look.

"They always say it's the heat, not the humidity." Turner Underwood, elderly Light Elf and retired Fixer, strode up behind her. His elegant cane tapped rhythmically on the blacktop.

"It's a wonder you ever snuck up on anyone, Turner. I could sense the portal opening."

The old elf laughed and leaned on the silver troll-shaped head of the cane. "I have no need to travel so quietly anymore. Trust me, though, I still have the goods." He winked and followed it with a deep chortle.

"You're a thousand-year-old dirty old elf. Like a crazy Santa."

"Now, *there* was a great Fixer. He still rates as one of the best." He sighed deeply and raised his cane and drew sufficient energy in through his feet to send a ripple of magic across the grounds. "You know, everything holds a memory of some sort, particularly when it involves death."

The enchantment settled on the grass and illuminated old trails of magic from the past months. Only a Fixer like Turner and a handful of other magicals could manage such a feat. Dark, pulsing lines of dark magic intertwined with the trails made by the elves, shifters, witches, and other magicals, The incandescent patterns shimmered in the heat.

These were the reminders of what had happened on the school grounds in the past, events that almost closed the school forever. "They nearly burned the place down," Mara said, her tone flat and regretful. The silence hung in the air between them. Turner broke it when he raised his arms again and electrical currents raced across the grass. They crackled and snapped and erased all visible traces of the magical history.

"You know why I'm here," the elf said calmly.

"That was a clever little trick. You made your point." Mara tightened her lips in faint disapproval. "I have an idea why you've arrived. Frankly, I'm surprised I didn't see you sooner."

"This is a chance for a fresh start. We can release the past and what the dark families almost managed to do to the school." He turned and looked at the manor. The old building now boasted a fresh coat of paint to hide where a hole had once blasted through the masonry. "Maybe we can help others forget as well."

"Don't say it." Mara looked down the long driveway toward the tall, iron gates. In her mind's eye, she could still see the waves of dark witches and wizards entering the grounds intent on destruction.

"It needs to be said one more time. Death and destruction are what everyone remembers about this school right now."

"Not everyone."

Turner shrugged. "True, but enough do to make it a problem. It's time we turn the page and start a new chapter —a fresh beginning for the school. A new class will enter those same gates soon enough."

"I heard about the girl. She's had no training, you know —the young witch. The magic's there, but she has no knowledge of what that means or even how to use it."

Turner tapped his cane harder against the ground. "When has that ever been a requirement? I'm telling you, she's exactly what we need here. How long have you been headmistress?"

"Twenty-three years, and you know that as well as I do."

"This place was founded by the government to—"

"Find a way to help magicals and humans work together. I know the legacy."

"A hardworking young witch whose family are all federal agents is precisely what we need. She'll set a good example."

"You act like one girl can single-handedly erase all the memories."

"It's a good start. Besides, you know I'm an optimist at heart." The retired Fixer opened a portal and Mara glimpsed the lush, green lawn of Turner's estate in Austin, Texas. A pang of desire to step through with him tempted her.

He saw the look on her face. "Come for a visit. Christmas is the perfect time. We can gather the entire family."

"Does this girl even know she's destined to attend the school?"

"Not yet. She's not even on the humans' radar but will be soon enough. Trust me, Raine Campbell is the beginning of a new day for the School of Necessary Magic. Have I ever been wrong?" He stepped through the portal which had already begun to close.

Mara recalled a few occasions where he had actually been wrong. Sparks skittered across the blacktop, and the gateway shimmered out of existence. She sighed and faced the inevitable. "All right, let the next chapter begin."

Raine and her friends laughed and joked with easy familiarity as they walked down the quiet street in Grand Rapids, Michigan.

"I can't believe you talked back to Mr. Hinton like that." The little blonde girl, Maggie, laughed again. "The look on his face was priceless."

Scott beamed with pride. "It's not my fault he was wrong."

Raine recalled the incident, torn between conflicting responses. On the one hand, Mr. Hinton had been wrong. On the other, she had been raised to respect authority. Her father had been an FBI agent, and she currently lived with her Uncle Jerry, another agency operative.

"You didn't have to keep talking after you'd made your

point, though." She gave Scott a stern look. "You did take it too far."

Scott rolled his eyes. "Spoilsport."

"I don't know how you didn't get detention." Amy grinned. "You will join the debate team in high school, right?"

"He's too hot-tempered for the debate team," the red-headed girl, Shannon, said with amusement in her tone. "He'd lose his temper and the debate."

"I'm not that bad." Scott huffed. "I can control my temper."

The group turned a corner and strolled farther into town.

"I hope we can get a corner table in Spoonlickers." Amy linked her arm with Scott's. "I like people-watching."

"I'll try strawberry balsamic yogurt." Amy scrolled through her phone to find the ad. "Here. Doesn't that sound amazing?"

"It sounds absolutely awful." Scott grinned at her. "But you've never had good taste."

"You'll get your usual black cherry gelato right, Raine?" Amy slowed to walk beside her friend. "Or will you try something new?"

Raine shrugged. "I'll see if there's anything new on the menu."

A group of older kids emerged from the alley up ahead and strode toward them. Amy and Scott slowed instinctively and closed ranks with the others. Raine watched the newcomers closely and assessed their balance and movement. Years of martial arts training had taught her to read potential opponents.

"It looks like we found ourselves some little piggy banks." A large boy sneered at the younger kids. "Hand over your money."

Amy opened her purse to retrieve her wallet, but Raine restrained her with a hand on her arm. The leader's sneer turned malicious and he lunged at Scott. Their friend stumbled back to avoid the large fist now on a collision course with his face. Raine pushed through the small group and prepared to sweep the boy's legs out from under him. She was half his size, but his balance was awful. If she applied her strike correctly, she could do it easily.

Her hands balled into fists as Scott crumpled to the ground. The leader turned to stare at Raine, and something shifted within her. A warmth tugged deep inside that she hadn't felt before. She tried to ignore it and shifted her weight, now poised for the attack. The older kids' eyes widened, and they collectively took a step back.

Rather than swing her leg around as Raine had planned, she moved her hands in slow, elegant patterns. An odd sensation of being almost outside her body surprised her. She sensed her own motions but had no idea why or what the purpose was, although it also felt entirely natural. The bully before her froze in place and swallowed hard. He tugged at his jeans and sweat beaded on his forehead when he realized he couldn't move.

Raine felt the pressure of his movements against the palms of her hands. It made no sense, but at the same time, it felt right. Lights flared and flickered around him. The air thickened and soft swirls of purple and yellow hovered around his trapped form. It was magic, she knew that, but how had she released what she didn't have?

"What have you done to me?" The bully struggled and his eyes widened in panic. "You're a crazy devil witch. Let me go."

By now, Raine felt as confused as he looked. She had been swept into a level of power she hadn't experienced before, and she didn't know how to stop it. Something burst from her hands and the group toppled like dominoes. They shouted in fear when they, too, froze in place. The same swirls of color formed and somehow held them immobile. They soon cursed up a storm and drew attention from the nearby houses.

Whatever flowed from Raine slowed a little, but it remained active and pinned the bullies in place. Each time they strained against the invisible force, she felt a corresponding surge in the palms of her hands—a sharp pressure that intensified until they stilled. Her breathing became short and fast and her hair clung in thick strands to the sweat that streaked her face. Finally, the power released, and the young thugs could move once more. Raine sagged and gulped air and wondered what on Earth had happened. Her friends whooped as the aggressors bolted.

"Since when can you do freakin' magic?" Scott stood and brushed himself off. "You could have told us."

She looked at her hands in confusion and felt a little light-headed as though she'd done a heavy training session without eating enough.

"Was that magic?" She turned to Scott. "It's never happened before."

Amy put her arm around Raine's shoulders.

"Let's get you home. I'm sure your uncle will want to hear about this."

"Woah, wait a second. She's a witch. Don't you think that's cool? What else can you do?" Scott blocked their path. "You have to show us what else you can do."

Amy glared at him and pushed past.

"She needs to rest. I'm taking her home."

Raine groaned. She did not look forward to the inevitable talk with her Uncle Jerry. He wasn't technically her uncle but had been her dad's best friend. Jerry had sworn he'd look after her if something went wrong, and he'd stood by that when her dad had been killed on a case.

Amy led her home, and Shannon and Scott trailed behind her. Raine was aware of the twitching curtains in the houses on either side of the road. Word would spread through the gossipers like wildfire. She wiped her hair out her face and sighed. No one had ever told her about magic. Still bemused, she ran the experience through her head to analyze everything that had happened and how it felt. She searched for the trigger in the hope that it wouldn't happen unexpectedly again.

It seemed the need to protect her friends had somehow set it off. That had been the moment when her magic rose up within her. She decided that there were far worse triggers. Still, Uncle Jerry wouldn't take this very well. Raine had no idea how to broach the subject and considered potential conversation starters in her head. None of them worked, at least not in her mind.

Hey, Uncle Jerry, it turns out I have magic.

I kicked some bullies' asses using magic.

So, er, how would you feel if I had magic?

She sighed. It should have been a quiet afternoon. Middle school had been blissfully uneventful, and they had set out for ice cream sundaes and to hang out. Now, she had to face the fact that she had potentially dangerous magic.

Scott and Shannon turned toward his house without Raine noticing. She was absorbed in trying to understand the experience. There had to be a way to control it. Other witches and wizards didn't have their magic spontaneously erupt from their hands, so there had to be people who could help her. And books, too. Raine felt comfortable with books. They usually held the information she needed. This time, however, she had to find out where to look.

To her dismay, a plain black car was parked outside her house. A small part of her had hoped her uncle wouldn't be home for a couple of hours so she had time to prepare herself. No such luck. Word had obviously traveled quicker than even she had anticipated.

"I got this." She smiled at Amy. "It'll be fine."

"You sure?"

Raine straightened her spine and prepared to face her uncle.

"Yep. I'm sure."

She walked slowly to the front door. The house blended perfectly with those around it with a neat lawn in front bordered by small hardy shrubs. The house itself was white-fronted with square windows and nothing at all to set it apart. She and her uncle liked it that way. Life was simpler when you blended in.

The dark wooden door opened before Raine could retrieve her keys. Uncle Jerry stood in the black suit he'd worn to the office that morning and looked at her with a sad smile that confirmed her suspicion that he already knew what had happened. Raine lifted her chin with a small smile of her own. They said nothing as she entered and followed him into the kitchen. A glass of milk waited on the breakfast bar. Jerry sat down opposite her with a fresh cup of black coffee.

"I'm not entirely sure what happened. I planned to use my martial arts to protect my friends from these bullies, but something shifted inside me. I think...I did magic." Raine sipped her milk and tried to collect her thoughts. "I didn't hurt them, though. They were only scared."

"Who saw? And were any of your friends hurt?"

Jerry was kind, but he carried the hard edges of his previous job as an FBI agent. He'd retired to give Raine a normal life after her father was killed. Raine knew that beneath his poker face were a brilliant smile and a wicked sense of humor that had carried her through some of the darkest days of her life. She wasn't intimidated by his quiet, firm tone.

"I'm not sure who saw. Shannon, Amy, and Scott were with me. I didn't recognize the bullies. It was on the corner of Gold Avenue SW. There are lots of houses there." Raine sipped again, conscious of his eyes on her. "Scott might have a black eye tomorrow, but he didn't seem concerned."

Jerry relaxed and allowed himself to smile. He had suspected this day would come, but he wasn't ready. Her father had been a wizard, so it made sense that she would have his magical bloodline. In all these years, though, she'd never shown any sign of it and he'd begun to hope that she wouldn't. He had known Raine since the day she was born and she felt very much like his own flesh and blood. That made this moment more difficult because he wanted only the best for her. While he knew the magic needed to be nurtured and she needed to step into what was her legacy, he also knew their lives would irrevocably change. He knew nothing about magic and had to accept that this was something he couldn't help her with.

"And you're okay now?"

She nodded and thought for a moment as she finished her milk. "I'm tired and hungry and I'd like a shower, but otherwise, I feel like myself."

Jerry watched her closely, but Raine had never lied to him. She had grown into a strong and honest young woman with a clear moral compass. He couldn't be prouder of her. Other kids would be shaken by the unexpected flow of magic, but she was calm and, if he read her expressions correctly, even analytical.

"I'd like to learn more about this. Do you know of any books?" Raine looked away, unable to hold his gaze. "I don't want to hurt anyone accidentally."

Jerry felt completely out of his depth. He had no idea how to train a young witch. He'd thought nothing of training her in martial arts and with guns and other weapons. Magic, though, was something else entirely.

"Not off the top of my head. I'll ask my contacts." He stood. "Why don't you take a shower and I'll make you mac and cheese?"

Raine's stomach growled and she realized she was hungrier than usual.

"Thanks, Uncle Jerry."

She hugged him tightly. He returned the gesture and

tried to push aside the feeling that he was losing his little girl.

Raine left the room and Jerry busied himself making her favorite comfort food. He ran through his mental list of contacts and tried to think who might possibly have relevant books for them to start with. This was a scary new journey, but he planned to hold Raine's hand through every step and help her fulfill her potential.

Jerry feared that this was the beginning of something much more dangerous. Dark wizards had killed his partner, Raine's father. Now that she had revealed power of her own, there was a chance they would look for her. He would give her what little peace and happiness he could before the police arrived. Life had taught him that the small moments were important and worth guarding.

CHAPTER TWO

A knock sounded at the front door. Raine and Jerry both stood, instantly alert for a moment, before Jerry raised his hand and smiled. "I'll get it."

He couldn't shake a bad feeling that this was related to the men who had killed Raine's father. Her coming into her magic could draw their attention. At the door, he braced himself for the worst. A tall broad man in a pristine black suit stood on the porch and greeted him with a polite smile.

Jerry tensed and hoped his fears hadn't come true. He'd kept Raine safe but had the killers finally caught up with her?

"We heard about your…Raine's magic. Someone caught it on their phone. Your old FBI unit raced to the police station and took over. I've worked closely with the PDA so I'm now handling this." The agent held out his hand. "Agent Bruce Connor. Can I come in?"

Jerry returned the handshake firmly and stood aside to

allow him entry. Bruce looked around the minimalist home and smiled. It looked very much like his own with pale neutral colors and very little personalization. The older man might have retired from the FBI, but no one would ever stop being an agent.

Raine stood in the kitchen with her arms folded and her posture strong and confident. A polite smile remained on her face as she studied Agent Connor.

"Someone took a video of your magic earlier, Raine. They posted it online."

Her shoulders slumped.

"Humans are still twitchy about magic, especially from teenagers who look out of control. You really scared those older kids."

Raine met his gaze.

"I simply protected my friends. I didn't intend to use magic, but I couldn't stand by and allow those bullies to rob and hurt the others."

"Would you like coffee?" Jerry went to the coffee maker when the agent nodded. "Raine, do you want a drink?"

"I'll grab a lemonade, thanks." She retrieved a can from the fridge and poured it into a glass. "Am I in trouble?"

Agent Connor sat on one of the slender stools arranged around the breakfast bar.

"Yes and no." He looked at Jerry. "Black, no sugar. Thanks."

Raine sat opposite him and waited for an explanation.

"It's clear that your uncle here isn't able to help you with your magic."

She gripped her glass a little tighter. Uncle Jerry had

been good to her and she didn't like where this might be headed.

"And what has the agency decided?" Jerry squeezed Raine's shoulder to reassure her. "I assume this was an agency decision."

Agent Connor nodded.

"There is a school in Virginia. It's government run and designed to help train young witches and wizards to use their magic. We have secured a spot there for Raine. I will accompany her to keep her safe."

Raine bristled at the keep her safe comment but couldn't help a grin at the school part.

"Virginia is a good distance from here." Jerry handed the coffee to Agent Connor. "Is there nowhere closer?"

"I'm afraid not. This is the foremost facility in this part of the world. She'll be trained by the best and all the students will be like her."

"They'll teach me to use magic?" Raine gave him her full attention. "And it'll be a boarding school?"

"Yes, to both. I don't have the full curriculum on hand, but you'll be taught magical history, potions, transfiguration, and much more."

Raine was torn. She didn't want to leave her friends and Uncle Jerry, but she was excited at the prospect of learning magic. There was so much potential there and so many new avenues to explore.

"When would I leave? What would I tell my friends? Do I get a choice? What do I have to pack? Will it cost a lot?"

The man laughed, and Jerry took the stool beside Raine. He was sad to see her leave him and the house would feel empty without her. Knowing that she would be somewhere safe with people who could release her full potential would be worth it, though.

"You will leave first thing next Sunday morning. It's a twelve-hour drive. Tell your friends you've transferred to an exclusive boarding school on a scholarship. Pack your normal clothes, notebooks, and such. I'll provide you with a wand—"

"I get a wand? They really use them?"

"Yes. They really use wands. I'll give you yours on Sunday morning."

"What else can you tell me about the school? I'd like to do my own research. Are there books I can read to bring me up to speed?"

Agent Connor was pleased to see she had taken this well. Her enthusiasm to learn would serve her well over the coming four years.

"It is called the School of Necessary Magic but you won't find anything about it online. I will speak to my colleagues about books."

Raine lapsed into silence, sipped her lemonade, and frowned as she thought everything through. Her friends would be shocked and upset, and there wasn't much time to say goodbye. Still, it was a once in a lifetime opportunity, and she could make a big difference. Her plan was to follow in her father and Uncle Jerry's footsteps and become an FBI agent. Surely the agency would be happy to have a witch on board. Magic would give her an advantage and allow them to make more progress against the dark magic users.

It wouldn't be pleasant leaving Michigan, but she was sure that this would be a fantastic adventure.

"I should break the news to Amy and Shannon." Raine finished her lemonade. "Can I do that?"

Uncle Jerry nodded. "Remember, it's a scholarship to an exclusive private school. No one knows that it's a school for magical kids."

Raine was used to keeping secrets. Her dad and uncle had told her things about some of their cases they shouldn't have.

"Got it."

Once she was out of earshot, Jerry turned to Agent Connor.

"Why is an agent sent to watch over a single teenager?"

The younger man sipped his coffee while he prepared his words.

"Raine is a legacy. A potential agent in training. She could be a real asset to the agency."

Jerry stared a challenge at the man and waited for the rest of the story.

"There has been a lot of promise for the future shown among the student body." He stopped his usual spiel and smiled. "Look. A lot of those kids will probably go on to work for the government, which is great. There have, however, been a few...incidents over the past few years, including a small battle centered around the school itself. A number of parents have called for agency presence on the campus to safeguard against these events."

Jerry knocked his coffee back and thought that over. It was true that Raine clearly had a lot of potential, but a battle at the school didn't sound very promising.

"And how frequent are these *incidents*?"

Agent Connor found his best smile.

"Not that bad. You know how teenagers are. Add magic in, and there will always be a little trouble."

It had been worse than that, but he wouldn't risk Jerry's refusal to allow Raine to go. The school was the best place for her.

Amy had clung to her like a storm-tossed sailor to a life raft when they said goodbye. Raine eventually had to peel herself away with promises to catch up over Christmas and to send emails and letters if she could. A small weight had settled into the pit of her stomach with the realization that this was it. She'd officially said goodbye to her friends and she'd head off to some strange school for magical people in the morning.

The internet had been useless, but she had tried as much research as she could into both the school and magic use. Agent Connor hadn't found her any good books either. She was dependent on what he'd told her, which wasn't much. Still, it was an adventure, but she'd feel better if she were more prepared. Raine wasn't the type of girl to go into things without adequate preparation.

The agent arrived barely after sunrise. Raine struggled to look more awake than she felt. She'd packed everything the night before and triple-checked that she hadn't forgotten anything. Now, she stood in the hallway with her bag at her feet, and Uncle Jerry hugged her tightly. "You keep in touch and take care."

"I promise."

It all felt horribly real as she released him. There had been a dream-like quality to it until then. Now, she had to say goodbye to the man who had raised her for the past few years.

Agent Connor held a thin black box.

"This is the wand I promised you. Keep it safe."

Raine opened it and felt a swell of excitement as she looked at the hickory wood wand. It was simple and pragmatic, made from a single piece of the gold-colored hardwood.

"Each witch and wizard's wand is made from a wood found in their home area." Agent Connor smiled. "Hickory seemed very fitting for you."

Strength and determination shone from the girl, even as she fought to maintain a calm facade while she said goodbye to her uncle. Bruce knew that she would make an agent to be reckoned with when she was ready. The agency needed people like her.

"You'd best get going." Uncle Jerry squeezed her shoulder. "Let me know when you get there."

"Will do." The agent held up his phone. "I'll text as soon as we're through the gates."

———

Raine managed to sleep a little on the long journey. The sun had already set when they finally arrived as the shorter days of autumn had set in. She sat upright and grinned as they drove through the ornate wrought iron gates toward an extravagant mansion. Elegant brickwork surrounded neat square windows and was topped with a dark slate roof. It was bigger than any house she'd ever seen before. They were able to house hundreds of people there.

Agent Connor turned in the circular driveway and pulled up behind an older woman who tried to wrangle her three boys into doing what she needed them to.

"Do you have your wands?"

"I left mine at home."

"Please tell me you didn't. Home is six hours away. Where is it?"

"This is Joe's bag. You packed my red sweater, right? I need it—it's my lucky sweater."

"You packed your own bag. If you forgot your sweater, that is on you."

"You're so dumb for having a lucky sweater."

"You're dumb for sucking at potions."

"Coming from the geek who loves history. You're such a suck-up."

With a smile at the family antics, Raine slid from the car and grabbed her bag. She followed Connor past a small family of what looked like elves. Raine tried not to be rude but she hadn't seen an elf before. They walked with grace and elegance like ballet dancers. Everywhere she looked, kids and parents surged and hustled one another. Small colorful orbs shot through the air and crashed against a grumpy dark-haired kid's head.

The girl glared in the direction the orbs had come from. A young blond boy with large blue eyes tried to look innocent but she raised her wand and whispered something. An older woman appeared in the doorway to the main building.

"Constance. You know better than to perform magic to win a disagreement."

The girl lowered her wand and her mouth puckered into a sour expression.

Raine didn't know where to look or what to think. Magic seemed so natural and normal to these people. She had stepped into a completely new world and that both thrilled and scared her. A sullen-looking dark-haired boy stomped from a pale blue car and pushed past her to walk up the front steps. A flicker of fire played along his fingertips and danced above his hair. Raine blinked and it was gone. Had she imagined it?

"You must be Agent Connor." A tall, imposing woman walked toward them. "I'm Headmistress Berens."

The man extended his hand. "A pleasure to meet you."

"And you must be Raine." She held her hand out to Raine who shook it politely. "You'll be introduced to the rest of the professors over the next couple of days. I hope this isn't too overwhelming for you."

"No. It looks wonderful." Raine smiled. "I'm looking forward to classes."

"Oh, look, another suck-up," someone whispered as a group moved passed.

"Have you finally brought an agent onto campus?" A tall, regal woman with long white-blonde hair looked from Ms. Berens and Agent Connor. "He has the bearing of an agent."

"I'm Agent Connor. And you are?"

"Mrs. Thyme. My son is a student here and I do not want him pulled into some awful battle."

"Your son will be safe here, Mrs. Thyme. You have my word." He smiled. "There's no place safer for magical students."

The woman pursed her lips and strutted off. Raine felt sorry for her son because she seemed unbearable.

"If you'll follow me, I'll show you to your room." Mara Berens turned toward the school. "I'm sure you'll find it satisfactory."

She took one last look at the car she'd arrived in. There really was no turning back now.

CHAPTER THREE

R aine stepped into the entryway of the school and the sight left her breathless. Dark wood paneled the bottom half of the walls, and the pale wallpaper above swirled with beautiful patterns. A large staircase filled the center of the room, perfect for anyone who wished to make a grand entrance. She had never seen anything like it.

"If you'll accompany Mr. Powell, he'll take you to your cottage." The headmistress gestured to a tall, older man with dark hair. "I'm sure you'll find your accommodation comfortable, Agent Connor."

"I'll catch up with you later, Raine." He smiled at her before he greeted the other man. "Agent Bruce Connor. A pleasure to meet you."

"Xander Powell, professor of dark magic."

Raine's ears perked up at that. She hoped she'd take his classes. Dark magic sounded very useful for her plans to become an agent.

"If you'll follow me, I'll show you to your room." The headmistress gestured toward the staircase. "It's not far."

She followed the tall woman up the stairs and tried not to stare open-mouthed at everything. Students bustled about and talked about everything from something called Willens to their favorite fashion brands. It was a whole new world and entirely unlike anything she'd experienced before. Amy would have loved it, she thought with a stab of nostalgia.

"To the right are the boys' dorms. Girls are not allowed in there, nor are the boys allowed in here." The headmistress looked sternly at her. "Don't let anyone tell you otherwise."

Raine nodded. She had no desire to have boys in her room and would far rather explore the library.

Ms. Berens led her through a large common room with an assortment of comfortable furniture and a large open fireplace to a hallway with many doors on either side.

"You're in here with three other freshmen." She opened the sturdy wooden door. "Come and find me if you have any problems."

Raine walked into the room and hesitated as she studied a trio of girls within. A slender girl with flame-red hair down to her waist turned to look at her and grinned. "I'm Sara, and you are?"

"Raine."

She placed her bag on the only empty bed. Raine suddenly felt awkward with introductions and such. She was usually confident but the exhaustion from the long trip had kicked in.

"Dinner will be soon, you don't want to be late. I've heard the pixies take your food away if you're late."

Raine turned to see a blonde girl with her hair swept into a complicated up-do. Her makeup was heavier than usual for girls her age, and she spoke with an undefinable accent. It made her think of country clubs.

"Don't be ridiculous, Paige. They wouldn't starve us." Sara rolled her eyes. "It's a school. There are laws."

"Well, you're welcome to risk it. I, however, will head down exactly at six." Paige examined herself in the mirror. "I can't believe how little wardrobe space we have. This school is supposedly exclusive. That mattress will need to be replaced too. It's far too hard."

Raine raised an eyebrow and folded her arms with irritation. The girl had been there all of five minutes and had already racked up a list of complaints.

"I'm Evelyn, but everyone calls me Evie." A dainty dark-haired girl held her hand out. "Which bloodline are you from?"

Raine frowned. She knew that must have magical relevance, but it meant nothing to her.

"Erm, the Campbell one? I guess." Raine shrugged and smiled. "I'm completely lost. I had no idea I had magic until a couple of days ago."

Sara and Evie exchanged a look.

Paige spun to look at Raine. "You're not from a well-bred family? You didn't even know you had magic?" She studied her disapprovingly. "I thought they only accepted good blood here."

Sara and Evie closed ranks.

"They accepted you so they're obviously not that fussy,"

Sara snapped. "You don't look like you have a scrap of usefulness in you."

Paige's eyes narrowed. "What are you anyway?" She sniffed haughtily. "I heard they'd allowed a kitsune, of all things, in this year."

Sara's smile was positively predatory. "That would be me."

Evie tried to stifle a laugh behind her hand and Raine bit her bottom lip hard to restrain her own laughter at the horror on Paige's face.

"They expect me to share a room with a kitsune?" Paige took a step back. "No. That's unacceptable."

"Don't worry, sweetie." Sara stepped forward. "You won't be missed."

"Did you threaten me?" Paige eyed the door. "I'll sue."

Sara adopted an innocent expression. "Did you hear me threaten her?" she asked Evie.

"Nope. Did you, Raine?"

"No, I merely heard a factual statement."

Paige huffed and stormed out of the room as the other three girls laughed uproariously.

Once they'd calmed, Raine looked at Sara. "So you're a kitsune?"

"Yeah. And Evie's a witch from an old Irish bloodline. Some people say they have fairy blood."

Raine tried to absorb the reality that she shared a room with a kitsune and someone who possibly had fairy blood.

"No, you can't call me Tinkerbell." Evie smiled. "I might let you call me Tink, though."

An older student knocked on the door and stuck her

head into the room. "Come on. The school tour for freshmen is starting."

They filed into the hallway where a group of other girls had gathered.

"We'll start with the labs, move into the library, and wrap up in the dining hall for dinner."

An older girl with a pair of braids that dangled down her back looked at the freshmen before her. She wasn't sure how she'd managed to be roped in as tour guide but she was stuck with it now.

The group moved down a set of stairs near the back of the house to the ground floor and followed their guide into a new wing of the house.

Raine noticed that the atmosphere changed as they approached what she assumed were the labs. She wondered if magic lingered around them or if something else caused the shift.

"On our left, we have the first of the potion labs. Plants for potions classes are also kept in there. Please try not to make the healing potions explode. Professor Fowler hates that."

A snicker rippled through the group.

They entered the lab and Raine felt a tinge of disappointment. Sturdy wooden tables with stools and a large board on the front wall behind the professor's desk looked much like her middle school classrooms. For some reason, she'd hoped to see big cauldrons or something equally witchy.

"Which classes are you most excited for?" Sara hooked her arm around Raine's. "I can't wait to take transfiguration and dark magic."

"I have no idea what classes there are. Am I supposed to know?"

"No. You're fine. If you're new to the magic world, it's perfectly reasonable that you don't know." Evie squeezed her arm. "I look forward to portals, myself."

"Have you guys heard that there's the most amazing kemana below the school?" Sara's eyes lit up. "We have to go there."

A brunette in front of them glared at her. "Freshmen aren't allowed there. It's against school rules."

Sara shrugged, and her grin widened. "Rules were meant to be broken."

"What's a kemana?" Raine looked at her companions. "Something really magical?"

"It's a huge underground city packed full of magic. All kinds of different beings live down there, and it's the best shopping experience you'll ever have." Sara leaned in conspiratorially. "We have to visit it. For Raine's sake."

Evie smiled. "For Raine's sake?" She shook her head. "We'll go because it'll be amazing. Don't try to pretend it's for Raine."

Sara shrugged. "Whatever works."

The tour continued through grand hallways and other rooms and finally reached the library. Raine gasped with delight as they stepped through the double doors and she gazed at the collection of books before her. The walls of two floors held floor-to-ceiling bookshelves. Farther aisles of shelves were evenly spaced throughout the area. It was far bigger than her previous school library and she couldn't wait to lose herself there.

A gnome dressed in a dark suit complete with a bowler hat and a red poppy stepped forward.

"This is Librarian Leo Decker. He is the head librarian."

The group laughed when his poppy blew raspberries at them. The gnome stood patiently with his hands behind his back and waited for the freshmen to focus on what he had to say.

"We take the management and protection of this library very seriously. Many security spells are in place to protect the books within these walls. Should any of you try to keep a book past its due date, you will find it vanishes and returns here. I strongly recommend against any attempt to hold onto the book when that spell begins. The magic will win, and we'd rather not see you in your pajamas."

That drew another laugh from the group.

"Is it true that there's another private library here? One with more interesting books?"

Librarian Decker's jaw tightened. "There are many fascinating books within this library. You'll find that every conceivable topic is thoroughly covered."

"What about dark magic?"

"We have tomes on dark magic relevant to your classes with Professor Powell."

"So, it's not true that there are some of the oldest and most dangerous books here?"

The head librarian exhaled slowly and searched for his inner peace. "The professors have a private library with their own personal collections. Students are not allowed there. Ever."

Whispers began within the group.

"What do you think they hide in there?"

"I heard Powell still practices dark magic and he'll teach you if you ask right."

"That has to be where the good stuff is."

"Dude, they're books. There's no such thing as good stuff when it comes to books."

Raine itched to break away from the group and explore the library. She edged forward a little and tried to see the plaques on the closest shelves.

Potions for defense.

Spells for defense.

History of battles fought on Oriceran.

Portals.

"The library opens at eight AM and closes ten minutes before lights out at ten PM," the guide said. "The gnomes are here to help you find whatever you might need."

"If anyone disrespects the books, they will suffer severe consequences." Librarian Decker looked sternly at the group. "And we do mean *severe.*"

"Oh, he's trying to scare us. They're merely books." Sara rolled her eyes. "I know gnomes are protective, but this seems extreme."

"As long as they're happy." Evie shrugged. "And they wouldn't have stuck around if they weren't."

Raine was seriously tempted to skip the rest of the tour and explore the library instead but Sara drew her away with the group. She knew she needed to see the school so she wouldn't get lost but left the library with real reluctance.

"There are many opportunities for extra-curricular activities here." The guide paused and gestured at a large board on a wall at an intersection. "We have everything from choir, orchestra, and volleyball through to student government, Entrepreneurs Club, and Debate Club."

"Is it true that Entrepreneurs Club is focused on mixing magic with technology?" a tall boy asked.

"I'm not a member but I believe so, yes." The girl turned and moved forward again. "We'll now walk out onto the grounds."

She checked her watch and saw there wouldn't be time to visit the various outside buildings, so she opted to simply point them out. It helped to remind herself that she never wanted to be the guide anyway. They should have chosen someone more interested if they expected the job to be done better.

Raine drank in the scene of gently rolling grass flanked by woods that faced a towering range which she thought was the Blue Ridge mountains. It was so unlike what she'd grown up with in Michigan. The woods wore their rich autumn colors of a range of golds and reds.

"Over there, you can see the stables. Students are allowed to interact with the horses and ride if they demonstrate knowledge and ability. Through those woods is a stream where you can sit in the hotter months. Be aware, though, that the professors' cottages are also over there, and students are not allowed anywhere near those. It has been rumored that Dorvu the dragon eats students who try. No one has confirmed or denied that yet."

A silver dragon flew from the far side of the barn and circled around overhead right on cue. He landed near the guide and grinned a toothy greeting.

"New students, I'm pleased to meet you. I'm Dorvu."

Gasps and whispers filtered through the group. Raine

pushed forward for a better look at the talking dragon. She'd never imagined such a thing existed.

"Dorvu is very friendly and is fluent in English. If you ask him very nicely, he might use his frost breath to allow you to sled in the winter."

The dragon preened and Raine smiled. The school was so much better than she had possibly imagined.

Agent Connor texted Jerry to let him know they'd reached the school without incident and he'd left Raine in the capable hands of the headmistress. He followed Xander along a road that crossed the wide expanse of lawn to a row of cottages. Each one clearly had its own personality. He assumed the one with the garden overflowing with flowers and herbs belonged to the potions mistress.

He exited the car and picked his bag up to follow the professor to his new home. The stream gurgled nearby, and magical lights were placed at even intervals to allow him to see without feeling like he was back in the city. There was a sense of peace around the place and he looked forward to the quiet and a slower pace.

Xander opened the small gate to the cottage at the end of the row. The garden in front was all grass and the walls were plain white. It suited him to a tee. He took the keys with a satisfied grin.

"Come and join us at the professors' table at dinner. I'll introduce you to everyone. I'm sorry I can't stop and chat but the first day is always hectic."

Bruce smiled. "Don't worry about it. I'll see you at dinner."

"Six PM."

He nodded and opened the door to his new home. The interior was cozy with plain off-white walls and well-worn wooden floors. He dropped his bag beside a large black sofa which stood in front of a wood furnace. A few old, faded paperbacks rested on a shelf beneath the window that overlooked the woods. He removed his shoes and walked over the thin blue rug toward the bare wooden stairs.

The upper level contained a single large bedroom and a bathroom with high water pressure. The agent grinned, satisfied that he'd be more than comfortable. It was actually better than the apartment he'd grown used to in Michigan. The placement at the school looked better at every moment. Raine seemed like a great kid, and the school was locked down tighter than Fort Knox.

CHAPTER FOUR

R aine stepped into the dining hall and paused for a moment to drink everything in. The ceiling had been enchanted to resemble far-off constellations that she didn't recognize. She smiled and stared in absolute awe. Sara tugged on her arm. "Come on, I'm starving."

They made their way between the tables where older students had already settled into comfortable conversation. The three girls chose a table near the edge of the room. She was happy to see Agent Connor with the professors. He looked relaxed. A pang of sadness hit her as she thought of Uncle Jerry and her friends. She hoped they would be okay. Her uncle would throw himself into work, she knew, and made a mental note to call him to make sure he was okay.

Plain white bowls sat at each place with a set of silver cutlery. Evie frowned at her empty bowl and looked at the other students who all seemed to have food.

"Do you have any idea how this works?"

Sara grinned as her small bread plate filled with fresh rolls and her main bowl with a rich beef stew. Raine made a mental note to visit the library to find out how the spell worked and where the food came from. She lifted her spoon with her first mouthful when a trio of guys their age stopped at their table.

"Do you mind if we join you?"

Sara's eyes met those of the attractive blond wizard and her smile widened.

"Of course. We'd love to have you." She pushed a chair out with her foot. "I'm Sara."

"Philip." He took the seat beside her. "Wizard. You?"

"Kitsune."

The dark-haired guy's eyes narrowed at that. Raine recognized him as the one who'd had a flicker of flames on his hair and hands earlier. She saw the fire dormant in his eyes when she looked at him.

"I didn't catch your name." She smiled politely. "I'm Raine."

"Half-Ifrit, and William." He lifted his spoon and frowned at the stew that appeared in his bowl. "Have you tried this?"

"Is it normal for people to introduce themselves with what they are?" Raine looked at each member of the group. "I'm not sure what I am. I guess a witch?"

She took a spoonful of her stew and smiled at the rich taste. It had been beautifully balanced with a soft herby aftertaste.

"How do you not know what you are?" The blond boy with the fine bone structure looked curiously at her. "Weren't you raised with magic?"

"No. My dad and uncle are—were—in the FBI. I don't know much about magic at all." She took another spoonful. "I'm looking forward to learning, though."

"Where are you from?" Sara glanced at the boy with high cheekbones and pointed ears. "You're an elf, right?"

"My name is Adrien. I'm from France." He bit into his bread roll. "And yes, I am an elf. Although I find the habit of asking people what they are to be very rude."

"Oh, France? How wonderful! I haven't been outside America." Sara sipped her water. "How long have you been in America?"

Adrien pursed his lips. "A week."

"What do you think of America so far?" Evie smiled at him. "I assume you've only seen the school."

He shrugged and ate his stew without answering.

"William, do you mind me asking what an Ifrit is?" Raine pushed her empty stew bowl aside. "I'm afraid I don't know much about anything."

He looked at her with suspicion etched on his face.

"Ifrit are fire elementals usually tied to the middle east." Philip leaned back in his chair. "It's very unusual to see them out in the main population, especially here."

Raine wanted William to open up a little. He guarded his stew as though someone would try to steal it from him. His eyes were hard, and his mouth had shifted between a scowl and a thin line of suspicion since he'd sat down. It was in her nature to draw him into her group and give him a safe space.

Evie had the same idea and smiled warmly at him. "Well, it's wonderful to meet you. I look forward to getting to know you better." She looked around to see what other people had done with their empty bowls. "Do you know what happens now?"

"The food is made by the kitchen pixies. They use their magic to put it on our plates and tidy it away." Philip glanced at the kitchen. "Although I've heard that if you take too long or make a big mess, they'll come out and scold you."

"Kitchen pixies shouldn't be underestimated." Adrien looked at the piece of apple pie and ice cream that appeared. "Is this apple pie?" The elf poked at it with his fork. "The crust is...different to what I am accustomed to."

A pixie appeared beside him. Raine was fascinated by her bright pink spiked hair with lilac highlights.

"Well if you don't want it, little French boy, I will take it for myself." She reached out as if to take the pie. "We wanted to give you students some comfort food."

Adrien stabbed the dessert with his fork and glared at her.

"I didn't say I didn't want it. I was merely...confused. It is unlike apple pie in France." He held the creature's gaze. "I'm sorry if I offended you."

The pixie folded her arms and watched as each of the students sampled the treat. The crust was thin and perfectly sweet with a spiced apple filling. Smooth vanilla ice-cream made the perfect accompaniment.

"This was wonderful." Evie smiled at the pixie. "Thank you very much."

She beamed at the girl and gave her a small nod.

"Is there anything we can do to help you?" Philip looked at the pixie. "It seems unfair that you do everything."

"We're good, thank you, but I might have a spare piece of pie for you. If you want it."

"I would love another piece." Philip's smile didn't quite reach his eyes. "Thank you."

Raine suppressed her grin. She'd met people like Philip before through her dad and uncle. He was someone who would treat his friends very well. She was sure he could be exceptionally charming, which would allow him to wrap people around his little finger.

"There you are!" Paige stomped up to them. "You cursed me, didn't you?"

They exchanged bemused glances and tried to work out what had the hysterical girl so upset.

"I have had the worst luck since I met you. I lost my favorite pen—a Swarovski pen, too. Then my favorite blouse formed a hole." She pointed at Sara. "That's all kitsune trickery. You did it didn't you?"

Sara grinned in a predatory way. "Oh, sure. You should see what else I've done." She maintained eye contact with Paige. "The best is yet to come."

The color drained from the girl's face and she stormed off toward the professors' table.

"Did you really curse her?" Adrien pursed his lips. "That seems a little extreme."

Sara shrugged. "No. I haven't worked a scrap of magic." She took a sip of her water. "But seeing the horror on her face was worth letting her think I had."

Evie and the others laughed. Raine had to admit that Paige was infuriating.

The headmistress approached the students as they stood to leave.

"Is it true that you cursed Paige?" Ms. Berens forced the frustration from her voice.

Sara rolled her eyes. "I haven't used any magic. I merely let her think I had." Sara folded her arms. "She's been a snotty brat all afternoon."

The woman sighed. There was always some trouble when the rooms were first allocated. She also noticed that Andrew was missing from the group of boys—a sure sign that yet another roommate might have to be relocated.

"Paige will be moved to a new room in the morning." She fixed Sara with a warning look. "Do not cast magic. You will survive one night together."

Paige huffed and muttered something under her breath but the headmistress ignored her.

"You are welcome to explore the grounds for one more hour until you're required to remain within the main building." The woman looked at each of them in turn. "I strongly advise against testing the professors' patience."

"We wouldn't dream of it," Philip said a little too quickly.

The headmistress left them and Paige stalked off toward a group of similarly primped and preened girls.

"You've heard about the kemana, right?" Philip turned to look at the girls in their group. "We plan to sneak in there soon."

"Do you know how?" Sara stepped closer to him. "I haven't put a good plan together yet."

"They do not watch the entrance as well as you'd expect." Adrien put his hands in his pockets. "We can slip in with some sophomores."

Evie wrinkled her nose. "We'd have to know some sophomores for them to cover us like that."

"Oh, I'm sure we can convince a couple of people." Sara looped her arm with Philip's. "I've only seen the kemana under New York. I've heard this one is amazing."

"Then it's settled." He led the group out of the dining room. "We'll make plans to go down there in the next couple of days."

"Did the guide say there were stables on the grounds?" Raine looked at Evie. "Or did I imagine that?"

"Oh, yeah. It's near the woods. You'll see the groundskeeper's fire, I think." Evie paused. "Do you ride?"

"Yeah. I had regular lessons and would love to keep up with it." Raine looked at the front door. "Do I go out there?"

"I think so." Evie looked around. "They didn't tell us about another door."

Raine chewed on her bottom lip and looked longingly toward the stairs that would lead her up to the library. The stables won. She knew she'd have an hour to wander those book-filled aisles once she returned. Without a word, she left the group and headed into the cool, dark night. The grounds seemed to stretch all around her. It had been a while since she'd spent this much time away from the bustle of the city.

She tucked her hands into her pockets and set out across the grass toward the barn and the small fire with a figure beside it. She hoped she hadn't broken any rules. The figure near the blaze stood and smiled as she approached. His hair matched the flames and had a slightly ruffled appearance but his kind eyes put her immediately at ease.

"Hey, is this the stables?" She gestured to the large red barn behind him. "I hoped I might be able to ride. Not now, obviously, but while I'm at the school."

The man held out his hand, "I'm Horace, the groundskeeper." He turned toward the barn. "I could give you a quick tour."

"I'm Raine. I've ridden English-style since I was a toddler." She followed Horace without reservation. "I assume you simply hack here?"

Horace opened the smaller door and led her into the barn.

"We do some training, and there are jumps available." He paused and looked at her. "Are you hoping for a project?"

Raine frowned, uncertain how to answer that. "I'm not sure."

The groundskeeper smiled and led her past the stalls which held horses in a variety of sizes and types. Smaller ponies put their heads over their doors in search of mints and carrots and tall thoroughbreds picked at their hay. They stopped at the last box which held a smaller black horse. He stood away from the door and watched the people with cautious eyes. His ears flicked back and forth and he remained wary and alert.

"This is Smoke. He's only two. The headmistress brought him here from a bad situation. I haven't had the time to work with him." Horace picked up a bucket with a handful of feed in the bottom. "He's too scared to be handled and has only been here a few days."

He rattled the bucket gently and the young horse stepped forward slowly and snorted at them. Finally, after surveying his visitors with nervous distrust, he sniffed in the direction of the bucket before he took the final step forward.

"We've reached a tentative agreement. He allows me to touch him, and I give him food." Horace handed Raine the bucket. "Why don't you try?"

She'd dealt with a few youngsters, but they had all been raised well. Smoke was clearly skittish and nervous of people. She extended her hand slowly and stroked his forehead gently before she held the bucket for him.

"He gives us what we want, and we give him what he wants." Raine pulled the bucket away once he'd had a mouthful. "Do you plan to back him next spring?"

"Well, if you're interested, and I'd have to see you with other horses first." Horace put the bucket down. "Then maybe you could do it."

Raine suppressed a broad grin. Smoke had the build and potential to be a real stunner and she'd dreamed of an opportunity like this. It would be a commitment alongside her usual school work, but the idea appealed.

"I'd love to." She looked at Smoke who now watched her closely. "I think he'll be amazing if we give him time."

"I think you're right." Horace gestured to the door. "But you should head inside. The headmistress won't want you to wander out here too late on your first day."

"Thank you. I'll see you tomorrow." Raine followed him from the barn. "Enjoy the rest of your night."

She walked across the grass and looked at the tall, slender lights illuminated with a pure white glow. There was no sign of electrical wiring and they stood suspended above the grass. The night had an unnatural tint to it that brought her reality home to her. She really was there in a school to learn magic.

Raine reached the main building of the house and tried to remember her way to the library. The hallways were so tall and imposing that she found herself a little over-whelmed. She walked past the potions labs twice before she recalled that the library was another floor up. A trio of gnomes sat at a small round table near the front and laughed while their poppies blew raspberries. She couldn't see any students in there, which seemed like a real shame.

She stepped in with a bright smile. "Hi, are you still open?"

The gnome she thought was called something Decker—the one who had addressed them on the tour—looked at her.

"It is, but classes haven't started yet." He raised an eyebrow. "You can't have any homework."

"Oh, no." Raine looked at the aisles which seemed to call her name. "I wanted to look around. I've never seen such a beautiful library before and I've been dying to explore it all day."

The gnomes looked at each other and whispered something.

"You have twenty minutes." The head librarian gestured to the books behind him. "You can check out no more than five books."

Raine looked at the plaques on the aisles and tried to pick a topic that really spoke to her. The problem was they all sounded far too interesting. She wandered down the center aisle and found a section devoted to elves and another on other magical beings. When she turned, she discovered books on transfiguration and curses beside a large and very colorful collection on mixing technology and magic.

"Oh, how am I supposed to choose?" She turned in a slow circle. "I want to read it all."

A soft laugh sounded behind her. One of the gnomes walked up to her with three leather-bound books, each in a beautiful oxblood color.

"I recommend these." He handed the books to her. "They're a good starting point."

Raine looked at them. Each was a beginner's guide to spells and magic.

"Oh, thank you." She clutched them tightly. "These are perfect. Do I need a card?"

The gnome shook his head and walked toward the front desk. "No. The magic knows who you are."

That sounded a little terrifying. It also sounded useful and she hoped she could learn how it knew that so she could apply it to her job as an FBI agent. It would be very handy when tracking criminals.

CHAPTER FIVE

Philip exited the bathroom after brushing his teeth. William sat on the edge of his bed and looked out the window over the grounds.

"Do you spend much time with your Ifrit family?" Philip pulled his blankets back. "You don't often hear of half-Ifrit."

William didn't look at him. His mouth tightened as Philip now trod on ground that should be better left untouched.

"No." He pulled his own blankets back with a sigh. "I don't."

"How did that happen anyway?" Andrew sneered at him. "Your mother can't have been very choosy."

Fire formed around William's hands and blazed over his hair. His eyes flared with the fury of an inferno. Adrien stepped between the two and held his hands up.

"That is enough." The elf turned his full attention to Andrew. "Why must you always make such snide comments? It is unnecessary."

"Typical frog avoiding conflict," Andrew sneered. "And an elf, no less."

Adrien exhaled slowly and sought his inner peace. He wouldn't be pulled into a fight on his first night in the school.

"What is your problem, Andrew?" Philip stood and faced him. "What's with the attitude?"

The other boy sniffed and flexed his arms.

"I don't like mixing with inferior beings." He looked at the other three boys and his lip curled disdainfully. "I'm already a master wizard and an accomplished fighter. I'll graduate early. You'll see."

Adrien felt his magic itch in the palm of his hand. It would be so easy to form a sword and show Andrew how accomplished a fighter he was himself. He had been trained in combat magic since he could walk. Instead, he calmed himself and saw the lack of balance and core strength in the arrogant wizard before him. Andrew was an easy target, but he didn't prey on fools.

"Graduate early?" Philip laughed. "And I'm half-dragon."

The belligerent boy's face turned pink with anger.

"You might mock me now." The wizard took a step forward and glared menacingly at the other boy. "But you'll eat your words."

Philip laughed again. "Dude, you're such a cliché."

Andrew balled his hand into a fist and launched a punch. He wanted to wipe the smug smile off his opponent's face. Adrien caught his wrist before the blow landed. Somehow, he swiped his legs out from under him and had his arm bent behind his back before he knew what had happened. Andrew whimpered in pain as the elf stood over him.

"You will settle down and sleep quietly now." Adrien spoke in a low, threatening tone.

Andrew tried to free himself, but the elf only held him tighter until he was sure his arm would break. He finally relaxed and accepted defeat.

"Lights out." The dorm proctor looked into the room. "What exactly is going on here?"

"Adrien was showing Andrew a self-defense move." Philip gestured toward them. "With the attacks on the school, we thought we could use all the advantages we could get."

The dorm proctor shrugged. "We have many layers of security measures around the school premises. You have no cause to worry. Get some sleep. You need to be up bright and early for classes tomorrow."

The man left without another word. Andrew glared at Adrien and balled his hand in a fist as he stood. The elf raised his eyebrow and dared him silently to try again. The wizard ground his teeth and went to his bed.

William had calmed himself and extinguished the flames. He returned his gaze to the view of the grounds beyond the window. The school was so unlike what he'd come to call home. He had hoped it would give him a sense of belonging but thus far, he had only received the same sneers and mockery that he'd endured before. His mother had fallen in love with an Ifrit man but she had died during childbirth.

His father, left to raise him alone, had been forced to choose between the Ifrit community who were very proud of their pure bloodlines and his son. He had chosen the community and sent William away to his aunt. The human woman resented William and blamed him for the loss of her beloved sister. The girl at dinner, Raine, had been the first person to look at him with any form of kindness. He closed his eyes and tried to find a comfortable position. The thoughts wouldn't settle, though, and he felt his fire rising once more in response to his frustration.

"We're sneaking into the kemana soon, right?" Philip looked at Adrien and William. "The girls seemed up for it."

"I don't think it will be too difficult. It will be a matter of timing." Adrien poked at his pillow. "I believe the professors are aware that freshmen sneak down there and some of them are less rigid with the rules. We need to see who will turn a blind eye."

"No. We can't get caught at all." Philip chewed his bottom lip. "The professor could turn on us."

"Then we need to go early in the morning." Adrien closed his eyes. "There is more bustle then."

"And less caffeine in their systems," William added.

He'd sneaked around a fair amount with his aunt and had mastered the art of slipping across the roof and down the drainpipe. Unlike the kids in the movies he sometimes watched, he didn't sneak to parties. He merely liked to wander the quiet woodlands near his house and see the stars. He wanted to see Oriceran one day.

Raine made it back to her room ten minutes before lights

out. The other girls prepared for bed while she flipped through the books the gnomes had given her.

"One of these has to have a light spell."

"What are those?" Evie looked at the books. "Did you seriously go to the library already?"

Raine shrugged and kept looking. "I have a lot to learn."

"Ugh, you're one of those." Paige climbed into her bed. "I'm so glad I'll move to another room tomorrow."

Raine ignored her and smiled when she finally found a simple light spell. They were beginner books and she hoped she'd master it. She retrieved her wand and said the words quietly to herself before she focused again. After a slow breath in, she said the words clearly and firmly and waited for the power in her to her move down the wand.

Nothing happened.

"You can't force your magic." Sara sat at the foot of her bed. "You have to allow it to flow."

Raine tried to relax and allow the magic to move forward. A flicker of light bloomed.

"Oh, for heaven's sake." Paige snatched her wand and cast a light spell to form a small white orb. "There."

Raine ignored Paige and her large light. She wouldn't give up that easily. Sara batted the other girl's light away and it careened into the wall where it shattered into a thousand tiny stars.

Still resolute, Raine made one last attempt and was delighted to see that it worked. Her orb was smaller and duller than Paige's but that was a good thing. She corralled the orb under her blanket and went quickly to the bathroom. When she returned, a hasty check under her blankets showed the orb was still intact. It bounced slightly when she climbed into bed with it and she hid it carefully when the dorm proctor came to ensure their lights were off.

Once the other girls had settled, Raine scooted under her blankets and began to read in earnest thanks to her little light. She discovered she needed to feel her magic within her. It was a natural part of who she was, and she needed to let it flow freely. Raine closed her eyes and tried to touch it with her senses. When she pushed really deep, she thought she could discern a warm flicker somewhere around her diaphragm, but she wasn't entirely sure it wasn't her imagination.

"We're going to the kemana with the guys the day after tomorrow, right?" Evie's voice sounded muffled. "It sounds absolutely awesome and we can't pass up an opportunity like that."

"Seconded." Sara poked at Raine's bed. "Will you come with us?"

Raine stuck her head out from under her blankets.

"Sure. I'm in."

"Do you do this every night?" Paige looked pointedly at them. "Some of us would like our beauty sleep."

"You're changing rooms tomorrow." Sara sat and glared at her. "What do you care?"

Paige rolled over and turned her back on the other girls. "Good riddance."

"Agreed," Evie muttered.

"Is there something we can help you with?" Evie looked at Raine. "I've grown up with magic, so maybe I can give you some pointers."

"I don't even know what I don't know." Raine shrugged,

a little embarrassed by her ignorance. "I don't really know what to ask or what I'm supposed to learn."

Sara and Evie shared a look.

"She kinda has a point." Sara wrapped her blankets around her and looked out the window. "Maybe we can help more once she has a better idea."

"What about your kitsune magic?" Evie scooted to face Sara. "What's that like?"

The other girl remained silent for a few minutes before she finally said, "I don't know. Kitsunes normally come into their magic by age twelve, but I haven't come into mine yet. Mom's desperately worried and my grandmother has considered disowning me."

Raine looked at her in horror. "Would she really?" She gestured. "Disown you, I mean."

"Probably." Sara shrugged. "Grandma is very old-fashioned and a kitsune without magic is thought to bring dishonor on the family."

Paige mumbled something, but everyone ignored her.

"Have you felt your magic at all?" Evie moved to sit beside Sara. "I mean, you know it's in there, right?"

Sara smiled. "Yeah. I've felt it." She turned to look at Evie. "It's a bonfire within me. I simply don't know how to access it."

"Well, feeling it is a great start." Evie squeezed her arm. "I'm sure you'll be able to use your magic in no time."

Raine shuffled under the blankets and read for a little longer. She reminded herself that she had to be up for breakfast in the morning, but it was all so fascinating. There was so much to learn. On many nights while growing up, she had stayed up far too late to read one book or another. Raine often preferred non-fiction so she could learn something new rather than escape to another world. Although now, it felt as though she had stepped into a book of her own.

She woke up with the book clutched to her chest and smiled. She'd dreamt she had found her magic and used it to hunt criminals. Uncle Jerry would be so proud of her if she could pull that off. A small ache of sadness coiled in the pit of her stomach as she thought about him and her dad. She wished they could see her now. She swallowed and reminded herself that Christmas wasn't so far away. She'd share a big celebration with her uncle and catch up on everything.

Paige was up first and spent far longer in the bathroom than was reasonable. The other girls had to rush to be ready for breakfast as they didn't want to risk the pixies removing their food because they were late.

They hurried to the dining room and darted around a pixie cleaning up someone's half-eaten toast. The girls sat with the guys who didn't look like they'd been there very long themselves. A pair of croissants appeared in front of Adrien. The elf smiled, apparently pleased with the quality of the pastries. Philip had biscuits with fresh blueberry jam, and William had sausages, hash browns, and bacon.

Raine took a sip of her orange juice and debated whether it would be horribly rude to ask the pixies how they decided who got what for breakfast. There had to be magic involved. A bowl of oatmeal with hazelnuts and dried red berries appeared at her place and she smiled.

The food was perfect, and Raine looked around for a pixie to thank once she had finished.

"Are you coming exploring?" Philip looked at the girls. "We didn't get much of a chance yesterday."

"There's the room we wanted to check out." William finished the last of his milk. "The one down near the basement area."

"I'm still not convinced there'll be anything interesting in there." Adrien pushed his empty plate away. "It's likely a storage room."

"There's one way to find out." Sara grinned. "I vote we head down there in a minute."

The headmistress stopped at their table and for a horrible moment, they thought they were in trouble.

"Your new roommate is arriving in your room as we speak." She looked pointedly at the door. "I suggest you go and greet her."

"I'm so glad we're getting a new roomie." Evie stood. "We had some snooty girl."

"Andrew is insufferable." Adrien led the group out. "He would not be quiet and tried to start fights."

"Is he moving rooms too?" Sara looked at the elf. "He sounds awful."

Adrien sighed. "Not that I know of."

"Not yet anyway," Philip added.

Raine looked longingly in the direction of the library as they started up the stairs. She didn't want to be rude, though, and accepted that their new roommate was more important.

"Why don't we meet here in an hour?" Sara gestured at the large window at the top of the stairs. "An hour's plenty of time to say hi to whoever our new roomie is."

The guys agreed, and they went their separate ways.

"I really hope she's nice." Raine pushed her hair behind her ear. "We'll have to spend a lot of time with her."

Sara opened the door to their room to reveal a blonde girl with a broad smile.

"Hi! I'm Christie. I'm from London and I'm a Sophomore. It's so nice to room with you. You must be so excited to be here. I was a ball of nerves when I first arrived but I met some really nice people. The professors are super too. And they have amazing extra-curriculars. Have you looked at those yet? They have everything covered so I'm sure you'll find lots of things you really enjoy. Try not to take too much on, though, as you don't want to get behind in your school work."

Raine blinked and tried to parse everything the girl had said. It had been a blur of words.

"Hey, I'm Sara." She pointed to Evie and Raine. "Evie and Raine. It's nice to meet you."

"Have you seen your class schedule yet? I just got mine and it looks absolutely amazing. I think transfiguration will be hard this year, though. Professor Hodges can be a real hardass sometimes. He's cool, but maybe it's a shifter thing? I haven't noticed any difference around the full moon. Oh, what a horrible thing to say. He's so nice, really. I hope I haven't put you off transfiguration. I'm sure you'll love it."

"Thanks...Christie, right?" Evie tried to hold back a laugh at the sheer rush of words. "I'm excited about transfiguration but I'm more interested in potions, myself." Evie put her hands in her pockets. "I'd like to learn healing."

The girls chatted to Christie and even managed to get a few words in sometimes. Raine was happy that the new addition was far friendlier and easier to get along with than Paige had been.

They left her to go and meet her own friends and headed off to meet the guys. Evie hooked her arm around Raine's.

"No disappearing into the library this time." She elbowed her gently. "We only get today and tomorrow to really explore. The library will be there all year."

Raine smiled and allowed her friend to lead her to the meeting place. Exploring did sound like a fun idea and Evie was right. The library would be there later.

CHAPTER SIX

Agent Connor greeted Raine and her friends halfway up the stairs. She felt a flush of embarrassment as he smiled and approached them.

"How're you getting on with everything, Raine?"

"Great." She looked at her new friends. "We're on our way to explore the school and grounds."

"Ah." He stepped aside. "Then I'll let you go."

He felt a little bad that he'd embarrassed the girl, which hadn't been his intention. He merely wanted to reassure Jerry that she had settled in well. The group of friends around her certainly seemed a good sign. He watched them for a moment or two, then headed downstairs and turned into a wide corridor he hadn't seen before.

Everyone had been very accommodating, and the professors were friendly. Xander Powell had promised to give him a tour of the magical defenses around the school. He couldn't use magic himself but examining possible weaknesses gave him something to do.

Raine followed the guys down the corridor. Sara looked at her from where she walked beside Philip. "Who was that?"

Raine flushed. "Agent Connor." She looked away. "He works for the FBI and is here to watch over me, I guess. At least partly. But apparently, a lot of parents complained about safety fears after the fights and things that happened here. They feel better with an FBI agent on the grounds, so I imagine that's the real reason why he's here."

"You must be pretty special to have an FBI agent watch over you." Philip raised his eyebrow at her. "Are you a secret princess or something?"

Raine laughed and shook her head. "No. My dad and uncle were FBI agents, so it's an extension of that, I think."

Adrien pursed his lips and studied her with what might be reservation. "Do you have ties to the human government?"

"I wouldn't call it ties." Raine shrugged. "I know a few operatives and I plan to become one myself."

"Why?" William slowed to walk nearer her. "Why an FBI agent?"

"I want to make the world a safer place." Raine put her hands in her pockets. "Being in the FBI means I can do that."

William assessed her quietly and said nothing more. The young half-Ifrit had been told to distrust the human government, but he more often than not ignored whatever his aunt said.

"I don't like the human government." Sara sighed.

"They'll cage us in the end. They kill or cage anything that scares them."

"I completely disagree." Raine stood a little taller. "I think the government wants to keep people safe and happy. They're not perfect, and you're right, a lot of people are scared of magicals. The government wants to unify everyone, though."

Sara glanced quickly at her but said nothing more.

"What about the rumors that they're trying to find a way to steal our magic?" Philip asked. "Is there any truth to that?"

"Of course not." She grinned. "You've read too many cheesy sci-fi books."

Philip relaxed a little and shrugged.

"She's got the inside scoop." Evie nudged Raine gently. "I say we can trust her."

Sara put her arm around Raine's shoulders. "It looks like you're stuck with us." She squeezed gently. "Sorry about that."

Raine matched the girl's grin and enjoyed the feeling that she belonged. It would have been so easy for them to reject her because she knew nothing about magic—and especially since her heritage was governmental, something they obviously distrusted—but they'd accepted her and she appreciated that.

Some of the older students had set up a fair to display the extra-curricular activities the freshmen could participate in.

Philip wandered to the Entrepreneurs Club table and began chatting with the dark-haired girl about the possibility of joining them.

"We focus on mixing magic with technology to produce a healthy profit." The girl pointed at a leaflet the club had made. "Last year, we had great success with butterflies that combined magic with various forms of music. The creatures were attractive, and the music could only be heard within a certain range."

Philip studied the leaflet.

"And how much of an hourly commitment is this per week?"

"Four hours a week until the big final project when it can get a little insane." The girl straightened the papers on the table. "It's worth it, though. It looks good on your college applications and you keep your cut of the profits."

"Where do I sign up?" Philip tucked the page in his pocket. "It sounds perfect."

He signed on the sheet and glanced at the meeting schedule. The first was next week on Monday after classes.

"I look forward to seeing you there." The girl turned to the blonde witch who had approached the table. "The Entrepreneurs Club broadens your options to many other advantageous programs."

Philip wandered around the rest of the hall.

Christie bounced back and forth between the Glee Club table and the orchestra table. She beamed at Raine when she glanced at the former.

"Hi. You'll love the Glee Club. It's really new but we already have an amazing group of people. Everyone's so friendly that you'll fit in right away. The professor is amazing too. She's so talented. I've been singing since I was little, but she's already helped me improve. I hope to get the lead part in the musical this year. It's rumored to be Beauty and the Beast."

Raine looked around her for an escape. "I've never really sung." She spotted the Language Club. "I'm sure you'll find some wonderful members."

She had almost reached the Language Club when she saw the student council from the corner of her eye. She had been student body president in her middle school and had hoped to do something similar there.

An older girl looked disapprovingly at her and her mouth thinned as she folded her arms.

"How do the nominations for the student council work here?" Raine looked at the empty table. "I assume anyone can run for the positions."

"You're the magic-less witch with the FBI agent, aren't you?" The girl looked down her nose at Raine. "Don't waste your time running."

"Don't be so ridiculous Kerry." A girl with short black hair with electric blue tips handed Raine a form. "Fill this out. Each candidate has five minutes to argue their case next Tuesday evening. Votes will be cast after the speeches."

"Thanks." Raine looked at the form. "Where do I hand this in when I've completed it?"

Kerry muttered something under her breath and pushed her braid over her shoulder.

"Hand it to the headmistress." The dark-haired girl glared at Kerry. "And be prepared for some stiff competition."

Raine found a quiet corner to read the form. Each year

had two officers, one girl, one boy. She could also apply to be the president, vice-president, or treasurer. She was very tempted to try for full president but given that she didn't know how everything worked yet, she decided it was sensible to simply aim for freshmen officer.

Evie wandered aimlessly around the extra-curricular fair and idly picked up a few leaflets, but nothing called to her. What she really wanted was a Baking Club. At home, she baked for relaxation and fun. She'd hoped for an opportunity to improve her skills and meet some like-minded people at the same time.

Finally, she walked to the professor who seemed to be watching over the proceedings.

"Hi, erm, I'd like to form a new club." She watched the professor's expression nervously. "How do I go about that?"

The older woman with white-blonde hair pulled into a bun and large glasses pursed her lips. "It's unusual for freshmen to start clubs."

Evie wouldn't back down, however. "I understand that, but I feel it's something that would be beneficial."

"Go on."

"I would like to start a bakery club. Baking is a skill that is often forgotten but offers relaxation, training in focus and attention to detail, and a productive outlet for those who may struggle in more academic pursuits. Of course, it also opens the door to basic cooking skills and potential careers including pastry chef and baker."

Professor Hudson smiled at the sales pitch. "Come with me. We will speak to the headmistress about this idea."

Evie restrained the desire to celebrate. She fought to

maintain a serious expression and reminded herself that she hadn't succeeded yet.

The professor led Evie out of the hall and toward the headmistress who rubbed her temples as a sophomore wizard tried to explain that he hadn't intended for the flowers to catch fire.

"You are the first student to receive detention before classes have even started Mr. Killarney."

The wizard beamed with pride, which only made the headmistress shake her head.

"Go. Detention will be in the usual time and place. You're very familiar with it by now."

She turned her attention to Evie and Professor Hudson. "And what can I do for you this morning? We don't have another student going to detention, I hope."

"Not at all." Professor Hudson smiled at Evie. "I didn't catch your name."

"Evelyn O'Connor, but my friends call me Evie."

"Evie here would like to start a Baking Club."

A smile spread slowly across Ms. Berens' face. "I'm sure the pixies will be delighted to hear that. We will go and speak to them now before they begin lunch in earnest."

Evie did a little victory dance in her head as she decided this would really happen. Not only would she get her Baking Club, but she'd work with the kitchen pixies. It would be far better than she had hoped.

The headmistress knocked on the kitchen door before she poked her head around. She didn't want to barge into the pixie's territory. There was a strong chance a ladle or other such implement would be thrown at her. They were very protective over their domain.

"Do you have a moment?" She looked at the team who had begun to set everything up for lunch. "I have an interesting new proposal."

They turned to face her. "Well, come in then." The leader with a shock of cotton candy pink hair ushered them in. "We'll start lunch soon."

A tea set appeared in the middle of the robust table in the center of the large kitchen. Evie looked at the numerous ovens and cooking stations. She'd dreamt of an opportunity to cook in a place like that.

"Miss O'Connor here would like to start a Baking Club. As it would have to take place in your kitchens, we wanted your thoughts." The headmistress sat down and picked up a small white cup of tea. "Your tea is the best I have ever tasted. It's always a delight to visit you."

The pixies gathered around the table and selected their own cups. Professor Hudson gestured for Evie to sit.

She tried to not look too hard at the pixies although she'd never seen them up close before. They were short with bright, colored eyes and short hair which revealed their pointed ears and ample curves.

"And have you done much baking?" The lead pixie looked at Evie. "Or will you want to learn the basics?"

"I baked each weekend with my mom and sister. I've mastered basic cakes and my croissant are a work in progress." She took a sip of her tea. "This really is wonderful tea. Thank you."

The kitchen staff exchanged glances and a silent conversation of small facial expressions and almost imperceptible hand gestures.

"We would be delighted to have a Baking Club. We can help you twice a week." The pixie knocked her tea back like a shot of vodka. "Come by tomorrow evening at seven PM and we'll start with cupcakes to see how good your basics are."

Evie grinned from ear to ear. "Thank you, I can't wait." She turned to the headmistress. "Erm, how do I go about adding other people to the club?"

"I'll make you a sign and find you a table." She stood. "We mustn't get in the way of lunch, though."

Raine slipped away to the stables to see Smoke again. She was pleased that she managed to edge her hand a little closer to his ears. From there, she headed directly to the library. But to her slight dismay, Sara wrangled her away and insisted that they accompany the guys to the mysterious room they had spotted the day before.

"It'll be amazing." She gestured with her hands. "We'll make it our own room. Philip thinks he can weave a few spells so no one else goes in there."

"Speaking of spells, we need to figure out stealth spells for tomorrow." Philip looked over his shoulder. "To go into the kemana."

"I'm sure I can find some in the library." Raine looked down the narrow corridor. "Would you like me to look?"

"Not yet." Sara put her arm around Raine's shoulders. "Not until you've seen our new hangout."

Philip led the way flanked by William and Adrien. Evie

walked on Raine's other side as they approached the plain black door. Raine couldn't work out why they were all so sure it would be their hangout. It looked like any old door to her. Given the narrow hallway tucked away from the main school, she assumed that it was a storage room.

William stepped forward and crouched before he whispered something and pressed his fingertips against the lock. He opened the door and flipped the light on inside. They followed him into the simple square room with no windows and a concrete floor. An older television complete with DVD player stood against the far wall.

A couple of old creaky couches had been pushed against the left wall and two armchairs that had seen better days sat in the corners.

"This will make the most amazing movie room." Sara went to the first couch. "Help me pull these out."

Philip obliged while William and Adrien dragged the other from against the wall. Raine and Evie moved the armchairs and arranged them on either side of the couches.

"We can watch cheesy old horror movies." Sara grinned at the rest of the group. "Come on, you know it would be awesome."

"You mean like *Night of the Living Dead?*" William raised his eyebrow. "And those Jason movies?"

"No." Sara pulled an expression of mock horror. "I mean the really old cheesy ones like *Curse of the Swamp Creature* and *The Blob.*"

Adrien exploded into a genuinely delighted laugh Raine hadn't thought the elf was capable of. He had been so uptight and quiet until then.

"I'm up for this plan." He poked at the couch closest to him. "I think we might need to get something better to sit on, though."

"You guys work on that." Philip sighed as a spring cut through the thin cushion on an armchair. "I'll get the snacks."

"What about the movies themselves?" Evie looked at the TV. "Are we sure that even works?"

"We'll make it work." Sara wouldn't give up on this idea. "I'll work with Raine to get the movies. Maybe her FBI agent can be useful."

"If we call it Movie Club, the headmistress might get the movies in for us." Raine jumped when something moved inside the armchair. "And maybe the groundskeeper can dispose of these couches. I think they belong in one of those horror movies."

The armchair moved again and the students decided it was best that they left before something they didn't want to deal with what might emerge from it.

Dinner was accompanied by laughter and wonderful food. Raine, however, was glad to have the chance to head back to the library while the others debated which stealth spells were best to use. She knew nothing about it but didn't want to remain ignorant. They could have shown her, but she found comfort in books.

The gnomes greeted her with cautious smiles and watched as she wandered the aisles.

"Were those books helpful?" one of the gnomes asked after a short while. "From last night."

"Oh, yes, they're fantastic, thank you." Raine frowned as the spells section seemed extensive. "I hoped to find something about feeling my magic, though. Those books all assumed I could do that."

"Ah, well." The gnome shuffled his feet a little awkwardly. "We assumed you could if you were here. Come with me."

He took Raine to a quiet corner full of slender but colorful books.

"You'll find books on the philosophy of magic and feeling your magic here." He turned to walk away but paused for a moment. "Don't be offended if they're aimed at a younger audience."

She ran her fingertip over the spines and stopped at one about finding your inner flame. It looked promising, so she took it and another on finding the magic within to a comfortable chair nearby where she curled up and began to read.

Sara and Evie marched up to her, and she looked at them in confusion, not sure how long she'd been there.

"I told you she'd be here." Sara looked smugly at Evie. "Come on, Raine. Lights out in fifteen minutes. We need to tell you the plan for tomorrow."

Raine reluctantly gathered her books and followed her friends from the library.

"Philip and Adrien have pinned down the perfect stealth spell." Sara checked to be sure no one was listening as they hurried down the corridor to the dorms. "We'll head there right after breakfast when people are busier."

Evie looped her arm with Raine's. "Don't worry. I'll cast your spell for you. We'll help you figure it out in the kemana so you can do it yourself on the way back."

"Yes." Sara averted her gaze hastily from a senior who narrowed his eyes at her enthusiasm. "You can practice magic in the kemana."

Raine smiled and felt excitement stir. Maybe she could make a little progress before classes started.

CHAPTER SEVEN

Sara buzzed with excitement at the prospect of sneaking into the kemana. She couldn't keep the smile from her face as she applied her make-up in the mirror. Raine used the spare minute to finish a chapter on feeling her magic. She'd practiced searching for the magic inside her. It felt like a strange warmth that slipped between her mental fingers but the book said it would become more solid and pliable with practice.

They met the guys at the bottom of the grand staircase and followed Philip outside and across the lawns. He'd boasted of his business skills which had enabled him to make a trade with a senior for the code. Now, all they had to do was stroll nonchalantly across the wide lawns and slip into the woods without attracting attention. It seemed to take forever, but the directions the young wizard had received were accurate and they found the cave without difficulty.

Once there, they remained hidden behind the trees while they watched and waited for a quiet moment. Frustratingly, it seemed many of the seniors had chosen that day for a kemana excursion, and their delay was a little longer than they preferred. Finally, though, there was a lull in the foot traffic.

"We'll need to move quickly as I can't maintain the stealth spell for too long." Philip gestured with his wand. "Who will cast over Raine? Evie?"

"Someone will need to check mine." Sara looked away and a soft blush colored her cheeks. "I haven't come into my magic properly yet. I have a little, but my full kitsune magic is still dormant."

Adrien smiled softly. "I'll check your stealth cover for you." The elf lifted his hands. "Are we ready?"

Philip, not happy that Adrien had stepped into a leadership role, cast his stealth spell with a flourish. He was still visible if you knew where to look and concentrated hard, but the moment you looked away, it was difficult to focus on him again. The rest of the group cast their spells. Adrien had had the foresight to add a little tag that meant they could still see each other. Philip's mouth tightened once he realized that, but he said nothing.

"We have about five minutes." Philip took a step toward the hallway. "We should move quickly."

They hurried to the cave and the wizard quickly pressed the carved symbols in the right order. He must have memorized them, Raine thought, because there was no hesitation. The hidden door slid open and they scurried inside. Her heart thudded with excitement and she and hoped the kemana was as wonderful as everyone had described it. She'd looked forward to seeing this incredibly magical place.

They reached the top of a set of twisting stairs and began their descent. One moment, it was a simple dark stairway, but they turned a corner and suddenly, an irides-cent ruby hue glowed like an enchanted ceiling over the underground city. Raine swore she could feel the magic in the air and a soft buzzing sensation when she stepped forward.

They reached the bottom of the stairs and gazed on the underground city. Paths lined with shops and market stalls stretched farther than their eye could see. Witches, wizards, elves, and beings that Raine hadn't seen before strolled casually down the walkways.

"That's a Willen." Sara gestured at the odd creature. "I wouldn't have any dealings with them if you don't have to."

Raine looked at the rat-type being and made a mental note to herself not to go into business with a Willen.

They stepped off the final step and Philip led them to the old trading post without hesitation.

"We have to change dollars for Ruby Falls coins if we want to pay for anything. They don't use earth money here." The others hurried to make the exchange, watching furtively for signs of anyone who might see them. This close to the stairs, they felt very visible and vulnerable. Finally, they left the store and found a quiet corner where they paused and looked around to decide on a direction.

"I vote we go left." William pointed. "It looks like it has the most potential."

"How do you figure?" Evie looked down each path in turn. "They're all colorful and packed with magic and people."

William shrugged. "It simply looks best to me."

The young half-Ifrit didn't speak much and Raine wanted to encourage him to gain a little confidence so she said, "I agree with William. Left looks good."

"Left it is." Philip strode off decisively. "Are we looking for anything in particular?"

"Exploring." Sara paused to look at a pendant a raven-haired witch was selling. "I haven't brought much money with me."

The witch glared at Sara who ignored her.

"We can practice magic freely down here." Philip drew his wand. "We should make the most of that."

William raised his hands and flames flickered and formed around them. He watched as they shifted slowly in color and spread down his arm. He clenched his fist and they vanished.

"Is that an Ifrit thing?" Raine pointed at his hand. "The flames?"

A pair of wizards stopped to glare at the group and mutter about Ifrit before they moved on.

"What was that about?" Raine nodded toward the rude wizards. "The muttering and death stares?"

"Ifrit aren't particularly well-liked." Evie touched his arm. "But William is one of us. It doesn't matter what everyone else thinks."

"They are considered to be dirty-dealing tricksters." Philip shrugged. "Much like kitsune, I guess."

Sara narrowed her eyes at his back but remained silent.

"Wizards are hardly perfect." Adrien lifted his chin defiantly. "It was wizards who created shifters against their will, after all."

"That was dark witches and wizards." Philip's hands clenched. "We are nothing like them."

"Mhm." That was Adrien's only response. The elf had quickly identified Philip's buttons. He felt that the wizard was a good guy at heart but would take control and be manipulative if given the chance.

They paused to look at a magical trinket shop. Raine was delighted by the sheer variety of things offered and everything was new and fascinating to her. She chuckled at a small, red carved elephant that walked back and forth across her palm. Sara rolled a silver disk over and over while she stared thoughtfully at it.

"It's supposed to bring out innate talent." She looked at Raine. "But most of the things that say that are aimed at those who are desperate and do nothing at all."

Sara replaced the disk and moved to look at wooden circles with small carvings on them. "These are for divination." She pointed at different groups. "Like Norse runes with the Elder Futhark."

Raine picked up a piece of oak with a lightning bolt carved into it. "Do they work?"

Sara chewed her bottom lip. "That depends on who you ask."

Down there amidst all the magic, Sara lacked some of her usual confidence. She should be like all of them, but her magic was buried deep inside her and refused to manifest.

Philip used his wand to levitate a set of small copper

balls. He spun them and moved them in intricate patterns. A small bead of sweat formed on his forehead and he lowered them after a short while. William smirked at the amount of exertion the wizard had to use in the little display.

They wandered past shops run by wizards, elves, fairy, and other beings Raine didn't even know the names of. White and blue orbs of light bobbed overhead, and a witch rippled her hair color through every hue in the rainbow and all shades between.

Evie made everyone wait while she went into a herbs and potions shop. That was where she was most comfortable as she had grown up with a hedgewitch family. Plants and potions were her happy place. While she had no idea what she wanted, if anything at all, she breathed deeply and reveled in the familiar scents.

A trio of bright pink bottles behind the counter caught Raine's eye. "Are they really love potions?" She nodded at them. "The pink ones?"

Sara snorted. "They might make someone notice you, but they'll do no more than that." She shook her head. "True love potions are dark magic. We must never work against free will or control someone. A love potion would do that."

Philip leaned against the doorway and sighed. "Do we really have to look at herbs and potions?" He looked pointedly at the blade store. "There are far cooler things to look at."

"I'll only be another minute." Evie chose some forget-me-not and a sprig of Valerian flower. "I'll mix up a sleep aid in case anyone struggles in the new environment."

"You could make some good money from that." Philip pushed away from the doorpost. "I'd be happy to help you market it. For a cut, of course."

Evie didn't look at him. "I won't sell it." She handed the herbs to a witch with green hair. "Just these, thanks."

"Why wouldn't you sell it?" Philip looked from her to the others as though he had missed something. "You could start a little business. That money could go into whatever you wanted."

Evie paid for her herbs and smiled at him. "That's not my style."

They stepped into the main walkway and almost bumped into a large man with thick, dark hair and yellow eyes.

"Sorry," the group said collectively.

The shifter merely nodded and moved on.

"Shifters put me on edge." Philip watched the man for a moment. "There's something weird about them."

"Don't be such a dick." Adrien glared at him. "Shifters are perfectly reasonable people."

"What got your panties in a twist?" Philip matched the elf's glare. "Are you dating one?"

Adrien rolled his eyes. "I don't have to date one to see them as people." He moved toward the blade store. "Anyway, I know a few through Louper."

"What's Louper?" Raine struggled to remember if she'd heard the term before. "A sport, right?"

"Yes. The players are put into a new environment and must find their way to the golden token before the rival team." Adrien stepped into the blade shop. "My brother, Etienne and I are on the school team."

79

"How did you manage to make the most awesome game sound so boring?" William looked aghast. "Louper is where two teams are placed into a difficult environment, like the elf said. They must fight many challenges from wild wolves, to skeletal warriors, to sentient vines, and so much more. I don't have enough control over my magic to play it, but you'll love watching it."

"Speaking of magic." Philip looked at Adrien who examined a short dagger. "We haven't seen yours yet."

The elf shrugged. "I have no reason to show off."

"You haven't mastered it yet." Philip folded his arms in an arrogant gesture. "No offense, Raine."

The elf merely shrugged and refused to rise to the bait.

They looked at the various bladed weapons, although none paid quite as much attention as Adrien did. He had been raised to wield weapons he formed himself as well as blades such as those. He found comfort in being surrounded by them. Nothing caught his eye—not that he could afford any of it even if it had.

"We should find some food." Evie looked around. "I'm starving."

"Agreed." Sara nodded. "I feel like I haven't eaten in days."

"Any ideas where we're going?" William turned in a slow circle and tried to locate something food related. "I haven't seen any food stalls yet."

"Then we keep wandering." Philip strode along the pathway. "We're sure to find something."

They paused to watch an overhead magic light display. A trio of witches threw orbs and ribbons of colors of pinks and purples through to greens and silvers. They danced across the space above the aisle and collided in showers of sparks, much like fireworks.

The shop owners didn't pay it any attention as it was a normal occurrence. For Raine, it was something to remember. Once the display ended, they continued along the walkway and squeezed past clusters of witches and wizards with the odd fairy amongst them. One smaller man with almost no hair and a large nose motioned with his wand and whispered an incantation. A stream of ice hurtled toward a younger man with golden eyes and spiked brown hair. He used his wand to turn the ice into an impromptu rain shower.

"You knew I liked her." The older man raised his wand once more. "You stole her."

His adversary laughed. "You have the wrong person."

The aggressor frowned and lowered his wand. "My apologies."

Five minutes later, the group of friends heard him shouting, "You knew I liked her," and laughed.

"He's having a bad morning." Adrien stopped outside what appeared to be an ordinary bookshop. "We should look in here."

Philip sighed. "It's a bookshop. We're supposed to be looking for food."

Adrien stepped inside anyway. "It's not what it appears."

They exchanged glances before they followed him. When William allowed himself to shrug off his surroundings and dig deep, he could feel something too. He joined the others in the small, bland shop. It was a study in brown hues. The mats on the floor almost blended into the wooden walls, and the narrow bookshelves were a slightly darker shade of grey. The spine on every single book in sight was yet another shade of brown.

Adrien paused when he sensed a tug of magic that almost felt welcoming. He explored it a little and decided it intrigued him, so he followed its source to the corner and focused. Instinctively he ran his fingers over the spines of the books there until he felt a tingle of real enchantment. He grinned as he pulled a tan-colored book from the row.

The shelf swung open and revealed a candlelit staircase which descended enticingly.

"That's so cool." Sara stepped around William to look. "We have to check it out."

Philip looked over Raine's head and had to admit it did look interesting. He didn't like the elf in the lead again, though.

Adrien stepped into the semi-darkness and they took the tightly spiraled stairs to emerge into a confection of pinks and lilacs with generous splashes of bright yellows. They stopped to allow their eyes to adjust to the sudden shift in light.

Before them sat the most brightly colored cafe-diner they had ever seen. A large sign hung over the archway acting as the entrance declared it to be Bubble & Fizz.

Sara linked her arm with Adrien's and led him around the small, round, bubblegum-pink and lilac flowered plastic tables. They chose a larger one near the left side where they could all sit together. Sara scooted around the bright gold, high-backed vinyl seat that surrounded a lilac and pink rectangular table.

Once they were all seated, a fairy with translucent wings and neon-pink hair pinned up in a complicated style bounced over to them with a large grin. "Good morning. Here are our menus."

They each took one decorated with a glittery border. Philip tried to look dignified and failed entirely. His expression was one of abject horror. Sara, however, appeared to have found her home away from home.

The bill of fare comprised only snacks, foods, and drinks that couldn't be described as even vaguely healthy.

"They have sweet potato pie with fresh vanilla ice-cream." Sara gestured dreamily. "Oh, and Twinkies."

"Black cherry ice-cream with Hershey's pieces sounds amazing." Evie put the menu down before she changed her mind. "I'll gain so many pounds coming here."

"I have no idea what most of these things are." Adrien frowned as though everything was written in Martian. "What is a dingdong? And why would you make a pie from coconut cream?"

"You should get the snack platter." Evie pointed it out on the menu. "It'll give you a whirlwind tour of American snacks."

"Sometimes, I miss France." The furrow between his brow deepened. "But I will try this snack platter."

Raine couldn't resist a large slice of pecan pie with a root beer on the side. The fairy returned with a bowl full of rainbow nerds. "Complimentary candy. Who's ready to order?"

"The snack platter please."

"Black cherry ice-cream with Hershey's pieces."

"Pecan pie with root beer."

"Cheez-its with a side of chips and salsa."

"The Hershey's experience."

"Beef jerky platter with a side of Fiery Habanero Doritos"

She jotted it down and bounced away again.

"You'll really have chocolate for lunch?" William looked at Sara. "Nothing savory at all?"

"Nope." She stretched her legs under the table. "We always eat something sensible for lunch. I'll embrace this while I have the chance."

"Speaking of snacks..." Philip leaned forward. "What type of snacks should we get for our movie room? And we need to protect it to prevent other people from going in there."

"Twizzlers." Evie grinned. "We can't have movies without Twizzlers."

"M&Ms." Raine fiddled with the edge of her menu. "I always have M&Ms when I watch movies at home."

"Reese's pieces." Sara ran her fingers through her hair. "And popcorn. No movie is complete without popcorn."

"We can secure all those. I've made a contact." Philip leaned back and allowed a dramatic pause which had little effect. "We should be able to get a good price too."

"What about the seating?" Adrien looked at him. "Have we made any progress with that?"

"The groundskeeper removed what was in there this morning." Raine wrinkled her nose. "He said they were infested with rats and we were lucky we didn't get bitten."

Sara's hand went to her mouth and her eyes widened in horror.

"Don't worry. We would have kept you safe." Philip put his hand on hers. "You wouldn't have been hurt."

William rolled his eyes.

The fairy brought their food and everyone watched Adrien as he looked at his selection of snacks.

"I think they've covered everything." Sara looked at it. "You have Hershey's, Dingdongs. Twinkies, Twizzlers—oh, and some taffy. I haven't had taffy in forever."

She stole a piece of saltwater taffy and popped it into her mouth with an expression of joy.

Raine savored her pie, which was by far the best she'd ever enjoyed. The root beer also seemed particularly good. She assumed it was the fairy influence. Whatever it was, she wouldn't complain.

"So, which movies will we get first?" Evie asked, waving her spoon in the air. "I think *Creature from the Black Lagoon*."

"That's a classic." Raine gestured with her fork. "We need to have *The Brides of Dracula* too."

"You can't do *Brides of Dracula* before *Dracula*." William finished his last chip. "That was the first Hammer *Dracula* film. They should be respected and watched in order."

"Respected?" Philip laughed. "Come on, they're ancient B movies."

"Just because they're old and cheesy doesn't mean they don't deserve a little respect." Adrien poked at his Dingdong. "I think they should be watched in order."

"How many should we line up?" Evie took a few nerds from the center bowl. "Four?"

"We need one more." Philip finished his ginger ale. "The *Curse of Frankenstein* gets my vote."

Everyone nodded agreement.

"We have to do *An American Werewolf in London* at some point." Raine pushed her plate away. "It's too good to ignore."

"I think we have a pretty good line-up to start with here." Philip smiled. "So, we start with the *Creature from the Black Lagoon?*"

"Absolutely." Evie brushed a crumb from her shirt. "I think it's the perfect starting point."

The waitress returned and they each paid their share.

"Where should we go next?" Evie stood and stepped aside to let Raine out. "And who will put some magic around our movie room?"

"Adrien and I can handle the magic on the room." Philip moved aside to let the elf out. "Don't you think?"

Adrien nodded. "It shouldn't take too much work. No one goes down there anyway."

They climbed the spiraling staircase and wandered through the bookshop. The main pathway outside had grown busier. The group scrambled into a jewelry store when they spotted someone who looked suspiciously like Professor Hudson. When it was safe, they darted out and chose a narrower walkway away from the main hustle and bustle.

The shops there were less uniform and contained more niche products like enchanted paints, and a shop was devoted to all forms of fizzing candies, chocolates, and some cakes. They peered through windows occasionally as they wandered aimlessly.

Slowly, the scenery around them began to change. The shops were fewer and farther apart and more houses appeared. The number of witches and wizards dwindled, replaced now by druids. Vines and trees flourished in abundance, and the sounds of hundreds of conversations faded into the rustling of an ancient forest. Raine looked around in absolute awe. She'd never dreamt that such a place even existed.

CHAPTER EIGHT

They made their way around houses formed in the trunks of great trees that arched their boughs overhead. Children played between the vines and skittered up into the lower branches with skill and ease.

"Another one disappeared last week. Elle, this time."

"Elle? My word!"

Raine frowned and slowed her pace to listen to the conversation. She knew it wasn't entirely ethical, but it sounded as though people had vanished.

"Yes. I heard that she went to bed as normal and was gone in the morning."

"Did she have someone on the side?"

"No. She loves Jake and has two little boys to think of. They were devastated."

Raine hurried to catch up with the rest of the group but the conversation replayed continuously in her head. They looked through stalls offering charms and ointments, but

Raine's heart wasn't in it. She was sure that people had vanished and that wasn't the type of thing she could simply ignore.

"Has Zoe arrived yet?" And older woman frowned at a younger one. "It's not like her to be late."

"I haven't seen her."

"Oh, please don't tell me she's gone too."

Raine couldn't resist. She walked up to the women and ignored the look of horror on Evie's face.

"Excuse me, but did you say people have disappeared?"

The older woman pursed her lips but the younger woman simply said, "You shouldn't eavesdrop."

"I'm sorry, I didn't mean to overhear, but people going missing is very serious."

The younger woman sighed and made a shooing motion at Raine. An older man waved her over. His long grey hair had been braided with green ribbons through it. Deep wrinkles surrounded his eyes and showed a well-lived life.

"Six druids have gone now." He leaned in a little closer. "No one knows why or how."

Raine's curiosity was thoroughly piqued now. "There's no evidence at all? Are there any connections between them?" She wished she had her notebook on her. "Are they all taken from a similar area?"

The old man smiled, and Sara tugged on her arm.

"One of 'em had an old holly leaf on her pillow in the morning. There's no connection that I can see. And they're taken from all over the community."

Raine tried to think what questions Uncle Jerry would have followed that up with. "And there are no suspects?

No one who's been removed from the community recently?"

The old man shook his head. "Not a soul."

"Thank you for your time." Raine turned to her friends. "I'm sorry."

She rejoined the group.

"That FBI instinct kicked in, did it?" William smirked at her. "Anything interesting?"

"I think so, but I don't know where to go next." Raine ran it through her mind. "Druids have disappeared."

"People vanish all the time." Philip took the next right turn. "They move on. It happens."

"One of them left two small children behind." Raine glanced over her shoulder to see a teenage druid watching them. "People don't up and leave small children."

"Does this mean you'll investigate?" Evie nudged her gently. "I think it could be pretty cool to look into it."

Philip picked up the pace a little.

"Are we going somewhere in particular?" Evie looked at the changing scenery. "I don't remember us discussing anywhere."

"We're going to find the Ifrit." Sara beamed. "For William. I thought it'd be nice for him to get to know some of his people."

He stopped dead in his tracks and glared at her. "Why would you?" He closed his eyes and exhaled slowly. "I appreciate the thought, but I do not think it's a good idea."

"Why not?" Philip turned to look at him. "It could help you learn your magic."

William clenched his jaw and moved beside Raine. "Do not forget that I warned you this was a bad idea." He stared at the other boy with a hard expression. "Because this will go wrong."

Philip continued and Sara moved to walk beside him. Raine and Evie walked on either side of William to offer him support.

"We don't have to if you really don't want to." Evie touched his shoulder. "We can turn around."

William shook his head. "I will not show fear to him."

Raine was tempted to march up to Philip and give him a piece of her mind, but she didn't want to upset William farther. She was sure that the wizard had a good heart, but he pushed too hard in his little quest to ensure he was the leader.

They walked in silence between the shops and around corners until flames flickered ahead. William slowed his pace and tensed as he watched the fire dance across the walls and along the edges of the pathway. He could feel in his blood that the Ifrit were close by. They would reject him for his impure blood once again.

The group walked between the flames. Sara tied her shirt around her waist in response to the increase in air temperature. Raine looked around for possible attackers. She could feel eyes watching her, but they were hidden behind the fire and within the dark buildings. Philip paused to look at a crystal shop with animated salamanders in the window.

A pair of large Ifrit stepped out of the shop next door and looked at the group. Their short hair flickered with flames that gleamed the reflection in their eyes.

"And what brings you here this fine morning?" The

broader of the two studied them casually. "Do you want to cut a deal?"

"No. We wanted to introduce our friend to his people." Philip gestured to William. "His father was an Ifrit."

The two glared at William. Their hair took on a blue hue as it danced and swirled furiously.

"Abomination." The first man said as they took a step closer. "You will never be welcome here."

Something snapped within William. He'd heard that for most of his life and could no longer tolerate the rejection and abuse. "I am no abomination. My father loved my mother." His hands balled into fists. "Ifrit blood runs through my veins."

Flames licked over his fists and hair and his eyes shifted to a dark orange. The two Ifrit were joined by three more of their kin.

"This child claims he is of Ifrit blood." The first pointed derisively. "His mother was a human."

Growls and muttered curses cut through the air. Raine assessed them for weaknesses in their stance. They were all far larger than her and on fire, but she wouldn't stand by and let them hurt William.

"You bring shame on the Ifrit."

"How dare you come here?"

"I have every right to walk here." William took a step forward. "My father was an honored Ifrit."

Evie tugged on his arm, but he ignored her. He wouldn't back down now.

"You will never be worthy of his blood," the leader snarled.

"I bear his fire." William held up his fire-swathed hands. "I will be respected for what I am."

A ring of fire burst from the ground. Sara gasped and leapt backward. Adrien formed a sword from thin air and Raine prepared to defend her friends by whatever means necessary.

The leader stepped through the fire and pointed at William.

"You will suffer for your disrespect and arrogance, part-breed. Never again will you step foot amongst our kind. Nor will you claim our blood."

The other Ifrit whispered something in a language Raine didn't recognize. The flames flared skywards and enveloped them in a flickering bubble of heat and smoke. Suddenly, it died away, and the Ifrit slipped into their homes and shops.

"We should leave." Evie pulled on William's arm. "Now."

"What happened?" Raine looked at where the Ifrit had stood. "What did they do?"

Adrien put his hand on her shoulder and pushed her gently in the direction in which Evie dragged William.

"I believe they cursed William." His gaze searched the shadows warily. "Hopefully, it was a small curse."

Raine wanted to go back and demand they undo whatever curse they had placed on him. It wasn't his fault that he had been born to the parents he had.

"This is your fault." Sara gestured at Philip. "He told you that it was a bad idea."

Philip stopped and folded his arms. "No, you can't put this all on me." He looked Sara in the eye. "You were as eager to show him his family, or community, or however you put it."

Sara threw her arms up in exasperation. "Fine. You know what? Fine." She turned her back on him. "I got him cursed too."

"Can we undo it?" Raine asked Evie. "Is there a potion or something?"

"We need to see what type of curse it is first." She looked at William for any obvious signs. "We can't do anything until we know that."

"Should we tell the headmistress?" Raine chewed her bottom lip. "A curse sounds serious."

"No way." Evie put her hand up. "We'd be in detention for the whole year."

Raine pushed that idea aside. There had to be something on curses in the library. Maybe there was a book or two on Ifrit curses specifically.

Adrien's sword vanished into the ether and he put his arm around William's shoulders.

"We'll help you with whatever it is." He guided his friend around a group of gossiping witches. "We're in this together."

"Look. I'm sorry you got cursed. I should have listened." Philip held up his hands. "Forgive me?"

William grunted and refused to look at him. The Ifrit could be very dangerous. Who knew what malediction they'd placed on him? He didn't feel like he was dying but that didn't mean much.

"We should head back to the school before they notice we're missing." Sara stopped to look at a pretty dress. "We'll never be able to come here again if we're caught."

They hurried back to the spiral staircase where Evie helped Raine form a stealth spell. Raine's own magic felt weak and sluggish but her friend helped her coax it out and wrap it around her in a weird bubble. She felt the spell against her skin and wanted to wipe it away but resisted the urge as they climbed the stairs.

Their spells faded as they emerged behind a group of juniors. Thankfully, no professors caught them, and they headed toward their soon to be movie room.

"What do we do about seating now?" Evie sighed softly. "I was looking forward to our movie night."

"I have us covered." Philip spread his arms wide. "I cut a deal with a senior who's giving us extra-large bean bags."

Raine raised an eyebrow. "And what are you giving them?"

"Don't worry about that." Philip shrugged. "I'm an entrepreneur. We'll have our movie room. That's what matters."

"We must remember to put magic around the lock. As we said earlier, it won't take too much." Adrien ran his fingertips over the smooth wood.

William walked with his shoulders hunched and his eyes downcast. The experience with the Ifrit had only brought back bad memories. Evie pulled a Twinkie from her pocket and offered it to him.

"No one can be sad when they have a twinkie."

He laughed, a short, harsh sound but it reached his eyes and relaxed him a little as he took the twinkie.

They entered what would be their movie room and found a set of brooms and dustpans waiting for them.

"I think the groundskeeper has left a message for us."

Sara grabbed a broom. "It would be nice to have it dust-free in here."

Raine took another and swept in the far corner while she thought over her experiences in the kemana. The vanishing druids were something she needed to know more about. Once they had cleaned the movie room, she would head to the library and have a look. She could also investigate the Ifrit curses while she was there but needed to make time to visit the stable. Horace had said she could give Smoke his evening feed that day. She enjoyed spending short periods with the young horse and looked forward to working with him come spring.

"Earth to Raine." Sara waved her hand in front of Raine's face. "Are you in there?"

"Sorry." She blushed. "I was thinking about everything."

"We were saying it'd be a good idea to go to the library and look into Ifrit curses." She put her hands on her hips. "We thought you'd be excited."

"I wouldn't say excited." Raine leaned her broom against the wall. "But yes, I had hoped to look into the curses."

"Of course you did." Sara put her arm around Raine's shoulders. "We have an hour before dinner."

"Oh!" Evie chewed on her bottom lip. "Did I tell you that I started a Baking Club? With the kitchen pixies. There are only three of us so far. Would you like to join us, Raine?"

"Why only Raine?" Sara put her free hand on her hip. "I might enjoy it, and William looks like he could be a wonderful baker."

"I could burn water," he said flatly and everyone laughed.

"All the more reason to join the club." Evie put her hands together in a pleading gesture. "Please?"

William sighed. "Fine. But don't blame me when I accidentally burn the kitchen down."

Evie threw her hands up and grinned. She went to hug him, but he narrowed his eyes and she stopped.

"You'll love it. And you can eat whatever you make."

"You're assuming I'd want to."

CHAPTER NINE

Raine climbed out of bed with a smile on her face. It was the first day of classes and hers started with potions with Professor Fowler. The girls raced to breakfast where they found the guys already eating.

"We have potions first." Sara sat quickly. "What about you guys?"

"Potions too." Philip stirred his oatmeal. "I'm more interested in transfiguration which is second period."

"Yes." Sara bit into her Danish pastry. "Potions looks boring."

"I'm looking forward to potions." Evie took a sip of her orange juice. "I find potion-making soothing."

Sara pulled a mock-disgusted face and grinned at her. "Each to their own, I suppose." She turned to Adrien. "Aren't the Louper try-outs later?"

"Yes." The elf finished his pain au chocolate. "I earned my spot on the team."

"That's arrogant." Philip looked sharply at him. "You're a freshman."

"And?" The elf shrugged. "I am aware of my abilities. That is not arrogance."

"How are you feeling today?" Raine smiled at William. "Any sign of the curse?"

"I'm not sure." William poked at his omelet. "Perhaps. I had nightmares all night."

"That was probably stress." Philip finished his juice. "It's the first day of classes. It's normal."

William nodded and finished his juice.

They left the dining room in record time and joined the throng of students in the hallways. Kerry and a dark-haired older girl Raine didn't recognize blocked their path and looked at the younger students.

"Ah, look, it's the mutts," Kerry sneered. "It's quaint that you've all joined together."

"I can't believe they let someone in who had no idea about her magic." The other girl looked pointedly at Raine. "The kitsune and half Ifrit are ridiculous, but at least they have some magic."

Raine rolled her eyes. "I'm sorry you're so lacking in talent that you're threatened by us." She smiled sweetly. "You must lead difficult lives."

Kerry narrowed her eyes but one of the professors intervened. "Come along, get to class."

"What was her problem?" Sara watched Kerry stalk away. "And how do they know about us?"

"Word spreads." Philip shrugged. "Knowledge is power and all that. Gossip is currency."

William sighed and put his hands in his pockets as he

hunched his shoulders. He had hoped for a little peace and understanding at the school.

The group entered the potions lab where Professor Fowler waited beside her desk. Her mane of bright red hair spread around her like a halo. The Light Elf smiled politely and looked pointedly at the remaining desks. Evie sat beside Raine and Sara took the seat next to Philip in front of them. William and Adrien sat to their left.

"Good morning and welcome to your first class on plants in potions. I am Professor Fowler. We will begin with a simple practical lesson where you will make a vitality potion. Please do not try to tweak the recipe. And please do not make something explode."

Raine looked at the dark marks on the ceiling overhead when the professor mentioned explosions.

A blond wizard raised his hand.

"Yes?" Professor Fowler nodded to him.

"Aren't vitality potions merely worthless colored water that scam-artists pedal in the kemanas?"

The professor's expression tightened. "I will not comment on those potions available in the kemana—which, I might add, freshmen are not allowed into. This potion is viable and efficient. If it's made correctly, that is. If made incorrectly, it will do nothing but turn your lips bright purple for a few hours."

She looked at the students who already looked around for distractions. "A vitality potion is used when someone feels rundown or is otherwise in need of an energy boost. They are sometimes used alongside healing potions to help a patient heal a little quicker."

Another wizard raised his hand.

Professor Fowler nodded to him.

"They're energy drinks? Like the caffeine-rich ones the humans use?"

"They have a more long-term effect and do not have the addictive qualities that the caffeine-based drinks do. They also do more than make the person more awake. They boost their overall energy levels and healing ability."

"I can see business potential here." Philip looked at Raine and Evie. "They sound perfect for exam time."

Raine had to admit that he had a point, especially for those students who didn't want to put in the effort to brew the potions themselves.

"You will need a permit to sell the potions to your fellow students, and each potion must be quality checked and confirmed to do what you advertise." Professor Fowler handed Philip his recipe card. "If you wish to attempt it, you'll need to fill out a number of forms, all of which are available from the administration office."

"Thank you." He took the recipe card. "That was very helpful and good to know. I'm sure you saved me many hours and headaches."

The professor smiled and continued handing out the recipe cards. Philip was already thinking of ways he could get around the forms and professors interfering in his business plans. There was money to be made there and he wouldn't let a little bureaucracy get in his way.

Raine and Evie looked at their recipe card. Evie smiled with relief. It was the same one she had made for a few years with her aunt.

Raine read the recipe three times to be sure she understood everything before she looked at the ingredients the professor had set before them. Each herb came in a neat little glass bottle with a handwritten label on it. She picked each one up and confirmed which was which before she set them out in the order they'd be used.

"Don't worry." Evie dragged the small cauldron closer to them. "I've made this hundreds of times. I'll help you through it."

"How much innate magic do you need for potions?" Raine set the stirrer down beside the cauldron. "It's a lower magic pursuit, isn't it?"

"It doesn't require as much as say transfiguration, but your magic definitely has an impact on the potion." Evie pointed to the recipe card. "See here... when you stir it, you add some of your own magic into the brew. That will make small alterations to the final product, which is why even if everyone follows the same recipe to the letter, the results will all be slightly different."

"Begin brewing." The professor sat behind her desk. "And please don't make anything explode."

Evie pointed to the recipe. "So, we start with holy basil and goldenrod." She picked up the two bottles. "We're only making a small batch so a teaspoon of each is all the recipe calls for."

Raine measured the holy basil out with absolute precision and placed it into the cauldron. Evie had a far more relaxed approach as she'd started brewing potions when she was eleven or so. She knew exactly how much she could get away with and how to get the best from her recipes.

"Now, we add the colloidal silver water." Evie handed

the water to Raine. "One drop at a time. Try to make sure each drop lands in the center of the cauldron."

Raine took her time and dripped the liquid exactly where she wanted it. Sara, on the other hand, folded her arms and glared at the bubbling cauldron as though it had personally offended her.

"It says we're supposed to simmer it." Philip looked at the sheet. "That doesn't look like simmering."

"It's simmering." Sara pointed at it. "There's a steady flow of bubbles."

"You should turn the heat down." Evie frowned. "A simmer is far gentler than that. You almost have it at a rolling boil."

"It'll go faster this way." Sara smiled. "And then it'll be over and done with."

Evie sighed and said nothing more. She knew their potion would be spoiled but if Sara didn't want to listen that was up to her.

She guided Raine through the following steps. They added the oak leaf and stirred it ten times clockwise while bringing it to a gentle simmer. They both watched it carefully and Evie began to relax when it took on the slightly sweet, heathery scent that meant it was almost done. Sara and Philip's potion had gone a sickly green and smelled of old cracked leather, a sure sign that it was thoroughly burnt.

William had allowed Adrien to take control of their potion making. He lacked faith in his magic to do much more than watch as the elf stirred and poured. Adrien handed him the stirrer, though, when it came to the second round of stirring.

"You should put some of your magic into it." He gestured to the simmering potion. "It will be good for you to get used to feeling your magic in a controlled environment."

William paused a moment before he took the stirrer. His magic writhed within him and he fought to keep it under control as he stirred the potion slowly. None of this felt natural to him. Ifrit were beings of fire and chaos. He refused to be caged by his heritage, though. With intense focus, he allowed a small sliver of his magic to enter the potion. To his relief, it didn't explode or change color.

Professor Fowler walked around the classroom and looked at the final products which the students had poured into beakers. She sighed when she looked at Sara and Philip's green ooze.

"And tell me, how is someone supposed to drink that?" She held it up to the light. "I'm not sure you'll even get it out the beaker."

"It's a new format. Instead of drinking a potion, we'll offer vitality bites." Philip turned his charm up to eleven. "Do you think it would work?"

The professor handed him a spoon and the beaker. "Take a bite."

He fought to keep the horror off his face but even he had to admit he'd brought this on himself. The spoon barely dented the ooze within the beaker, but he managed to break a small piece off. The green stuff tasted of old leather and rotting leaves. Philip looked wildly for some water to wash the taste from his mouth.

Evie handed him her beaker of potion, which was the correct pale golden color and liquid consistency. He gulped it down and felt the soft buzzing sensation as it immediately took effect.

"Well done. That was a beautifully brewed potion," the professor said to Evie and Raine.

Raine wanted to say it was all Evie, but her friend squeezed her arm and whispered, "It was a joint effort."

Professor Fowler was a little disappointed at the number of potions that had not met the required standard. The recipe was very simple, and the results didn't give her much hope for the future of the class. To her surprise, the young half-Ifrit had worked well with the elf and produced something close to perfect. A flicker of fire could be seen in the gold, but she suspected that would only make the potion dissipate faster, which wasn't a disaster.

"I must remind you to read the recipe very carefully in the future. As we have ten minutes left, we'll cover some basic terms that I had wrongly assumed you understood." The professor wrote on the board. "A simmer is a gentle point below a boil. It should not produce lots of bubbles or, as the term rolling boil suggests, roll."

She continued to explain basic cooking terminology that they would need to know for future potions. Sara watched the clock closely and itched to move on to the next class. Raine, however, took careful notes even though she knew most of the terms. She wanted to be sure.

While the rest of the students practically ran out of the potions lab, Raine hung back and approached the professor.

"Would you mind recommending some books I can read in the library to help me better understand potions?"

She shifted her book bag. "In particular, how to weave my own magic into them."

The professor looked absolutely delighted. "I will pass a note to the gnomes for you. They'll have a list waiting for you after your classes."

"Thank you."

Raine hurried into the hallway where her friends waited for her.

"Did you seriously ask for extra reading?" Sara looked aghast. "Why would you do that to yourself?"

"I want to succeed." Raine shrugged. "And reading will help me do that."

"I wouldn't mind never seeing another potion again." Sara led the way to the transfiguration class. "They're so tedious."

"Potions are very useful and often overlooked." Evie dodged an elf who peered at a poster on the wall. "There are plenty of times when you can't throw a fireball, for instance, but a potion will resolve the problem."

Sara didn't look convinced.

Professor Hodges leaned against his desk as he watched the students filter in. They all had a look of excitement about them, which they would quickly lose when they found out this was strictly a theory lesson. Everyone was energized by the thought of transfiguration, but they didn't understand how complicated it was. They simply wanted to change one thing to another without putting in the hard work it required.

"Good morning. I am Professor Hodges and I will teach you transfiguration. Pull out your notebooks as we have a lot of ground to cover today."

To Sara's dismay, he handed out textbooks.

"We'll begin with page five. Read pages five and six and we'll discuss the information you acquire there in fifteen minutes."

Raine was quite happy to read. She opened her textbook and sank into the world of knowledge. The pages in question related to the ethics of transfiguration, which made sense to her. It seemed like a valuable starting point.

"Today, we will look at the ethics of transfiguration and then move into the magic involved."

A green-haired witch raised her hand.

"No, we will not do practical work today." The professor shifted his weight as the students moved restlessly. "Transfiguration is the act of transforming one thing into another. The most obvious is that of shifters like me. We have the ability to change from a human into a wolf and back again."

He looked around the room and waited for any sneers or comments. Shifters weren't well regarded among the magical community. No one spoke, however, so he continued.

"This year, you will work with small changes such as the transformation of a rose into a lily. However, we must first investigate the ethics of changing things to begin with. It is considered dark magic to transform a living, sentient being into another form unless it is, of course, yourself."

Another witch raised her hand. "Will you teach us how to transform ourselves?"

"No. That is beyond the scope of this school. You will need to study that at a higher education facility."

Professor Hodges heard the mutters about shifters that

time. He brushed it all aside and simply smiled. He'd grown up with such commentary and it wouldn't affect him now.

He continued with a familiar talk on the ethics of transfiguration that he had given many times over the years that he'd taught the class. Most of the students developed a glassy-eyed expression after a few minutes but one listened to his every word and took many notes. He thought it was the girl Agent Connor had accompanied.

Once he moved into the actual magic behind transfiguration, the students seemed a little more alert.

"So, you're telling us that magic is a living thing?" a Light Elf demanded.

Professor Hodges smiled politely. "That is something for your philosophy of magic professor to cover. I am telling you to think of it as a living entity. That way, you will treat it with respect and approach it in a way that will enable you to use it for transfiguration. If you try to beat it into submission, the object will resist you and the magic will lock down, thus ensuring it does not transform at all."

"Do we really have philosophy of magic classes?" Sara whispered to Raine and Evie. "That sounds hideous."

"I haven't seen it on our class schedule." Raine retrieved her roster to check. "I think it sounds interesting, though."

Sara rolled her eyes. "I'm interested in practical magic."

"Would you care to share with the class?" Professor Hodges looked pointedly at Sara. "I'm sure we'll all find your thoughts fascinating."

"I merely said how interesting the process of transfiguration is." Sara straightened her spine and smiled. "And how much I appreciate you taking the time to teach us."

"Then you'll have no problems acing the test next week."

Sara cringed as the other students glared at her. One day, she'd learn when to keep her mouth shut.

Once class was over, Raine approached the professor and asked for a list of texts she could read to better help her understand the mechanics of transfiguration. He smiled for the first time all day and gladly gave her a rather long list. Raine hoped the gnomes wouldn't mind that she spent so much time in the library, but she wanted to understand how everything operated. She hoped that if she understood the inner workings, it would help her to get to grips with her magic.

Raine hurried across the grass toward the stables after dinner as she'd promised Horace she would work with Smoke every morning and evening when he was fed. She felt as though she had made progress with the young horse and was grateful for the opportunity.

Smoke had his head over his stable door when she walked into the barn. He watched Horace give the big chestnut thoroughbred opposite him his hay for the night. Raine stepped into the feed room and picked up the bucket. He leaned his head a little farther over the door when he saw her approach.

"You know how this works." She held the bucket out of his reach and stretched her hand toward his forehead. "You let me touch you, then I give you food."

She could run her fingertips around the base of his ears

and now edged down his neck. If things continued at that pace, she hoped to be able to enter the stall with him and touch his withers and back.

"He's coming on nicely." Horace stood next to her. "I reckon he'll be a fantastic horse next year. He simply needs time."

"I agree." Raine held the bucket for him to take his next mouthful. "He has fantastic conformation. I think he'll make a good jumper."

"He has a good kind eye, too. I think he'll give his all to the right rider."

Horace wandered off to finish bedding down the other horses for the night, leaving Raine to finish up with Smoke. He showed far more interest in the world outside his stall now, and Horace said he was calmer when they mucked out. Raine hoped to get a halter on him next week and lead him.

She added a mental note to find some books on groundwork positive reinforcement training for young horses once Smoke was finished for the night. Her list of books was almost as long as her forearm. The gnomes would either be very happy to see her or upset that she hoped to conquer so many texts. Raine still hadn't quite figured out their relationship with the books. She knew they guarded them, but she wasn't sure how they felt about other people using them. It seemed like a very rude question to ask.

Horace settled himself on the bench in front of his fire as the stars emerged. "Good night, Horace." Raine gave him a little wave. "I'll see you in the morning."

"Enjoy your evening in the library."

Raine hurried to the main building, determined to start on her reading. She knew the others were setting up the bean bags down in the movie room and felt a little guilty at not being there with them. Still, she had a lot to get through. Unlike them, she didn't have a firm grasp on her magic or how to summon it, so she had to learn about it first.

"Don't forget Baking Club later," Evie called out from across the main hallway.

Raine had completely forgotten. There went her plans to spend the entire evening in the library. Still, she wanted to support Evie and baking sounded as though it would be helpful in improving her potions.

"I'll be there," Raine called back.

She had one hour in the library and intended to put it to good use.

CHAPTER TEN

Raine claimed a table to herself. Three stacks of books waited for attention as she scribbled in two different notebooks. She'd settled into her classes and her professors had formed the habit of sending a list of relevant texts to the library after each class. The gnomes were now accustomed to her cheerful smile as she arrived each afternoon and began on her latest collection of books.

It was a Saturday and she currently divided her time between potions, the history of the druids, and Ifrit magic. She refused to ignore the vanishing druids. Sara and her friends planned to return to the kemana that afternoon. The kitsune desperately wanted to go to Bubble and Fizz, and Raine would use any excuse to get more details from the druids.

William took the seat opposite her and peered over the stacks of books. He looked exhausted with deep circles around his eyes and a small frown on his face. He lifted the top book from the Ifrit stack and his frown deepened.

"I suppose I should be glad they've only given me night-mares so far." He flipped through the book. "They could have turned me into a salamander."

Raine looked up at him in alarm. "Are they any worse? The nightmares, I mean." She put her pen down. "I hate to say it, but you look absolutely awful. Have you spoken to the nurse about a sleep aid?"

William closed the book and hunched his shoulders. "The sleep aid didn't do anything. Evie gave me one her family swears by and it helped a little more." He raised his eyes. "They're still getting worse though. I can feel their fingers around my neck when I wake up."

He rubbed his throat subconsciously and Raine checked for red marks there. She didn't see any, but she'd read that Ifrit magic could be insidious. People assumed it was all fire and some trickery, but they worked on people's minds too.

Adrien flopped down beside William and looked at the stacks of books. "How can you possibly read all of these?" He gestured at them in bewilderment. "There must be fifteen here."

"Magic." Raine grinned. "I alternate between topics when my mind freezes. It's more efficient that way."

Adrien huffed.

"How was training?" William studied the elf as he sprawled in his chair. "You look like you've run three marathons."

"I think I did." Adrien ran his fingers through his hair. "The captain wants to work on the wizard's stamina, so we were sent around the assault course. Three times."

William smirked. "Poor elf, having to work for a change." He folded his arms. "Such a hard life."

Adrien ignored the little dig and returned his attention to Raine. "What are today's subjects of interest?"

"I'm trying to understand what went wrong in potions class. Evie said that the plant growth potion is a very simple one and she has no idea what happened. I followed the recipe to the letter, so it must have something to do with my magic." She pointed to the middle stack. "I'm sure there's something we can do to help the druids, and we have to help William."

Adrien ran his finger down the spines of the Ifrit stack. "Hand me an Ifrit book. I'll see if I can find anything." He held his hand out. "I'd rather my friend stopped suffering."

William allowed himself a small private smile. Things hadn't been easy for him at the school. Between the curse and the other students' response to his heritage, he'd had a hard time. Hearing the elf call him a friend gave him a small sense of belonging, something he hadn't experienced before.

Raine handed Adrien the fourth book from the top. "I haven't been through that one yet."

"How's the horse coming along?" Adrien opened the book. "Have you started leading him yet?"

"Yes." Raine beamed with pride. "He accepts a halter now and we've begun leading and moving away from pressure. We're going far slower than we would with a normal youngster because he's so scared of humans. He's coming on beautifully, though."

"Will you ride him in the spring?" William took an Ifrit book. "Or will he still be too wild?"

"Horace has said I can bring him on myself." Raine picked up her pen. "We'll have magic to make sure I don't break any bones."

They each began reading their respective book and sat in a comfortable silence for a while before Sara and the others arrived. Philip turned his seat backward and sat astride while he smirked at them all reading.

"Has she converted you to her bookworm ways?" He lifted the cover on William's book. "We've finally finished the movie room. We should be able to have our first movie night soon. The DVDs are on their way."

"Have you seen Professor Powell?" Sara leaned closer conspiratorially. "He looks awful. Rumor has it he's been cursed."

Raine closed her book and looked sharply at her. "He did seem pale in the last class, but I'm sure he's simply ill." She brought her other notebook closer. "Why do they think he's been cursed?"

"Because he never gets ill." Philip flipped through the book closest to him. "Are we ready to head down into the kemana later?"

Evie squeezed Raine's shoulder. "I'll help you with your spell. You got really close last time."

One of the gnomes headed in their direction.

"Can you believe it's almost time for the big Halloween dance?" Sara played with a strand of her hair. "I've already chosen my dress. What about you?"

"My uncle is sending a dress for me." Raine chewed on the top of her pen. "Something black and suitable."

Sara's mouth dropped open. "You won't choose it yourself? This is your first big school dance."

Raine shrugged and didn't look up from her book.

"My aunt has made me something." Evie fidgeted with the cuff of her sweater. "I designed it but I'm awful at sewing."

Sara shook her head in disappointment at their nonchalance. "I've found something in this quaint little boutique. I have a list of spells I'll use to make everything perfect." She looked at Philip. "Are you ready for the dance?"

He shrugged. "It's easy for guys. We only need a black suit."

"Will they do anything with the The World in Between?" Adrien closed his book. "In France, we usually offer up small orbs of light magic in the hope that it will help those stuck there move to where they're supposed to be."

"People get stuck there?" Raine looked sharply at him. "In the World in Between?"

The elf looked solemn. "I don't believe it is too frequent, but it happens. If the stories are true, the headmistress was trapped there for many years."

Raine glanced in the direction of the door and considered whether Ms. Berens would tell her what it was like in there. She had been called a black hole for knowledge by her father and that particular topic was no exception.

Xander sat on Mara's couch and tried to take a deep breath. It didn't matter how much he attempted to calm himself, his lungs would not expand enough. The nurse had given him a full exam, much to his chagrin. He hadn't been ill in three decades thanks to a healthy lifestyle and magic. Then suddenly, he woke up one morning feeling lethargic and it only got worse from there.

A set of four black circles had formed on his ribs. He had researched that in books and asked the nurse about it, but no one seemed to know anything helpful. Finally, he had no choice but to see Mara in the hope that perhaps she had some idea what was happening.

He sat shirtless and vulnerable as she prodded gently at the black marks. He felt the familiar cool edge of her magic and happy memories welled up. There had been a time when he looked forward to her hands on his body, but that was not one of them. He had broken her heart many years before and they had kept secrets from each other ever since—big secrets tied their pasts and their families and things that couldn't be pushed aside easily.

Mara's magic pressed against his own as she probed for the source of this mysterious malady. Her mouth pressed into a thin line when she finally caught a thread of something. A sliver of dark magic. Of course, she had suspected as much. It took a great deal to make Xander Powell ill, but feeling it now made it real.

"I know it has to be dark magic, Mara. Do you know what type?" Xander used frustration as a shield against his fears and vulnerability. "A curse?"

Mara pulled away and ran the sensations of the magic through her mind.

"No. I believe it's a poison." She stood and went to her bookshelf. "I may need to look in the private library and even the books in the vault."

Xander squeezed his eyes closed. Poison meant that someone close to him had slipped it into his food or drink. He had been so careful with whom he allowed close to him, and yet he had still been betrayed. The list of potential enemies who would want him harmed or dead was far longer than he could remember. It would take him months to write down every name, and even then, he would be sure to miss a few.

"Have you—"

"No. I haven't eaten or drunk anything unusual. Nor has anyone given me any gifts."

Xander regretted cutting her off when he saw the storm in her eyes.

"I am trying to help you." She exhaled slowly. "Must you be such a stubborn ass?"

He looked away. "I do not allow people close, Mara, you know that." He licked his lips. "I prepare all my own food or drink, or the kitchen pixies do. We trust those pixies with our lives. Their loyalty to us and the school is unrivaled."

"Which means that someone slipped something into your own supplies." Mara sat at the edge of the sofa. "We must find out which poison it is so we can counteract it."

She hated seeing him like this. He sat tall and proud, but she could see the slight rounding of his shoulders and the soft glassiness in his eyes. Xander Powell was the strongest, most passionate man she'd had the pleasure to meet. Now, however, she could see him slowly losing his shine and she didn't know what to do about it.

Xander pulled his shirt on and drank the last of his water.

"I will go to the private library and see what I can find."
He gave her a soft smile. "Thank you. I don't say that often
enough."

Mara stood. "I'll join you." She walked to where she had
left her boots. "I won't lose my dark magic professor that
easily. You're a difficult breed to replace."

He snorted and tried to hide his smile. He had never
gotten over Mara. They had been separated for decades
now and his heart still fluttered when she smiled at him.
There would never be another woman for him.

The sun hung low in the sky when they stepped into
the daylight. Dorvu flew slowly overhead and puffed small
clouds of frosty air as he amused himself. The dragon had
missed the seniors who recently graduated and the newer
students hadn't given him as much attention as he would
have liked.

The dragon planned to make them an ice-rink the
following day in the hope that they would see him as a
friend and spend more time with him. There was only so
much hunting and sunbathing he could do after all.

Xander and Mara walked slowly across the swathe of
grass toward the main building. His breath labored and she
grew more concerned. He walked with a stubborn pride
that almost covered the weakness that filtered through
him, but she knew him well enough to see his steps falter
and the strain on his face.

They entered the main building and made their way
past the bustling students who laughed and joked about
something Mara didn't quite catch. A pair of freshmen
whispered and pointed in the direction of the dining hall.
She hoped they hadn't planned to mess with the pixies.

They would regret it for a very long time if they did. The staff were incredibly kind and generous to those who respected them but would make a student's life very uncomfortable should they feel badly treated.

Xander paused for half a beat at the bottom of the second flight of stairs before he ascended. Mara continued, knowing that to stop for him would only wound his pride more.

They reached the heavy, dark wooden door and she used the special and frequently changed combination of magic to unlock it. The private library contained the dangerous and very rare books that professors and faculty had gathered between them over the decades. When they had opened the school, they had combined their resources into the library that stood before them. There were several tomes that many people, including the dark magic families, would very much like to acquire. These, however, were kept in the restricted section and she'd leave that for last as a gnome had to be present. Perhaps they might find something here to make that unnecessary.

The room was far smaller than the main library but still contained floor to ceiling bookshelves packed with books of every shape, size, and color. Mara made her way to the section on dark magic poisons which contained a great many texts.

They made an unspoken agreement to split the section into two halves. Mara took the left while Xander took the right and worked in a comfortable silence to study the spines to discern which might be most relevant. Mara selected six books to begin with. Each covered a variety of poisons from all around the world.

It would be a very long afternoon.

Librarian Decker looked at Raine and her friends. He'd watched the girl come to the library every day since school had started. She'd been diligent in her reading and covered every topic that her professors gave her and more. He'd never seen a student quite as committed as she was. The girl had started to grow on him and he didn't know how he felt about that.

"I'll make you a wager." Joe, his second in command stood beside him. "I bet you that red-haired kitsune wears her down and she becomes like the other students by Christmas."

The head librarian laughed, and his poppy laughed along with him.

"Not a chance. She's devoted to books, this one." He looked at Joe and grinned. "What do you bet, though?"

"An extra slice of the pixies' Christmas cake."

That was serious business. The pixies' Christmas cake was notoriously good and it wasn't unusual for scuffles to break out over the last piece. He wasn't sure how they did it, but it was heaven on a plate.

He held his hand out to Joe. "Deal."

They shook on the wager and the head librarian smiled to himself. There was no way that Raine would give up her books. That slice of cake was as good as his.

CHAPTER ELEVEN

Raine huddled beside Evie and held her wand with determination. She had practiced feeling her magic and summoning the stealth spell. Closing her eyes, she sensed her magic within her and nudged it out toward her wand where she could focus it into the spell. It felt stubborn and thin. When she'd asked the others how theirs felt, they had described it like a river that needed to be channeled. She was sure her magic would become like that but it obviously needed to be coaxed.

Finally, the enchantment slid into her wand and she opened her eyes and smiled. She whispered the words and felt the bubble form around her. In her mind, she saw it wrap her feet and lower legs but it stopped at that point. It was better than the last time they had snuck into the kemana, but it still wasn't the complete spell.

Evie whispered the words while Raine added her magic and the bubble completed. The others accomplished their own stealth spells with a flourish. William had become more comfortable working simple spells as he grew to understand his fire. The nightmares still left him haunted, though, and his classwork had begun to suffer.

Philip was determined to return to the Ifrit to try to have the curse lifted. He didn't show it, but he had come to see the stubborn half-Ifrit as a friend, and he was loyal to his friends. The elf and the wizard exchanged a short staring contest before Philip stepped ahead and led the little group down the stairs into the kemana.

Saturday was a very popular day in the underground city and they hoped that the hustle and bustle of the crowds would hide them. Raine couldn't help but slow her steps and admire the view of the city with the magic arcing overhead. She swore that it was even more stunning than it had been before.

They stepped off the stairway as their stealth spells burst. A startled creature turned to look at them. Raine automatically lowered herself into a fighting stance as she looked at the large hairy beast. It bared its big teeth in something between a snarl and a smile and the students froze and waited to see how he would react to them.

He finally lumbered off. Evie relaxed and Raine turned to her. "What was that?"

"A Kilomea. They're very war-like on Oriceran but they tend to be calmer here." She turned to see it step behind a stall selling dainty trinkets. "They even own businesses down here. They react very badly when they think someone has cheated them or tried to steal from them, though."

Raine could certainly see how they'd be warlike. Their big bodies and large teeth gave them a definite advantage over the more lithe elves and wizards. She tapped out a hasty note on her phone to look them up in the library.

"We're going to Bubble and Fizz, right?" Sara looked over her shoulder at Raine and the others. "I'm dying for some mac and cheese and I swore they had that on their menu."

"Comfort food at its finest." Evie laughed. "I think I need to try one of their pizzas. Don't get me wrong, the pixies spoil us rotten but sometimes, you need something unhealthy and not necessarily good."

The group remained close together as they wove between groups of witches, elves, and a few more Kilomeas. Raine thought she saw a Willen snatch a pendant from a stall run by a Wood Elf. Its hand moved so quickly she wasn't entirely sure whether it had happened or not. The rat-like creature stuffed its prize in the fold of its skin and merged with the crowd without so much as a backward glance.

"Don't get too near a Willen if you don't have to." Sara nodded toward the creature. "They'll steal anything that isn't pinned down."

"They're very nice once you get to know them." Evie chewed on her bottom lip. "And they're very devoted to their families. They're very blunt though, so don't talk to one if you have a thin skin."

"Are they related to the big rats at all?" Raine looked to Evie. "The ones in the New York subways?"

"Yeah." Evie put her arm around Raine's. "They're cousins."

"So, does that mean there are crocodile creatures too?" She stepped aside to let a shifter with her small boys running around her feet go by. "Like the crocodiles in the sewers, I mean."

"I haven't seen any, but I've heard there are all sorts of weird things on Oriceran." Evie brushed her hair from her face. "I hope I never bump into one if they do exist."

They took their time and paused to look at shops offering everything from clothing to short-term spells.

"How do those work?" Raine pointed to the spells written on paper. "They say they're only short spells?"

Sara rolled her eyes. "They're a waste of money." She picked one up. "They have weak magic woven into the ink. You add a touch of your own magic to release the spell and it only lasts an hour, two if you're lucky."

"The defense ones can be useful in an emergency." Evie rifled through the variety on display. "They can be enough to get you out of a sticky situation."

"Why not simply use your own spells?" Philip looked at them with disdain. "We're witches and wizards after all."

"Sometimes, a situation is dangerous and you freeze." Evie compared two spells side by side. "Or you don't have the knowledge to use the spells you need to get out of the situation."

She handed three spell notes to the stall owner, a slender Light Elf.

"Just these, please." He took the money and she tucked her purchases in her pocket. "I'd rather be prepared." She took Raine's arm once more. "You never know what you might run into."

Philip shook his head and muttered about a waste of money before he moved on.

They took a few wrong turns before they found the

little bookshop that housed Bubble and Fizz. Sara strode to the shelf, pulled on the book, and darted down the stairs. The others followed closely behind her. Raine was relieved to find the cafe was only half full and the corner booth they had chosen before was available.

The fairy fluttered beside them and placed a large bowl of M&Ms in the middle of the table.

"Complimentary snacks. We have a deal on the Hershey's platter and the mac and cheese today. There is also a secret prize for any table that orders the right combination of foods." She handed everyone a menu. "I have a good feeling about you."

With that, she flew away and left the group feeling a little confused.

"Well, there's a deal on the mac and cheese, so it was clearly meant to be." Sara put her menu down. "I think a large Mountain Dew too."

"Do you want to split a pizza?" Raine looked at William. "I'm happy with all the toppings they have here."

"Meat feast." William ran his finger down the menu to the extra toppings section. "With pineapple."

Sara's mouth fell open and Evie laughed. "You can't. That's blasphemy." Sara looked aghast. "Pineapple on pizza is wrong."

He smiled and shrugged. "I'll have to get extra pineapple now." He looked at Raine. "Will you eat that?"

"Sure." She shrugged. "I'm happy with pineapple on pizza."

"Who are you?" Sara shook her head. "I can't believe I'm friends with such blasphemers."

They each ordered something savory and the sugar-rush banquet for after.

"We're still on for movie night later, right?" Philip brushed a crumb from his chips and dip off his shirt. "I have the snacks ready and waiting."

"Seven o'clock." Sara pushed her plate away. "I can't wait to see this B-movie. It looks absolutely ridiculous."

"That's the fun of it." Raine finished her root beer. "They're far too silly to actually be scary."

William watched the horror on Sara's face as he ate the last slice of pizza which had even more pineapple than the rest. He relished every last bite and Sara's reaction along with it.

The sugar-rush feast lived up to its name. It came with three types of Reese's, two forms of Hershey's chocolate, and four types of ice-cream complete with marshmallow fluff, sprinkles, and three different sauces. The students lounged in the booth and waited for the room to stop buzzing.

"I think we might have gone a little too far." Adrien closed his eyes. "I don't think my body was meant to consume that much sugar."

William looked at his friends as he felt completely fine. He had noticed that he tended to eat more than he used to.

"Raine." He waited for her to look at him. "Do Ifrit have different metabolisms than wizards and such?"

"Yeah. People think that it's the fire." She shifted in the seat. "They burn through food much quicker and don't get drunk either."

William thought about the not getting drunk part for a moment. That seemed like an important part of college life, and he hoped his metabolism wouldn't interfere with his social life too much.

Once they had all recovered, they left Bubble and Fizz and stepped into the main walkway once more.

"We should go and see the Ifrit again." Philip pressed himself against the wall to let a Kilomea past. "To try to lift William's curse."

"I really want to see the druids." Raine watched as a witch tried to win a game of chicken with the Kilomea. "I'm not sure the Ifrit is a good idea."

"We can't let William continue to suffer." Sara put her hands on her hips. "We have to make them take the silly curse off him."

"Why don't we split up?" Philip looked at them with a raised brow. "Raine, Evie, and Adrien go and bug the druids. Sara and I will help William with his curse."

Raine ground her teeth at the implication that she chose not to help William, but she let it slide.

"We can't stay down here too long," Evie warned. "The longer we're here, the more likely we are to get caught."

"It sounds as though it's best we split up then." Adrien took a step in the direction of the druids. "We should meet by the Kilomea stand in forty-five minutes."

Philip nodded and turned on his heel, leaving Sara and William to follow him.

"I really hope they don't make things worse." Evie followed Adrien as she walked beside Raine. "Philip can be very bull-headed when he chooses."

"The Ifrit really do need a careful approach." Raine glanced at the ground when a bone shard protruding from under a wooden board caught her eye. "I'm sure they'll be fine, though. Do people die down here?" She gestured to the bone shard.

"People die anywhere there are more than two people." Adrien put his hands in his pockets. "This is a city. There will be murder and crime as with any city."

Evie tugged on Raine's arm. "It's a bone shard. It means the owner is already too far gone to care."

Raine let it go and wove her way between shoppers and inhabitants alike, staying close to Adrien and Evie as she did so.

The surroundings changed subtly at first, but she noticed the slender vines that crept along the ceiling and the change in scents around her. They approached the druid neighborhood now, and she prepared her questions in her mind. A good agent knew what they were getting into and how best to get what they needed from their suspect.

Raine's reading on the druids had told her that they were usually a very peaceful people who prized balance and nature above all. That made it even more odd that they had disappeared as doing so threw off the balance of the place. Their magic worked as a community to maintain the forest around them.

They reached the main area of the druid neighborhood and Raine noticed it was far quieter than it had been when they were last there. She decided that there was no time like the present and approached a middle-aged druid with long, dark-brown hair tied back in a series of braids.

"Good afternoon, I'd like to ask a few questions about the missing members of your community." She pulled out a notebook and pen. "How many have gone missing? And when did it all start?"

The man narrowed his eyes at her. "That is none of your business. Run along home, little witch."

Raine wouldn't give in that easily. She asked another three druids, each of whom brushed her off with more vigor than the one before. Finally, an older woman with thick streaks of steel-grey through her dark hair emerged from one of the homes.

"Do not come into our community asking questions you've no right to ask." The old woman made a shooing gesture with her hands. "Leave now."

They were aware of innumerable pairs of eyes that stared at them from windows and doorways. The feeling of being very unwelcome settled between Raine's shoulder blades and she had to admit defeat. They wouldn't talk to her and she had no authority to push the issue. There had to be someone else with the information she needed. People had vanished, which meant they needed help.

Adrien put his hand gently on her shoulder and guided her to the edge of the neighborhood where a younger druid waited for them. He leaned against the bough of a tree, partially hiding himself from the view of the locals.

"A weird figure has snuck around in the middle of the night." He looked furtively around before he continued. "It wears odd robes and walks in a way no person should be able to."

With that, he ducked between the tree and the building and vanished into the shadows. A sense of victory filled Raine. She now had something she could investigate. There was a lead

William held back and wished it was Evie and Raine who accompanied him to the Ifrit community. He appreciated Philip's dedication and Sara's fire had its moments, but he feared they would only make the delicate situation worse. Still, he found he didn't want to say anything for fear it might upset them. Friendship was a new concept to him, and while he hated feeling weak, he didn't want to ruin the tenuous bond they had formed. He thrust his hands into his pockets and straightened his spine. The Ifrit were his people and he wouldn't crawl on his belly like some pathetic puppy.

Philip walked deep into the Ifrit neighborhood before he came across someone whom he felt was suitable for the discussion he wanted. The Ifrit was a large middle-aged man with dark horns that curled from his temples.

"Good afternoon. There seems to have been a misunderstanding." He plastered his most charming smile on his face. "One of your brethren placed a curse on my friend here. If you could remove it, we'd be very grateful."

The Ifrit bellowed a laugh that echoed mockingly around them. "You think you can walk in here with the mutt and simply ask to have the curse removed?" The Ifrit brushed tears from his cheeks. "You are more of a fool than I thought."

Sara stepped forward. Something stirred within, a burning fire that she hadn't experienced before. She felt as though her ears flattened against her skull before she said, "Do not mock us. William has done nothing wrong and you dared to curse him?"

William groaned. This was even worse than he'd imagined.

The Ifrit bared sharp white teeth and stepped forward to tower over Sara who refused to shrink away. "You have the nerve to walk into our neighborhood and speak to us like that, fox?"

She lifted her chin in defiance. "Remove the curse from William."

"Or what?" A new Ifrit stepped beside the first. "Will you bark at us?"

Sara narrowed her eyes and folded her arms. Philip held his hands up in a placating gesture.

"It is all a misunderstanding. Surely this can be undone and we can all walk away?" He hoped his wording had been careful enough. "I'm sure my friend here didn't mean any harm."

"Oh, I meant—" He squeezed Sara's arm hard.

"You have ten seconds to leave our neighborhood before we demonstrate how cursed you can be." The Ifrit took a step forward. "Nine seconds."

They ran.

Philip stopped two streets away from the edge of the Ifrit neighborhood and gulped air. He didn't think he'd ever run so fast in his life. A small group of witches, each with matching white-blonde hair, paused to point and laugh at them. William calmed himself and resisted the urge to shout and scream at them both. Who knew how bad the curse would be now, and there was nothing to stop the Ifrit from cursing them too as they ran.

A small crystal salamander in fire-orange with golden dots down its spine skittered along the edge of the shop they leaned against. William stomped on it and shattered it into small pieces. He ground it with his heel for good measure.

"Next time, listen to me." William glared at Sara. "I get that you tried to help, but you really screwed up back there."

She had the good sense to lower her eyes and apologize and William allowed his anger to dissipate rather than consume him. He would not become his aunt.

"We should go and meet the others. We're drawing a lot of attention." He turned toward the Kilomea stall. "And thanks for trying. I guess."

They squeezed between groups of gossiping elves and darted around a Willen who stared longingly at a particularly sparkly necklace. Raine and the others waited for them at the stall. The Kilomea watched them with deep distrust and he deflated noticeably when they hurried to the stairs.

"What happened to you?" Raine looked at her friends with concern etched on her face. "You look like you sprinted all the way here."

"We kind of did," Sara formed her stealth spell. "I'll tell you back at the school."

Evie helped Raine once again and they jogged up the stairs. Their spells ended with a small pop and they all laughed.

The friends hurried to the main common room where older students lounged on the couches and read magazines. They claimed the last cluster of armchairs and couldn't keep the grins off their faces.

"So. Spill." Evie gestured to Sara, Philip, and William. "What happened?"

Sara looked down and away.

"We might have upset them." Philip straightened his shirt. "Our wording was imperfect, and they might have chased us out of the neighborhood."

"Are you okay, William?" Evie touched his arm. "Did they hurt you?"

He smiled in response. "No. I don't think they did anything more than chase us off." He sighed. "It looks like I'm stuck with this curse, though."

"What about you?" Philip settled himself into his chair. "Any luck?"

"I have a lead." Raine flapped through her notebook. "It's not much."

"But it's enough for you to spend a few hours in the library with," Sara teased.

"I believe so." She read through her scribbled notes. "There's nothing wrong with the library, you know."

Sara pulled an expression of displeasure. "Not for me."

"Each to their own." Raine shrugged. "We'll fix your curse, William. Somehow."

CHAPTER TWELVE

Raine wrapped her arms around herself as she settled on the stand overlooking the Louper field. She sat between Evie and William, with Philip and Sara beside the half-Ifrit. Philip passed them a small bag of hard candies.

"Firebugs." He popped one in his mouth. "They'll warm you up."

Evie took one and smiled. "They're safe." She unwrapped hers from its simple white wrapping. "They taste like strawberries and cream and contain a little fire magic to warm you through."

Raine took one and offered it to William who shrugged, "I have my own fire magic."

Evie had been right. Raine savored the rich strawberries and cream taste as the warmth began to spread through her. The ache in her fingers and the stinging pain in the tips of her ears faded away and left her comfortably warm.

The crowd quieted as the Louper team walked onto the

field. Adrien walked with his head high and his eyes looking straight ahead. He didn't acknowledge the crowd as he focused on mental preparation. This was the first game of the year and it was against a long-term rival, the Cincinnati Lions.

Matt was a junior and a shifter who was still settling into his new role as captain. He turned his dark eyes toward his team and steeled himself. This would be a difficult match and it was even harder given that it was their first match together. Cody and Daniel were talented wizards with solid experience, but they occasionally lacked confidence and that could hinder them at the worst possible moments. Adrien provided a hidden advantage, though. The elf's steely demeanor and talent with combat magic would give them an edge over the Lions.

"We're in this to win it. Put aside any worries and fears." Matt straightened with resolve. "This is only a warm-up match, but it will set the precedent."

The others nodded in understanding. Cody shifted his weight from one foot to the other while they waited for the scene around them to change. He hated the wait after the crowd's attention had settled. It felt almost anticlimactic after the rush of welcome he enjoyed so much.

Silence descended, and the field slipped away and became something very different. The short green grass gave way to cracked and crumbling concrete. Old high-rise buildings towered before them. A soft breeze whispered and rustled the hardy grass that had forced its way through the cracks in the concrete and the piles of rubble around them.

The city looked as though it had been something to be

proud of once upon a time. The building still held hints of the sleek edges and shiny surfaces they must have once had. Matt ignored all that, sniffed the air, and allowed his instincts to come forward. As a shifter, he could sometimes feel where the gold token was, a talent that manifested at a young age and which no doubt pushed him quickly through the player ranks and gave him an advantage.

Raine frowned and leaned a little closer to Evie. "Remind me how this works." She looked at the small Louper team in the middle of a bare area between tall buildings with missing roofs and broken walls. "They have to find a gold token?"

"There's another team somewhere in that city. We'll be able to see them once the Cardinals get closer. Both teams will try to reach the gold token first but there will be traps and things along the way. It'll come down to which team is the fastest, the most cunning, and best with their magic." Evie watched as Matt led the Cardinals at a jog around a collapsed wall with metal girders that poked out at awkward angles. "The Cardinals have a great reputation. I'm sure they'll win."

Adrien remained alert for any potential traps or signs of the gold token. The two wizards jogged in the middle of the group. Cody tried to form a tracking spell, but something hindered his magic. The elf narrowed his eyes as he felt something press against his own power. That wasn't a normal part of the games, but they did like to throw in new and interesting challenges.

Matt slowed and scrambled up a pile of concrete slabs for a better look. He turned in a circle and peered at the horizon. The Lions were out there somewhere, and he had no idea how close they were to the token. They needed to make some real progress, but his instincts remained dormant.

"We need to go north." Adrien pointed to the tall buildings which were in slightly better repair. "That will get us out of this magical dead zone."

The shifter smiled, jumped off the concrete pile, and set off at a quick jog. They vaulted over fissures in the ground and swerved around sharp shards of glass that protruded from grey mounds and wispy grass. Finally, his instincts kicked in and he felt as though he could breathe clearly again.

Adrien relaxed visibly as his magic returned to his fingertips. A rustling sound came from their left and everyone turned to face it. The elf called his swords and they formed in his hands as he settled into his fighting stance. Cody and Daniel each formed fireballs in their hands, and Matt bared his teeth.

A vaguely human-shaped being forged of twisted metal girders and broken glass rushed at them from the tall grasses. Adrien cursed under his breath. His swords would be no use against that metal monstrosity.

The crowd gasped as they saw the metal beast surge from the greenery toward the team. The wizards paled when they realized their fireballs were futile. Matt did the only thing he could do.

"Run!"

The team raced down what had once been a wide road. They darted between abandoned cars and looked for some way to rid themselves of their pursuer. The metal man charged after them. With each step, the metal feet clattered and crashed as they collided with the road. A squeal cut through the air when the metal joints scraped against one another. Daniel stopped abruptly and turned to face the being. He held his wand up and whispered something. Cody hurried to join him and together, they formed a water spell to rust the creature's joints so it could no longer move.

It fell onto the ground with a deep groan and the crowd roared in celebration.

"That was really close." Sara put her hand to her mouth. "I wasn't sure they would make it."

The team didn't pause to celebrate but continued to jog down the road while each searched for some clue as to where the gold token might be. Finally, Matt saw something. He climbed the broken remains of what might once have been a post office and perched on the edge of the upper wall. A glint of gold caught his eye and he knew he'd spotted the token.

"Do you see the rusted-out frame?" He looked at his team as he pointed. "The token is on top of that."

Cody dragged his fingers through his hair. He didn't mind heights, but Matt hadn't exaggerated when he called it a frame. It looked as though a construction crew had erected the towering metal skeleton and never completed the structure. It loomed above them, easily thirty stories high. From where they stood, the wizard saw nothing to hold onto and definitely no comfortable elevator to ride. Metal struts provided the only way to climb.

"Only one of us needs to get to the token." Adrien sent him a comforting smile. "You and Daniel can remain below and cover our backs."

"What a fantastic plan." Daniel sighed with relief. He'd obviously shared Cody's reluctance to venture onto what appeared to be a challenging climb "We can keep our feet firmly on the ground."

The crowd hushed as the Lions appeared. They headed directly for the token on its lofty pedestal. The Cardinals pushed into a sprint. Adrien and Matt threw themselves at the first strut and climbed frantically.

Cody and Daniel raised their wands and formed a simple glamor that made the ground floor level of the metal frame look as though it was surrounded by a tall stone wall. It wouldn't last long but it would give their teammates a head start.

The Lions stopped dead in their tracks and looked suspiciously at the wall. Their shifter stepped forward and sniffed. He shook his head and ran when he determined that it was nothing more than a glamor.

Adrien and Matt were already on the third floor when the Lions began their ascent. Louper matches were never that simple, though. The metal girders shivered warningly before they twisted and became like flexible tentacles. They struck at the beam Adrien and Matt clung to and it shook and wobbled. For a few seconds, all they could do was hang on until their perch stabilized and they began to climb again as quickly as they could.

One of the Lions was caught off guard and slipped off his beam to land on the Louper field back at his school.

"Was he badly hurt?" Raine frowned. "The magic protects them, doesn't it?"

"He might have a couple of bruises but nothing his

nurse can't fix." Evie squeezed her hand. "The schools are careful to look after their Louper players."

Matt used his shifter strength and speed to pull ahead of Adrien. Unfortunately, the shifter captain of the Lions managed to close the gap between them. The elf stayed as close behind his teammate as he could to try to guard his back and increase their chances of winning. The token was only two stories away now but both teams were tired and had slowed in response.

The Lions captain was only one story below them. He used that knowledge to help him dig deep and push on to close the gap. Matt, not one to accept defeat, gave it everything he had.

The three players pulled themselves onto the final level. The other team's leader balanced on the beam to Adrien's right. They all had to teeter across the narrow beam to reach the token that hovered over the center. One wrong step and it would all be over.

Matt rolled his shoulders and moved confidently. He kept his gaze level and trusted his own balance. The opponent tried to move quickly but his foot slipped and he almost toppled off the beam. He caught himself and took a slow, shuddering breath as he saw the open air below him. They were a long way up. His teammates looked like tiny ants from that height and he realized he shouldn't have looked down.

Matt and his counterpart were both halfway across the beam when the frame rocked. It started as a small motion but rapidly became a movement that resembled waves crashing on a beach. The shifter closed his eyes and felt the rhythm.

With his eyes closed, he allowed his body to flex with the motion as he took one careful step after the other toward the goal. They were so close and he wouldn't lose now.

The opposition player didn't have the inner calm that Matt had and instead, opted to crawl along the beam and keep his body weight as close to the metal as possible. He tried to speed up when he saw Matt edge closer to the token with an infuriatingly calm expression on his face.

The shifter opened his eyes and smirked as he lunged forward and snatched the prize. He held it up for all to see and the crowd exploded into applause and cheers.

The city faded away until the Cardinals stood in the middle of the field with huge grins on their faces. Matt slapped Adrien on the back. "Thanks for watching my back there."

The elf shrugged and said nothing.

"That was exhilarating." Raine clapped enthusiastically. "I couldn't play myself, though."

"Me neither." Evie looked to Sara and Philip. "We'll have to congratulate Adrien."

They made their way through the crowd which still cheered and whooped in celebration. Max Regency, the Louper coach, congratulated the team. "I knew you could do it. The championships will be ours."

Raine and her friends managed to squeeze through the crowd and run to Adrien. Evie pulled him into a hug, much to his alarm. "You were amazing." She released him when she noticed his discomfort. "What a fantastic first game."

The elf smiled and shoved his hands into his pockets. "Thank you. We're a good team." He nodded at the coach. "And we have a strong coach."

"Flattery will get you everywhere." Coach Regency lifted his glass of untouched scotch. "Except out of training. Make sure you're here bright and early tomorrow morning."

The wizards groaned. "Please tell me it won't be the assault course." Cody looked at him with wide, pleading eyes. "We deserve better."

The gnome snorted. "I'll think about it."

CHAPTER THIRTEEN

Xander struggled to hold the glamor together. He closed his office door behind him and felt it fizzle around him. He didn't need a mirror to know he looked like death. The poison had taken its toll now and was slowly killing him. He walked to his comfortable chair and collapsed into it, coughing as he did so. His energy levels had waned considerably, and his eyes had developed a glassiness that frightened him. Yet, despite their research, they still weren't sure what the poison was or how someone had managed to administer it.

Mara had interrogated everyone who might have come near his food and found nothing. The pixies were livid that someone had managed to hurt one of their faculty. They had sworn vengeance on whoever had dared to hurt Xander, and he appreciated the sentiment and the support.

He had eaten in the kemana a couple of times and even in Charlottesville before the poison began its work. It could have been in his system for a while before the symptoms manifested. Whichever enemy had done this knew what they were doing.

Mara came into his office with an armful of colorful vials and books tucked under her arm. She placed everything carefully on the desk and studied him with her lips pursed. He made no attempt to wear his glamor around her. She would only chastise him for wasting his energy.

"Lucy has made you some more vitality potions. There are some new healing potions here too." She handed him a pair of lavender-colored vials. "We think we've narrowed down which type of poison they've used. That means we're a step closer to the cure."

Xander pulled the stopper off the first vial and finished the contents in one large swallow. To his surprise, it tasted like fresh orange blossom, a vast improvement on the last one which had resembled old pond water.

The soft fizzing sensation of the vitality potion coursed through his veins and made him feel slightly more alive again. The room shifted into clearer focus and he allowed himself a small smile. He was surrounded by good friends and talented magic workers.

Mara handed him two more vials but didn't specify what they were, which meant that he likely didn't want to know. The second burned like cheap whiskey but he took the last two from her anyway.

He closed his eyes and enjoyed feeling a part of the world again. The poison had made him feel oddly ethereal, as though he were losing touch with the physical world around him. It was a deeply unsettling and disturbing sensation.

"We haven't given up yet." Mara put her hand on his

shoulder. "We will find whoever did this and bring them to justice. Are you sure you don't have any idea who it could be?"

Xander smiled wryly. "My list of enemies is far too long to whittle it down to even twenty."

Mara shook her head and leaned against the edge of his desk. "Why couldn't you have left it at dabbling?" She folded her arms. "Why did you have to keep digging into things that weren't your concern?"

It was an argument they'd had many times over the years. "Because they needed to be someone's concern." He met her eyes. "I helped a lot of people, Mara. I know you don't approve of my methods, but I did help people."

"At what cost?" She gestured to him. "Was it worth it?"

"Yes." Xander spoke without hesitation.

He missed her and he hated the distrust that had grown between them, but he didn't regret the fact he had helped many people over the years. He had taken lives using dark magic, but they had been dangerous people who did more harm than good. His understanding of dark magic had allowed him to protect others who were less capable.

There had been a time when the dark magic threatened to consume him, but even then, he never regretted his decisions.

Mara tried to understand his views and actions, but he had never given her the details. How was she supposed to trust him and really understand when he brushed her off?

"Lucy is bringing some rare plants in from Europe. They should help her make more efficient healing potions, so you'll feel better for longer." She stood. "I suggest thanking the pixies for their support after dinner tonight."

With that, she left.

Xander sighed softly. It wasn't his intention to push her away, but he feared that if he brought her into his world and told her everything, he would simply paint a target on her back. Mara already had her own enemies and she didn't need to draw the attention of his as well. He closed his eyes and wished he could see her smile—the genuine bright smile she had given him when they were together—one more time.

Sara hadn't been able to sit still all morning. Her dress had waited in their dorm room and she hadn't had a chance to look at it before breakfast. The big Halloween dance was the next day and she planned to be the belle of the ball. She'd never attended a school dance before as her family didn't feel that such things were appropriate. That only made her more determined to make the night exceptional.

The moment Professor Hudson allowed the class to leave, Sara raced out of the classroom to her room. Evie sighed and let her go ahead. Raine, predictably, remained behind to speak to the professor about what they had discussed in the class. Professor Hudson already had a list of books on hand for her to check out of the library. Raine smiled and took the list.

"I hoped to ask you about Professor Powell. He seems to be very ill." Raine glanced at the list. "Is it true that he was poisoned?"

She knew that there was a chance the professor would reprimand her for the question, but Professor Powell had been good to her. He had taken the time to give her a few extra lessons to help her really feel her magic. She appreciated that and wanted to help him if she could.

Professor Hudson pursed her lips and looked at the doorway. Seeing no one else and trusting that Raine would be sensible with the information, she simply said, "Yes. I'm afraid it's true."

"Is there some way I can help? If you give me some idea of what to research, then maybe I can help find a cure." Raine tucked her list in her pocket. "I know you have your own library, but one more set of eyes might help."

Professor Hudson nodded, her expression thoughtful. "I will speak to Professor Fowler. We will consider it extra-credit." She closed the door to the classroom to stop others from eavesdropping. "It seems to be a class that attacks his very essence directly. It's slow-acting and inflicts a great deal of pain on the victim, but we haven't yet determined what it is or exactly how it works, or even how to treat it."

Raine scribbled that down. "I'll go to the library now. I'll give Professor Fowler my complete findings after potions class tomorrow."

The girl's enthusiasm brought a smile to Professor Hudson's face. She knew that Xander would appreciate it, even if he wouldn't approve of including a student in researching his cure.

Raine hurried to the library where she bumped into Christie.

"Hey! It's Halloween tomorrow. You must be really excited. Did you hear that last year, some of the dead came through the veil and had to be corralled back into the World in Between? It was a real test of our magic and negotiation skills. I'm sure this year will be far smoother. The dance looks as though it'll be amazing. You have some say in that, don't you? Being on the student council and all. I thought about applying for that, but I don't think I have the right personality for it. I'm not sure how I'd fit it in either. I started violin lessons this semester. I already play the flute and the piano, but I do love the violin."

Raine tried to organize the questions and statements into a logical order in her head.

"Yes, I had heard about last year's Halloween. Yes, I had a small say in the decorations we'll use, but the seniors will put them together. And I think the violin is beautiful, even if it sounds like a strangled cat when you're first learning."

Christie seemed ready to say something else but thankfully, one of her sophomore friends approached and distracted her. She liked Christie. She was very friendly, but she talked so much and Raine really wasn't in the mood for chitchat.

She greeted the gnomes with a smile and Librarian Decker responded cheerfully. One of the seniors saw it and did a double take. He'd never seen the gnome smile before and had been sure his face wasn't capable of the expression.

"Good afternoon, Librarian Decker. I have quite a long list today, although I'd like to start by researching poisons." She handed him the list from Professor Hudson. "Do you have any suggestions on where I should start?"

The gnome stepped closer and whispered, "Is this about Professor Powell?"

Raine nodded. She didn't want to say anymore as she didn't think the other students were supposed to know.

"Well then, come with me. I'd be happy to help you." He led her to the very back of the library where the students rarely went. "I have a little spare time. I'll sit with you and help you compile your notes."

"Thank you, that's very kind." Raine took the first book the gnome offered her. "Do you know much about poisons?"

"A little." He gathered four more books and passed them to her. "My expertise is more history and military strategy."

"Would you mind if I asked you some questions for my history class tomorrow?" She shifted the weight of her books. "I know you're busy, so I understand if you say no."

"I'd be happy to help you." He took the final book and pointed to a spare table. "We'll sit there."

The head librarian arranged the books in an orderly fashion and formed a notebook and pen from the ether. He opened the first book and made notes in neat handwriting. Raine watched with a feeling of awe before she opened the book closest to her and searched for something on poisons.

Sara practically leaped on the red satin box sitting on her bed. She had been desperate to see the dress in person for a month now.

She took her time carefully undoing the ribbon and placing it to one side before she opened the box and folded back the delicate tissue paper. The fabric shimmered a deep obsidian black with small threads of pumpkin orange. Sara lifted it and squealed with delight. It was absolutely perfect. The skirt was trimmed with black and orange ribbon and the underskirt gave it enough volume to add a retro flair.

"Is that the dress?" Evie sat down on the edge of her own bed. "Can I see?"

Sara turned and held it up. It really was a work of art with a multitude of small details at the neckline and over the bust. At first glance, it was a simple black satin dress with small shimmers of orange, but when Evie looked closer, she saw the black roses embroidered onto the left side and the way the orange ribbon at the bottom flickered like fire.

"It's stunning," she said honestly and Sara beamed.

"Oh, you'll look amazing. A couple of the seniors will be so jealous. What type of magic will you use to finish it off? I can help if you like. I've practiced my hair and make-up magic." Christie took a step closer to see the dress better. "With your beautiful red hair, I think a simple look would work best, and we can focus on bringing out the green in your eyes."

Evie shook her head and began her homework while the other two gushed over their preparation for the dance. She did look forward to it, but really only the fun with her friends part. Dances weren't her thing and she would rather bake or play in the garden than swoon over pretty dresses. She considered heading into the library to join Raine. At least it would be more peaceful down there.

CHAPTER FOURTEEN

R aine's Uncle Jerry had shipped the dress in time for the Halloween dance. She had opened it after class and been very happy with the result—a simple black dress that ended above her knee and with a straight neckline. It had no sleeves and shimmery black stars were embroidered onto the simple skirt. She paired it with a pair of black lace gloves and low black pumps with small orange bows on the back.

Christie bustled around and helped the younger girls with their make-up and hair magic. Sara took forever in the bathroom and the others squashed around the mirror on the wall in the bedroom. Evie wore a form-fitting red dress with a black lace overlay. She listened to Christie's instructions and used her magic to gently bring out the green in her eyes and add some shimmer to her cheekbones. She wanted to keep it simple.

Raine remained still as Christie's magic washed over her. She felt her long, dark-blonde hair lift and twist into a complicated up-do. When she opened her eyes, they shimmered with a pale gold eye-shadow that brought out the blue and her lips were painted with a soft dusky pink.

Sara emerged from the bathroom looking like a queen. Her dress fit perfectly, and her hair had a soft golden glow to it that glistened in the light. She twirled gracefully and couldn't keep the grin off her face. This was an important night to her. It was her first dance ever, and she intended to make sure that it went perfectly.

"You look beautiful." Evie squeezed her hands. "I'm sure you'll turn every head."

Sara blushed and turned her attention to Raine. "How do you make such a simple little dress look so stunning?" She put her hands on her hips and smiled. "You'll show me up."

Christie finished up her own make-up and turned to face the others.

"Wow. You look incredible." Evie put her hand to her mouth. "Is there someone special?"

Christie blushed furiously. "Well. Maybe. There's someone I like but I don't know if he knows I exist. I mean, we share a bunch of classes, so he must know I exist, but does he think of me in a way that means he likes me? I don't know. I should talk to him, but what if he says no? I don't think I could live the humiliation down. It's so ridiculous. I make myself pretty for me but also hope he sees me."

Raine took that as a yes, there was someone.

A knock sounded on the door. Christie opened it and was greeted by a collection of compliments and happy noises. She embraced a tall, dark-haired girl with a grin and was enveloped into their group and whisked away to the dance.

Sara put her arm around Evie's shoulders. "Will you give William a dance tonight?"

Evie's eyes went wide. "I guess. I mean, he is a friend." She blushed. "If he'd like to dance, I won't say no."

Raine stifled a laugh. She'd never seen Evie quite so flustered before. "Come on. We should go and meet the guys."

As Philip had pointed out, it was much easier for them. They each wore a simple black suit. William had to barter to get enough money together for his, but Evie noticed that he looked particularly smart in it.

The school buzzed with excitement. A small group of seniors strutted past in elaborate dresses woven with magic and silk. Sara glanced at her own dress and walked a little taller with her chin out. She wouldn't spend her night comparing herself to them.

"You look very pretty." William smiled at Evie. "I mean you're always— I don't know how to dance."

"I'm pretty sure you stand and move your hips to the music." Sara shrugged. "Or simply sway."

"Does anyone our age know how to dance?" Philip looked at the others. "I mean really dance, the waltz or whatever."

"I do." Evie didn't look at him.

"You'll have to teach William." Sara gave her a smirk. "I'm sure he'd love to learn."

"I would like to at least make sure I don't step on anyone's toes." William shoved his hands in his pockets. "It doesn't have to be anything fancy."

Evie took his arm. "We'll see what music we have."

The half-Ifrit relaxed a little. This was the first time he'd attended anything like that and he had no idea what to expect or do with himself. Everyone else seemed excited and perfectly at ease but his nerves jangled.

They reached the dining room and paused to take in the scene. Raine smiled, pleased that the seniors had stuck closely to the agreed decoration scheme. She had suspected that some of them planned to ignore it and do as they pleased. They had bridled at any input suggested by the lower years.

Black cobwebs hung from the corners and glittered in the soft moonlight that shone from the center of the room. Pumpkin patches had been placed around the edges. Each pumpkin glowed softly from magical fire at its heart and their terrifyingly contorted faces moved sufficiently to make them look alive. Whispers drifted under the popular music and gave the impression that the spirits were all around them.

As they moved into the room, they saw the cemetery in the far corner near the live band. They had decided to go for a very human theme this year and based it on the over-the-top decorations humans often opted for. The gravestones creaked and rocked as groans issued from the freshly dug soil. Every now and then, a bony hand emerged from the soil, only to sink a few seconds later. A few juniors were startled and jumped away when they first saw it.

"This is amazing!" Sara was wide-eyed with excitement. "How did you convince the Phoenix Flames to play?"

Philip looked particularly pleased with himself. "We struck a deal."

Sara dragged him to the middle of the dance floor where she proceeded to dance to her favorite song. It was a rock tune that brought a smile to everyone's faces and filled the room with vibrant energy. The others found the luminescent green punch bowl that bubbled and gurgled. William narrowed his eyes and stared hard as he could feel the magic within it.

Adrien, having concluded the magic did nothing more than make it glow, took the first cup. He smiled when the taste of fresh blueberries and vanilla ice-cream hit his tongue. The dance floor had filled with happy students all dressed in black and orange.

"It feels so alive." Raine chewed her bottom lip nervously. "It seems a bit weird, given the thinning of the veil."

Evie put her arm around her shoulders.

"We celebrate a closeness with those who have passed and the lives they lived. This is a time to drive out the darkness." Right on cue, shadowy figures crawled along the ceiling. "It is a time of light and laughter in preparation for the dark side of the year."

Raine liked that interpretation.

"Then we should dance." Adrien held his hand out to Raine. "Would you dance with me?"

She took his hand and followed him onto the dance floor beside Evie and William. Raine was sure her dancing wasn't up to standard, but it didn't matter. The music flowed through her and she hadn't trodden on anyone's toes yet. Slowly, the concerns over the druids and

Professor Powell slipped away and she allowed herself to enjoy the night. She was amongst her new friends with great music, so for now, at least, there was nothing to worry about.

Seth walked away from the main dance to get some fresh air. He felt as though something was calling to him, a familiar voice he couldn't quite place. As a junior, he hesitated to ask one of the older students what it could be. They looked down on the younger students most of the time, or at least that's how he perceived it. Besides, he'd never really been popular and didn't want to encourage a perception that he was a little odd.

The music was so loud and he assured himself he simply needed a few moments alone. He leaned against the wall and looked out the window at the grounds. The grass glittered silver with a heavy frost and the full moon hung low overhead. He was sure there was some superstition about a full moon on Halloween night, but he couldn't recall it off hand.

"Seth? Come to me."

He spun and his gaze searched the shadows for who or what had whispered to him. The words were clear that time, but they sent a chill down his spine.

"You're so close, Seth. A few small steps."

He frowned and tried to pinpoint the source of the voice which seemed to echo around him. Tentatively, he pushed away from the wall and stepped forward. Professor Powell's voice seemed to ring in his head.

"Don't trust anything. The dark families hide in the shadows. Never step into the shadows." He repeated the words aloud but they seemed to bounce back with no effect.

"Seth. Over here."

Something tugged at his bellybutton to leave a weird sensation of a string that encouraged his feet forward. It felt wrong. Something had to be very wrong. He knew that the thinning veil allowed the darker creatures from the World in Between to slip through. Another chill shivered down his spine. That must be what he faced here.

He raised his wand and formed a light orb to banish the darkness that seemed to creep closer. The moon slipped behind a cloud and the darkness consumed the room.

Something tugged on the invisible thread to his belly-button and Seth's feet moved of their own accord.

Suddenly, everything shifted around him. The air became thick and viscous and he struggled to walk. He tried to shove his way through it toward the doorway. If he could find a professor, they would help him through whatever this was.

Everything changed again. The darkness congealed into what felt like a thick, glutinous substance that resisted moved. He swallowed his panic and tried to recall if he'd covered anything like this in classes. When he turned, he could see the room he should be in through a thin mist. He tried to reach it but couldn't penetrate the enchanted haze.

Panic rose within him. He had been pulled into the World in Between. He dragged in a steadying breath and tried to remember what he knew about it. The veil would remain thin until sunrise. He needed to find a weak spot that would allow him to cross into the school.

Seth proceeded as quickly as he could through the thick air but it felt as though the floor sucked at his feet like heavy mud. Every step was a struggle, but he couldn't allow himself to be trapped there. He wouldn't age and could linger in shadowed nightmare for an eternity, slowly going mad while he searched desperately for a way out.

Mara's head jerked as she sensed the moment when someone broke the veil. Xander and Eleanor both looked in the same direction. They'd felt it too. Without speaking, they hurried toward the small room at the back of the building with the bay window.

Memories flooded Mara's mind as she ran. She had been trapped in the World in Between for four years and wouldn't wish that fate on anyone.

Eleanor Hudson cast a bright light spell over every corner and space within the room. Xander could almost see the slight crack where something had been pulled through the veil. Mara approached it and stretched her fingers out slowly to the air. The crack was now too small for someone to return. It had sealed itself.

"Eleanor, can you cast a—"

Her companion raised her hand to stop Mara, already working on the necessary spell. The witch slowed her breathing and calmed herself. It had been a while since she'd needed to cast such a large enchantment. She exhaled slowly, called her magic, and spread it through the school. Her next step was to push it to make hidden things visible.

When she opened her eyes, she could see the desperate expression of one of her juniors. His dark hair stuck up at every angle where he'd obviously dragged his fingers through it. He pressed his palm against the veil and clawed at the thin wall of mist between them while his eyes begged them silently for help.

"We need to guide him." Mara squinted at the veil as she tried to find a place where they could penetrate. "There must be a weak spot we can work with."

Xander put his hand on her shoulder to steady her. Her protective instincts toward the students and her memories of the time in the World in Between made her heart and her thoughts race.

"I will stay with him," he said. "You and Eleanor find Max. He has a thin place in his classroom, if I recall correctly." He put his hand against the veil near the boy and called his thinning magic. "We will get you out," he said to the terrified boy although he wasn't sure he would hear him.

His own weakened condition meant he might not access sufficient magic to make real communication possible but he forced himself to relax. Xander felt useless thanks to the poison. If he were at full strength, he could have ripped the boy through the veil, but now, he struggled to form what had been easy spells only a few weeks before.

Eleanor and Mara left the room and hurried to find Max who would hopefully know a suitably frail place in the veil.

"Max!" Mara shouted to the gnome. "We need you to help us find a weak spot in the veil."

He saw the urgency vibrate through the headmistress, emptied his scotch in a potted plant, and led them to his classroom. He immediately called his magic and with his eyes closed, confirmed that the enchantment thinned noticeably near the window. Mara sent the rest of the professors to watch over the students and ensure that no one else was pulled through the veil.

It was one of her worst nightmares. She could not leave that student trapped in there.

It took them almost two hours, with Xander and Max working together, to guide the student to the place where they could pull him through from the World in Between.

To his credit, the boy remained calm as he forced his way through the thick, featureless shadows. When a dark creature lurked ahead of him, he put his shoulders back, raised his wand, and spoke a spell Xander had taught him only two weeks before. A swell of pride swept the professor as he watched the dark creature skitter away to where it had come from.

It would have been so easy to lose control and panic in that situation, but the student remained calm and strong. It was almost sunrise when he finally reached the classroom. Mara and Eleanor had woven the required spell to break through but didn't dare release it until Seth was in place for fear that it would allow something else through.

Together, the professors set up a protective circle and dragged Seth back into their world. He landed with a thud and gulped with tears in his eyes.

"Thank you." He swallowed hard. "Thank you."

Xander helped him to his feet and put his hand on the boy's shoulder.

"You made us proud tonight." He looked at the other professors who nodded in agreement. "You performed that spell under difficult circumstances and you were precise and calm."

Seth tried to smile but now that he was safe, his legs shook and the reality of his narrow escape overwhelmed him. Eleanor put her arm around his shoulders and guided him back toward the dining room.

"What happened?" she asked gently.

"I don't know." Seth wiped at his eyes. He would not let the other students see his tears. "I looked out the window when I heard someone whisper. I cast a light spell, but something tugged at me and the next thing I knew, I was in the World in Between."

"I'll take him to the nurse," Eleanor told Mara. "We'll watch over him for a few days."

Physically, she was sure he was fine, but mentally, he would need to heal.

Mara pursed her lips and looked at the students who should have been in bed. They had all gathered in the main entryway and surrounding corridors. Expressions of horror vied with admiration on their faces.

"You should be in bed," she said sternly but with a gentle undertone. "You will not be given time off classes."

A groan spread through the crowd before they shuffled off toward their dorms. She watched to make sure everyone ascended the stairs before she turned to Xander. He looked pale and drawn.

"I'll cancel your classes today. The students can use the

time for study." She glared firmly at him. "I will not take no for an answer, Xander."

"Can you believe someone was pulled into the World in Between?" Sara changed into her pajamas and hung her dress carefully. "That's the stuff of nightmares."

"I'm so glad they got him out." Evie shuffled under her blankets. "I hope he isn't too scarred from the experience."

"Does anyone know how it happened?" Christie brushed her hair. "I thought there were numerous spells and defenses in place. This won't be another one of those attacks, will it? I don't know what it is about this school, but there is always something going on. Oh, don't tell your FBI agent friend that, Raine. I'm sure he'll have a heart attack. It's not so bad. Well, I suppose the school did sort of have bits of it blown up a couple of summers ago, but that sounds awful."

"I'm sure it was simply a fluke." Evie squeezed Raine's hand across the gap between the beds. "Did you have a nice Halloween anyway?"

"It was mostly perfect, thank you." Raine pulled her blankets a little higher. "Although I will miss all of those hours of sleep."

CHAPTER FIFTEEN

Philip held the backpack full of movie snacks when Andrew entered the room and everyone tensed. The boy had established his own friendship group away from the others, but that didn't stop him from making jibes at every opportunity.

He looked at the backpack and squared his shoulders. Adrien's fingertips itched with the desire to summon one of his blades.

"What have you got there?" Andrew pointed at the bag. "I think you should show me."

Philip laughed. Adrien and William moved to stand at his side.

Andrew's faced turned red with anger. He wasn't used to refusals. He tried to rush Philip, who side-stepped, and Adrien swept the bully's legs out from under him. The elf pinned him down with a foot between his shoulder blades.

"I recommend against trying to take something from

us." He pressed a little harder with his foot. "We have boobytrapped everything."

The three guys had used their spare time over the past few days to ensure that Andrew couldn't rifle through their belongings. They'd suspected that he'd done so for a while, so they took action. They couldn't go to the professors without proof, but if or when Andrew showed up with bright pink hands and neon blue-and-green striped hair, they'd have the evidence they needed.

Andrew cursed colorfully, but the friends ignored him and left. They had their first movie night to attend.

Raine had looked forward to their movie night for the past few days. She'd pushed ahead with her reading to ensure she could relax and enjoy the evening. Sara made sure her hair was perfect before they headed down the stairs.

Christie was away with her friends, so they didn't need to find an excuse. They'd made a good effort to place wards on the room to prevent other students from claiming it as their own. Horace knew they were in there, but Raine had a good feeling about the groundskeeper. He'd helped them find some comfortable couches.

They met the guys at the corner of the hallway that led to the room. Philip raised the backpack with a grin on his face.

"I got the important things. We can get others next time if we want." He looked around to be sure they hadn't been seen. "Shall we?"

They followed him to the space they had claimed.

Philip opened the door with a flourish which earned him an eye-roll from William. The room had been swept clean and now contained a pair of large couches in a pink-and-green floral fabric that the wizard had somehow found. They were ugly, but they were soft and comfortable enough to sleep on and preferable to the bean bags he'd originally suggested.

Philip closed the door behind them as Adrien headed to the TV and DVD player.

"Tonight, we have *Curse of the Swamp Creature*." He slid the DVD in. "It was quite a feat and involved a fair amount of magic to get something this old onto a DVD.."

Raine curled up at the end of the slightly larger sofa with a happy sigh. Evie and Sara sat beside her and Philip set the small, scruffy coffee table near them. He opened the backpack and emptied its contents onto the table.

"Twizzlers!" Evie grinned and grabbed the pack. "You can have some if you ask really nicely."

Raine laughed. "Sara picked up a bag of chocolate M&Ms and some sweet popcorn." She looked at William. "Would you mind?"

The half-Ifrit had practiced controlling his fire and was happy to demonstrate how far he'd come. He focused and pressed it into the corn, which popped almost immediately. Once it was done, he handed the bag back to Sara.

"It's perfect!" She poured the M&Ms into the bag and shook it. "Thanks."

William popped a few more bags of popcorn for the others as no one wanted the same flavor. Adrien wanted cheese whereas Philip shared his toffee popcorn with

William. Once everyone had settled with their preferred snacks, they started the movie itself.

Sara laughed after a minute. "The acting is so bad." She calmed herself with effort. "He's like a robot."

"The melodramatic way of removing his glasses was amazing." Philip took some more popcorn. "It was like an old-school CSI moment. What was his name?"

"Horatio Caine." Evie bit into a Twizzler. "He's the one with the sunglasses."

They all fought to keep straight faces through the music but finally, Adrien broke. "Are those bongos?" He frowned at the TV. "Are they really playing the soundtrack on bongos?"

Sara could no longer restrain her laughter. "I think they are."

Raine smiled as she took a Twizzler from Evie. The laughter had done her a world of good. She hadn't expected anyone to take the movie seriously, but the joy and simple pleasure brought a smile to her face. The bonds with her friends had grown and she looked forward to spending time with them. Even though she spent most of her waking time with Evie and Sara, she still enjoyed their company.

"She looks like the bride of Frankenstein." Evie pointed at the woman who'd come onto the screen. "She only needs a white streak down the side."

"She does." Philip chuckled. "Really? That's his line? You meet so many interesting people?"

Sara smirked at him. "Since when are you the expert on pickup lines?"

Philip didn't look at her. "I know all sorts of interesting things."

William and Adrien exchanged a look and stifled their amusement.

"Oh, come on." Evie pointed at the TV. "She'll so clearly drag him off to the swamp monster."

Raine had to agree. The woman looked as though she tried to seduce the guy from out of town, and that always ended in a gruesome death in movies like that. She took another bite of her Twizzler and watched the cheap cinematography with great amusement.

"Wow! Check out that room décor." William said around a mouthful of popcorn. "I don't have words to describe it. Did people really decorate like that?"

Raine wrinkled her nose at the awful brown-and-white smudged walls and wondered why those particular colors had been so popular in those days.

"Damn. I thought the woman would kill him." Sara sighed dramatically. "We knew he'd die, though. That type always does."

"I'm sure there's some social commentary in there somewhere," Philip said and sipped his coke. "I'm not in the mood to dig into all of that, though."

"Agreed. I want to watch a movie for light entertainment." Sara popped some more popcorn into her mouth. "I do like how it's the woman who's the brains of this operation."

The group watched as the woman in question plotted to take over from the out of town guy to investigate oil in the swamp. They were completely fascinated by the stilted cinematography and faded colors.

"They don't make horrors like this anymore." Evie sighed and took another Twizzler. "Which is a bit of a shame, really. They're fun in a completely different way."

"It shows how things have changed." Adrien shifted his weight. "This was scary back when it was new. Now, people mock slasher movies and like the really psychological stuff."

Evie wrinkled her nose.

"I'm not a fan of the psychological horror." Raine frowned at the scene on the TV. "I don't really want to be scared. I like the more outrageous horror you can laugh at. Slasher movies can be a lot of fun."

"Psychological movies play on what could really happen." William blew some hair absently out of his eyes. "I think you have to be a certain personality type to really enjoy those."

They quieted down again as the movie moved to the next part of the plot and the soundtrack took on a foreboding tone.

"What's going on with you guys and Andrew?" Sara asked. "Is he still being an ass?"

"We've put boobytraps on everything, so he'll be caught red—or should I say pink?—handed if he tries to steal something." Philip grinned at her. "Hopefully, he'll be moved or even kicked out of the school soon."

"That bad?" Evie frowned a little. "I haven't seen Paige since she changed rooms."

"We can only hope for the same result." Adrien shifted a little. "He is a difficult personality. I don't want to hurt him, but he keeps pushing and I won't have a choice if he goes much farther."

"And you know you'd be the one in trouble if you did hurt him." Sara shook her head. "It's always the way with that type."

"It sounds like you have experience," Philip commented. "Did you get in much trouble in middle school?"

Sara shrugged. "Not a ton. I learned how to play the game pretty quickly."

"I'm glad I don't have to play those games here." William looked at his hands for a second, his expression tense. "People can be cruel."

Adrien smiled sympathetically and noticed the dark shadows under his friend's eyes. "Your potion is wearing off." The elf stood to find another vitality potion for William. "I'll get you another one."

Evie had brewed potions to help William through the ongoing Ifrit curse. His nightmares had reached a peak and he habitually wore a harrowed look. Evie researched a way to break it through herbs, and Raine had read every book she could find on Ifrit curses and come up empty-handed. They wouldn't let him continue to suffer, though.

William thanked the elf for the potion and they returned their attention to the movie. The soundtrack had turned dramatic with a heavy timpani undertone which indicated that something bad was imminent.

"Are they seriously beating out a warning beat on logs and things?" Sara raised an eyebrow. "This is…uh, something else."

"They were very different times." Evie shrugged. "You have to ignore the…less pleasant parts."

"Does this mean we'll see the swamp monster soon?" William looked at Evie and Raine who seemed to be the experts. "They're showing crocodiles and things in the swamp."

"No." Raine smiled. "The monster won't show up until after dark."

"It's a rule," Evie added.

William frowned at them. "Are there really rules for horror?"

The group all turned to look at him.

"Absolutely." Sara put her popcorn down. "Do you not know the rules of horror?"

"No."

"First, no sex. Ever." Philip smirked. "That's sure to get you killed in the most horrific way possible."

"Oh, look, he's sacrificing people." Evie pointed to the TV. "You know he'll die horribly. Sorry, we were talking horror rules."

"Do we mean rules horror lives by?" Raine frowned. "Or rules to survive a horror?"

"They're tied together." Adrien stretched his legs. "You can't survive a horror if you don't know the rules."

William looked from one to the other, more confused than ever.

"No swimming. Especially in a movie involving something watery in the title." Sara held up her finger. "You'll be eaten by something awful."

"Always trust the crazy looking local at the beginning." Philip leaned forward a little, his eyes dancing with humor. "They'll tell you how to survive."

"The monster only shows up in the dark," Evie added. "It's scarier that way."

They looked back at the movie as the tone of the music changed.

"Oh, look at him, a real badass with his sunglasses on indoors." Sara laughed. "I bet the swamp creature enjoys killing him."

"He needs big frizzy hair, though." Philip frowned at his lack of popcorn. "Mad scientists need big frizzy hair."

"There! The monster." Evie pointed at a clawed hand that emerged from the fog. "Damn, it's not showing it clearly. I thought it would break the rules for a second."

"You know that it'll come to life in the darkness and go on a rampage." Raine took another Twizzler. "The doctor will try to control it but he'll get eaten. And he'll deserve it."

"And that is why I'll never go camping." Sara pointed at the TV. "They're lying on the ground and don't even have a nice fire with marshmallows. No, if I go out into the wilderness, it'll be glamping."

"What is glamping?" Adrien looked at Sara for an explanation. "It sounds painful."

Raine laughed and tried to suppress it with her hand. She'd enjoyed camping with her dad and uncle. Admittedly, they did have a fire and marshmallows, though.

"Glamping is glamorous camping." Sara brushed her hair back. "It's where you have a nice tent with a comfortable airbed and sometimes, a little electricity for the essentials. But we have magic."

"What's the point?" Adrien frowned at her. "Camping is about being with nature."

She snorted. "You're an elf." She waved at him with a smile. "Nature is different for you."

Adrien shook his head and looked back at the movie.

"Wait, what did I miss?" Philip looked at the TV. "Is he turning that guy into a swamp creature?"

"No, I think swamp creatures come from crocodiles?" Evie chewed her bottom lip. "I'm not sure if they explained that. The creature did have a human-like hand though. So maybe?"

"That guy looks like he's animatronic." Sara pointed at the man on the screen. "Look at how he talks. It's really weird, like a robot reciting words."

Everyone burst out laughing when one of the employees made a vague motion of a karate chop on the other's neck and the recipient dropped, unconscious.

"That was the most ridiculous thing I've seen in forever." Sara wiped tears off her cheeks. "He didn't even touch the guy's neck."

The group settled and tried to focus on the movie once more. Raine hoped there weren't too many fight scenes as she couldn't stop herself from laughing. They were so ridiculous.

"Do you know what those flowers are?" Evie leaned a little closer. "They look familiar. I think they go in a luck potion."

"Sorry, plants aren't my thing." Sara shrugged. "They're pretty, though."

"How is he supposed to see if the guy nods his head?" Evie gestured at the scene on the TV. "He's completely hidden under that thick fog."

"That poor tortoise." Sara looked away. "Why couldn't he give him a fish?"

Evie put her arm around the other girl's shoulders. "I'm sure the tortoise was fine."

William shared his glances between the movie and his friends who all grinned as they watched. He had expected them to enjoy the movie for itself, but he now understood that they liked laughing at how cheesy it was. At first, he'd been unsure about horror movies as they weren't his thing at all, but he could see that they were a lot of fun.

"She has a curl in the middle of her forehead so you know she's trouble." Evie put the empty Twizzler packet down. "There once was girl who had a little curl right in the middle of her forehead. When she was good, she was very, very good, and when she was bad, she was horrid."

"What was that?" Philip looked curiously at her. "The rhyme."

"Something my grandma used to say when I was little." She smiled and shrugged. "Although I never had curls. I think it's an old Irish rhyme."

They watched for another twenty minutes or so before the finale started. Everyone laughed uproariously through the next fight scene.

"His fist definitely didn't touch that guy," Sara said when she'd gasped a breath. "And he went down like a log."

They watched as the finale escalated and the doctor's enemies gathered around his home in preparation to attack.

"Wait, was that the monster?" William asked. "That bug-eyed, sharp-toothed thing?"

"How did that come from a man and a crocodile?" Philip peered at the TV and waited for the next frame of the monster. "It looked...screwed up."

"Wait, wait, that was the ending?" Evie looked at the rest

of the group. "That little fight and the crocodiles, and then it's done?"

Philip rewound the movie a little.

"It looks like it."

"Well, damn. That was really anti-climactic." Sara slouched disapprovingly. "They kinda killed it at the end there."

"It was a great laugh, though." Evie stood and gathered the empty packets. "Do we know which movie we'll watch next?"

"Something werewolf-y." Adrien said. "I can't remember what we said before, but I'd like something with a werewolf."

"Sounds good to me." Raine helped Evie clean up. "There are some classic werewolf movies."

"Well, name a couple and I'll see what I can do to secure them." Philip shoved the empty packets in his backpack. "When do we want to do the next movie night?"

"Next week?" William stood as well. "We could make it a Friday night thing."

"I like the sound of that." Raine smiled. "It will give us something to relax with at the end of the week."

"That's a date, then." Philip slung the backpack on his back. "I have a few business dealings to see to. Catch you later?"

"Take care."

"Don't get caught!"

CHAPTER SIXTEEN

Philip entered their room first. Andrew had been suspiciously quiet all morning and he hadn't made a single dig at William since Adrien pinned him down. Philip now understood why. The boy glared at them, his hair a mix of neon green and blue streaks and his hands bright pink.

"You did this to me," he accused resentfully.

"Technically, you did it to yourself." Philip slid his hands into his pockets and smirked. "You shouldn't have tried to steal from us."

Andrew tried to rush him but both William and Adrien acted too quickly for him to even get close. The half-Ifrit tackled him to the ground and Adrien pinned him with a foot to the throat before he could recover.

"We'll take you to the headmistress now." The elf's smile was cold and ruthless. "You will be lucky to stay in the school."

The boy's expression darkened but he said nothing.

William hauled him to his feet and Adrien grabbed the collar of his shirt and marched him from the room. Philip smiled. He wasn't a fighter, but he knew how to make friends with people who were.

Other students paused to stare as the elf marched the thief to the headmistress's office. He was only an inch taller than Andrew, but his presence made it feel as though he towered over the wizard. The boy glared at everyone and dared them to ask him what had happened. No one did until they bumped into Sara.

"I take it that's the thieving ass you room with." She folded her arms. "Did he manage to take anything?"

Adrien shook his head. "Our magic was efficient. He won't have had the chance." He nudged Andrew forward. "We're presenting him to the headmistress."

"There's a new guy." Sara looked down the stairs toward the front door. "I bet he'll be your new roomie."

Adrien sighed softly. He had quietly hoped the three of them wouldn't have another roommate.

Philip knocked on the headmistress' door and William stood on the other side of Andrew. Fire flickered over his knuckles as a quiet warning not to try anything.

Ms. Berens told them to enter. She wasn't all that surprised to see the boys as she was aware they'd had trouble with Andrew for a while.

"He tried to steal from us." Adrien pushed the culprit forward. "His hair and hands prove that. We wove wards around our stuff that would produce that result should he try."

Ms. Berens pursed her lips and stared at Andrew. The boy lifted his chin, entirely unapologetic.

"Andrew will be removed from your room immediately, and I will discuss the matter of his punishment and continued presence at this school with the faculty."

The boy's eyes narrowed. He came from a good bloodline and his parents would be livid to hear he'd been kicked out. The headmistress wouldn't dare, he decided arrogantly.

Professor Hodges stepped into the office. The shifter towered over Andrew and glared at him with the gold shine of his wolf in his eyes. The boy tried to step away and found he had nowhere to go.

"You'll stay with me for the rest of the morning." The boys didn't miss the growl in the professor's words.

"Thank you, Professor Hodges." The headmistress smiled. She looked at Philip and his friends. "You're excused."

A pair of gnomes ran up the stairs toward the dorms ahead of them and students paused and whispered as they passed.

"Is it true you turned Andrew's hair green and blue?" a blonde witch asked.

Philip shrugged. "He had it coming."

She turned to her friends with a grin. Philip wasn't sure how this would affect his reputation. He had been careful to cultivate the persona of an astute businessman with enough charm to sell ice to a polar bear.

The gnomes passed them at the landing. This time, they carried two bulging bags and a sleeve poked out from one of them.

Adrien smiled when he recognized Andrew's belongings. He was gone. Now, they had to see what the new

guy was like. He hoped for someone quiet and unob-
trusive.

Cameron glared at the gnome who had led him to his
room. He walked in and found it sparse but livable. He'd
been in worse, he decided, and dropped his bag on the now
empty bed recently made with fresh linen and sniffed the
air. He wrinkled his nose when he smelled elf and Ifrit.
Still, it was likely easier than trying to share with another
shifter.

He had begun to unpack when the elf and Ifrit in question walked in. Everyone stopped and looked at each other.
Cameron narrowed his eyes a little and allowed them to
shift to yellow to make it clear what he was. He came from
a very long line of shifters and was perfectly aware of the
prejudice against his kind.

The wizard grinned and held out his hand.
"Philip. You?"

Cameron looked at the proffered hand and then at the
wizard. "Cameron."

He continued to unpack and ignored them for as long as
he could. The pressure of their gaze on him burned into his
back but he ignored it. He had been through four schools
already, and this would make number five. Cameron knew
better than to try to make good friends. It never worked
out. He should be back with his pack and with his own
kind. No one understood his need to run or guard his food.

It always followed the same disappointing pattern. He'd
start off as a novelty and people would be friendly enough.
Then, somehow, as word spread that he was a shifter,
they'd treat him like a freak and that would make him

angry. In the last magical school, they'd tried to drive him out as an inferior. He'd actually attempted to set the head professor's car on fire so that he could move on.

His pack insisted that he get a good education, but he was sure that if he was expelled from this school, they'd give up and homeschool him. Then he wouldn't need to worry about the looks and the whispers and would be among his own kind where he belonged.

"Why were you transferred?" William studied the shifter curiously. "You must have screwed up."

Cameron turned to face him. His dark hair was messy and hung to just above his ears, his dark eyes were narrowed, and a soft growl sounded in his throat. The half-Ifrit raised an eyebrow and allowed his fire to coat his hands and hair. Two could play at that little game.

The shifter changed tack and lifted his chin and straightened his spine.

"I set the headmaster's car on fire." He folded his arms and mimicked William's stance. "It turns out they hate that."

Adrien tilted his head slightly with obvious confusion. "Why did you do that?"

Cameron glared at him. "You're not a shrink. I did it because it was fun. End of story."

The elf didn't believe that for a second. The shifter had clearly had a goal in mind and he suspected it was to be free of the previous school.

"Was it a human school?"

"No. Magical. Not as nice as this place, though."

Adrien exchanged a look with Philip. They felt as

though they had a pretty good understanding of the newcomer.

The wizard leaned against the wall and crossed one leg over the other.

"I bet they treated you badly because you're a shifter, right?" He didn't wait for a response. "They claimed you don't have magic, so you don't belong. You, being weak, decided to get out of the situation."

Cameron began to shift as he bared his teeth. Philip remained entirely unmoved. He knew that Adrien and William would handle him if they needed to.

When the guys didn't flinch or react at all, Cameron pulled himself under control. Normally, people would have tried to fight or backed off if he had bared his teeth like that. He didn't know quite how to handle the situation now.

"I was not weak," he ground out after a short silence.

"It seems weak to me." Philip shrugged. "You're all bark and no bite."

With that, he pushed off the wall and walked around Cameron to sit on his bed. "We're heading down to the kemana again soon, right?" He looked at William and Adrien as he stretched out on his bed. "I have a craving for an ice cream sundae from Bubble and Fizz."

"I think we agreed on next Saturday." Adrien sat on the edge of his bed. "Raine wants to dig into druids a little more first."

Philip snorted. "She won't let that go, will she?"

"She plans to be an FBI agent like her dad and uncle." William picked up a notebook. "It's logical that she wants to help them."

"And I admire that, really I do." Philip put his arm over his face. "But I won't spend hours with her in the library. Wake me when it's time to eat."

Cameron sat on his own bed and frowned as he studied his roommates surreptitiously. They didn't give a damn about his growls or his attitude. No one had ever simply not reacted like that before. The wizard's jab about him being weak had hurt, too.

"Will you come to the kemana with us, shifter?" Philip lifted his arm to look at him. "We can weave a stealth spell for you."

Cameron held back a smile and fought to keep a scowl on his face. "Sure."

No one had invited him to accompany them anywhere before. He'd been in the school for less than an hour and already had a little hope. That was something he hadn't felt in years.

Raine sat in her usual spot in the library hidden behind a carefully constructed wall of books. The gnomes watched her with a paternal pride as she flipped between two notebooks and compared her scribbles with what she'd found in her latest book.

"Do we know what she's researching today?" Librarian Decker asked Joe.

"Something to do with druids. She's worked through all the druid books, but they are not part of any of her classes."

The head librarian's poppy blew a raspberry while he rocked back on his heels and debated whether or not to approach her and ask. After a minute, his curiosity won out and he walked over to the girl.

"Good afternoon, Raine, and what are you looking at today?"

She looked up and greeted him with a broad smile. The gnomes were extremely likable and she found their passion and dedication to the library admirable.

"I'm looking into druid history and culture. I saw a few marks that looked like runes somewhere close to those of druids, and I want to find out what they mean."

"Ah, well then, you need to add some symbology books." He turned and headed toward the relevant section of the library.

It was a less-trodden area as the professors didn't really cover those subjects. The gnomes insisted on maintaining the area as symbols were very important, particularly in magic. They had tried to have them added to the curriculum and failed. Mara understood their arguments, but they only had so much time in the day and wanted the students to learn practical magic.

The head librarian pulled out a little stool and climbed on it to retrieve a blue-covered book with silver font down the spine. He made his way along the bookshelf and selected three more.

"These should give you better insight." He placed them gently on her table. "Shout if you need anything else."

"Thank you so much, Librarian Decker, you're so helpful."

He bowed his head a little to hide his smile. The students were usually polite, but none were quite so grateful or eager to learn as Raine was.

She opened the first of the symbology books and searched for chapters relating to runes or druids. In the quiet of the library, she was in her element, lost amid the words and knowledge.

Time slipped away from her and Raine realized she must have read for a couple of hours or more. She'd fallen down a rabbit hole and researched sigils for her own education rather than the druid quandary. Luckily, that led her to exactly what she had searched for. She was about to close the book on ancient sigils when a drawing of the marking she'd seen in the kemana caught her eye.

She made a note of the name and looked for it in the other texts as excitement blossomed within her. Now, she had made real progress. With the relevant books spread out around her, Raine made notes on everything she could find about the symbol.

A frown crept in when she realized that it was a mark of territory and hiding. If she understood it correctly, someone with an understanding of druid magic claimed that part of the kemana as their own and also hid something from outsiders. That wasn't quite what she had hoped for, but a note about the fact that every sigil had a unique signature woven into it gave her a farther spark of hope. She now needed to learn how to see that signature.

Evie watched the pixies with awe. She had baked with them for a few months now and remained enchanted by their efficiency and grace. The leader, Victoria—or Tori as the other pixies called her—mixed batter with a flick of her wrist. The beater moved in neat, rhythmic circles while she gently kneaded out some dough for pastries.

The pixies had taken her under their wings and allowed her to really learn how to bake. She loved the Baking Club, but this was something else.

"Come and help me make pain au choc." Tori nodded to the fridge next to her. "The dough will be ready to be worked. Remember to put your strength into it."

Evie removed the large batch of pastry from the fridge and placed it at her usual spot on the countertop. She smiled at the knowledge that she had her own area to work in. The pixies hadn't let anyone cook with them before and she had earned a place on their counter.

She peeled the clingfilm off and set it aside carefully before she worked the dough. Her strength and the definition in her arms had improved from the intense work that went into making the breads and pastries.

Tori smiled with a flicker of pride. Evie had really come into her own as a baker. She'd known the basics when she first arrived but now, she learned to weave her magic into the baked goods too. She'd needed to be coaxed a little, though, and Tori thought that perhaps someone in her family had been too harsh on her. The girl touched Tori's maternal instincts and she wanted to have stern words with whoever had made her nervous to use her magic.

"These will be for Mr. Powell, so weave some vitality and health into the dough." Tori fluttered to Evie. "Remember what I said about stretching the threads of magic out with the mixture. You want it thin and tender. That will add a slight sweetness that compliments the dark chocolate."

The chocolate they used for Professor Powell's pain au choc had been sourced from France where it had been imbued with a difficult healing spell. It wasn't cheap, nor was it easy to work with, but the professor had gained a little energy since they'd used it.

Evie smiled and nodded in understanding as she selected the small vial of golden liquid from the potion rack in front of her. The pixies often added a little magic to their food, although they didn't tell the students that. During exams, they added a little focus and calm to help them through the difficult time.

Evie had come to appreciate the pixies more and more as she got to know them and saw the little touches they put into everything. She added six drops of the golden potion to the pastry and closed her eyes to focus on the magic. As she stretched the dough and folded it back on itself repeatedly, she pulled the enchanted threads thin and taut. The professional chefs in France took nine months to learn how to make good croissant, so she was thrilled to have achieved the delicate, thin layers in only two months. They weren't quite perfect, but her last batch had received compliments from the pixies and professors.

Evie immersed herself in her work. She was at home in the kitchens. There was something wonderfully soothing about the act of baking. Everything was so simple and yet so incredibly precise. Each confection used a similar flour, butter, and yeast recipe, but they became something completely different depending on how the ingredients were handled and combined. That simple fact on its own was enchanting.

When the dough was ready, she stepped aside to let

Tori finish them. She wasn't quite ready to handle the chocolate. The magic it contained was delicate and temperamental, and the price tag meant that Evie shouldn't use it to practice. The pixies had promised they'd teach her once Professor Powell was healed, though.

Philip and the others insisted that Cameron joined them for dinner. The boys knew that the shifter was in desperate need of good friends and had decided to provide that for him. Cameron had glared and growled but they ignored it for what it was—habit and a fear of forming a connection with someone.

Adrien rolled his eyes and put his hand on Cameron's back. "Don't be a grumpy puppy and come to dinner with us."

The shifter's face literally gawped at the words. Philip and William had to look away to hide their laughter.

He shoved his hands in his pockets and didn't say a word as he followed the others into the dining hall. No one so much as looked at him as he walked down the corridors. He saw a couple of other older shifters who both acknowledged his presence and nothing more. They knew what he was, and they accepted it. Cameron grudgingly conceded that maybe the school wouldn't be so bad after all.

CHAPTER SEVENTEEN

Mara smiled for the first time in weeks as she pointed to a gilt-edged chapter in a very old book.

"We've found it. We know what the poison is. Now, we can work on finding the cure." She handed the book to Xander. "It's the shadow spirit poison. A truly vicious concoction, but we've done the right thing so far."

She placed her hand on top of his.

"We can cure you. Does this help you know who did this to you? It must have been administered via a drink on the night of a full moon."

Xander leaned back in his chair and rubbed at his temples. It had become more difficult to focus as the poison slipped deeper into his mind and magic. There were so many people he'd upset over the years. Many of them were talented with dark magic, so that didn't really narrow it down at all. He could list perhaps twenty or so who excelled at dark magic poisons and potions. None of the names came to him then, though.

Bruce stepped into the small cottage living room.

"You wanted to speak to me?" He looked at the two professors. "About the cure?"

Mara nodded. The agent didn't know much about magic, but he'd been a willing student since he'd taken up residence on the school grounds.

"We will need a number of things from Charlottesville." She handed him a list. "There is a magical supply store there that will expect you."

He nodded and left, happy to finally be able to help. His lack of magical knowledge had made him feel useless, and Xander hadn't been able to provide a short list of suspects. That, however, hadn't stopped the agent from digging into the professor's past as he tried to narrow it down himself.

Bruce had ten names that he needed Mara to look at, but there hadn't really been an appropriate time. It was clear that she and Xander had a past together, and a very intimate one if he read the situation correctly. Still, he didn't know how to broach the topic of Xander's enemies with her.

The agent walked to his car, a black sedan like those most agents drove. It was entirely unmemorable and blended into any situation. He wondered if perhaps someone in the agency had added a spell to make people's eyes slide right over it. It wasn't impossible, but he didn't think the few witches or other magicals who worked with the agency would worry about mundane things like cars. They were very interested in Raine and had high hopes that she would bring the magical community a larger presence within the agency, so their sights were set a lot higher than agent transport.

Once behind the wheel, he checked the address on the back of the list. He'd spent a fair amount of time in Charlottesville and had never seen a magical supply shop. A smile flickered when he realized it was hidden in a flower shop. He had to admit he would never have suspected a florist.

It was already late in the day and the shops had closed and the streets were quiet. Most people were tucked inside watching TV and eating dinner. Bruce didn't mind this time of evening where things were peaceful but full night hadn't quite arrived.

He pulled into a small parking lot and checked the name of the place. Don's Florist and Gifts occupied a small, neat, brick building with a green awning. It was modern and clean, and he wouldn't have associated it with magical supplies at all. He had expected something old and perhaps a little ostentatious.

Bruce peered past the vases in the windows for any sign that someone was still there. He knocked on the door and rocked back on his heels as he waited. Mara had been adamant that someone would be around, and he wouldn't let her down.

An older gentleman with a wisp of pale silver hair in the middle of his head opened the door.

"Good evening, sir. I'm hoping to purchase these." He handed the list to the man. "Do you think you could help me?"

"Lila! One of yours here," the old man called.

He thrust the list at a younger blonde woman with tight curls and a small, tense smile. "Well now, these are a little costly. They're quite rare." She looked at him and narrowed her eyes. "What did you say you needed them for?"

"They're for Mara Berens."

She relaxed immediately and ushered Bruce into the shop. He followed her past the large arrangements of flowers and realized he'd had no idea that daisies came in so many different colors. Lila led him into a small back room where every wall supported pale wood shelves bursting with jars and vials full of what he thought were dried herbs.

"I'll put it on Ms. Berens' account." She selected three small vials and one large jar and scooped the herbs into small cardboard containers. "That'll be okay, I assume."

"Yes. Perfect, thank you."

Mara hadn't told him how to pay for the supplies, so he assumed that would work out fine. Lila handed him the small boxes and ushered him out of the shop. He wasn't entirely sure what he carried but he knew they were important. Bruce secured his purchases in a larger bag which he placed carefully in the passenger footwell before he returned to the school.

Now, they could finally help Xander to heal.

Raine frowned at the book and sighed as she lifted her wand once again. She practiced the light orb spell her friends achieved so elegantly. Her magic was closer to the surface now and she was more aware of it, but she still struggled. It didn't help that she'd managed it relatively easily the first time she tried or that the spell books all made it sound so simple. She had to move her magic gently through her wand which would focus it and then visualize the light orb.

Her power pulsed through her wand and formed a small spark that fizzled out within two seconds. She went back to her books and read them again but found nothing new. She did exactly what it said but for some reason, it simply didn't work. Maybe she didn't have as much magic as people thought.

Librarian Decker wandered over to her. His poppy greeted her with a soft raspberry that wiped away her frown.

"Is there something I can help with?"

Raine sighed.

"I'm trying to form a light orb. I managed it once but have failed ever since, and everyone makes it look so easy." She gestured at the books. "I do what the books say but it doesn't work."

He frowned. "Well, try it and I'll see if I discover what goes wrong."

Joe walked around a bookshelf and came to watch. Raine raised her wand and tried to visualize the light orb. The spark barely made it out the wand that time. Her frustration level rose significantly.

"She's doesn't release enough magic." Joe smiled. "You need a little more faith in yourself."

Raine restrained a sigh. That didn't sound like something tangible that she could work with. She liked philosophy in principle, but she was far too pragmatic to deal with it in situations like that.

"Take a deep breath and feel your magic." Librarian

Decker moved his hands in a yoga-style gesture to demonstrate taking a deep breath. "Then, once you have a good grasp on it, release it into your light orb."

Raine rolled her shoulders and closed her eyes to try to feel it. She was aware of a liquid-fire sensation deep inside, but it was far deeper than all the books suggested it should be. A gnawing doubt made her wonder if there was something wrong with her magic.

"Push aside whatever doubt that is." He folded his arms. "You're holding yourself back."

Raine mentally boxed the doubt up and pushed it to the back of her mind. She was in the school, so she clearly had magic. It was time to get on with things.

The power pooled within her and trickled into her wand. It was more than the little thread she'd released last time, and the progress cheered her. The image of the light formed more easily in her mind. When she opened her eyes, she saw a small orb the size of a golf ball. It didn't provide much light, but it was definitely better than a spark.

"Progress!" Joe clapped. "Now we can get somewhere."

"He's right. If you take yourself out of your own way, we can really help you." The head librarian smiled. "Now, you need to clarify the image in your mind."

He was proud of how far Raine had come during her time at the school. She had worked very hard to achieve every little step and she wouldn't give up despite the difficulties. What the other students considered easy, Raine had to work for, and she never once backed away from the challenge.

They spent the next hour guiding her through light orb

formation and by the end of it, she was able to form a large, bright, white one. It would rival Adrien's which could light up a large barn. She grinned with pride as the globe bounced and hovered before her. A little regretful, she mentally squashed it and closed the spell books.

"Thank you. Both of you." She thought about hugging him, but it seemed a little forward. "Your help is very much appreciated."

"It was our pleasure. You're welcome to practice magic with us any time." The gnome tipped his hat. "Don't be late to dinner now."

CHAPTER EIGHTEEN

Sara lifted her paintbrush and looked at the base she had laid in the last Art Club get-together a few days before. It had dried slightly darker than she had anticipated and she now paused to evaluate how to proceed. The piece had been intended as a majestic phoenix rising from the ashes. She chewed on her bottom lip and debated how best to make the flames and colors shine as she had originally visualized.

"If you use the spell-cast gold, it'll brighten the highlights and draw out the shadows more and give it more drama."

Sara looked at Rachel in surprise. She'd forgotten other people were in the room with her.

"You're right. Thanks." She grinned and picked her palette up once more.

When she painted, she felt as though she were someone else. The act of drawing out the colors and adding the layers to create something beautiful gave her peace from her own mind. Her magic still hadn't emerged as well as she had hoped, and it began to worry her. The rest of her family had come into their kitsune magic early. There were increasing rumors that perhaps she had no real fox magic.

Philip scanned the business plan one last time and frowned. The numbers didn't add up. He was in Entrepreneurs Club which specialized in mixing technology with magic. His plan had been a simple one. He wanted to use a glamor to aid the creation of holographic adverts. Humans hadn't been able to shrink their holographic technology to a size that would fit in a pocket, but magic would enable them to do so.

He had thought that if they could create small portable ads for businesses, it would help forge bonds with humans. Their view of magic was still suspicion at best, and that really wasn't very good for business, for them or for the magicals.

They had managed to combine the magic with the technology, but the numbers still didn't tally. The materials they needed to hold the magic for more than a day were very costly, enough so that no one would be willing to pay for the ad. He had argued that it would pay for itself and that the curiosity of such small and precise holograms would draw people's attention and make them memorable. The rest of the club hadn't been so sure.

"Well, what if we change out the copper thread—"

"No. We've established that it needs to be copper.

Bronze isn't pure enough. The magic rebels against the impurities and causes the hologram to disintegrate."

Philip sighed. There had to be a solution.

"What if we looked at a different market? We could target the high-end market which would be willing to pay for something new and unusual." He looked at the group gathered around him. He was the only freshmen present. "What if we don't use them as ads but as something more appropriate to high society?"

A murmur rippled through the group and Philip knew he was onto something. He wasn't quite sure how exactly they could alter the concept for a new purpose, but he had complete faith that they would figure it out. The hologram idea was too good to give up.

A timer sounded and the club dispersed. Philip was the second to leave. He needed to speak to Evie whom he knew was in the kitchens with the pixies. He didn't like dependence on one business and he had an idea that he was sure would make them a small fortune.

He pushed past a small group of elves who discussed some obscure band or TV show, he wasn't entirely sure which. Evie would be finished in two minutes and he had to catch her while she still rode the high of working with the pixies. He knew she'd be in the best mood then and much more amenable to his ideas.

She stepped out of the kitchen as he arrived. Her dark hair had been pinned back from her face with a series of bobby pins, each with a small butterfly on. Flour marked her collarbone and cheek, but her smile was radiant.

"Hey, Evie, can I have a word with you?" Philip put his

hands in his pockets to make himself look less threatening. "It'll only take a minute."

She shrugged. "Sure. What's up?"

"I have a new business plan that I'd love your help with." He watched her reaction. "Everyone loves snacks, particularly cookies. I thought we could sell some. All money goes into the group social fund."

Evie thought it over. She really did like baking and Philip was right that everyone loved cookies. There were some new recipes she wanted to try out too. "The group social fund, huh?"

"Yes. I thought it might be a nice idea to have a collective pool that we can put toward group activities. Movie night, trips into Charlottesville, and so on."

Evie had to admit it had a nice ring to it. She enjoyed hanging out with the group of friends she'd gathered, and even Cameron had begun to soften a little.

"Okay, I'm in." She held her hand out. "You handle the business side, and I'll do the baking."

Philip shook her hand enthusiastically. "Deal."

He was confident they would make a fortune and he had discovered a small potion that would ensure their customer base couldn't resist coming back for more.

Raine led Smoke into the all-weather arena and rubbed his nose gently. She'd done a lot of reading on how best to approach the next stage of his schooling. It was time to begin his in-hand training in earnest. He walked beautifully on the lead and would follow her happily anywhere she went without one. Now, it was time to get him bending and moving sideways.

The young horse's ears flicked back and forth as he listened to everything around them. Raine drew his attention back to her and moved him around in a large circle while encouraging him gently to bend and turn. He tensed at first, not entirely sure what she demanded with her gentle pressure. It took patience, but he finally moved around her and relaxed. Raine changed direction to avoid too much work on one side which might make him unbalanced. He was receptive and eager to do as she asked.

Horace watched from the sidelines with a smile on his face. Smoke was growing up to be a beautiful horse and he had developed a strong bond with Raine. She had worked with him morning and evening for the past couple of months and it showed. The horse focused on her and did his best to do what she asked of him. He was eager to learn and that would make backing him in the spring far easier.

Once Smoke started to show small signs of tiring, Raine began to play games with him to get him used to things he'd need later. She ran over colored poles that she'd placed on the ground and he followed her without so much as a glance at them. Many young horses snorted and acted as though colored poles were predators. Smoke had such faith in Raine that he showed no alarm whatsoever.

They finished with a nice back rub and a handful of carrots. Raine couldn't keep the happiness from her face. Working with the horse gave her a feeling of joy and satisfaction that she couldn't get elsewhere. He was an absolute pleasure to work with and seeing him progress from a terrified little thing into the increasingly confident horse before her made her heart swell with pride.

Cameron sat on the edge of his bed and looked out the window at the forests and the mountains beyond. The full moon approached and the need to run consumed him. He desperately wanted to be at home with his pack in his familiar surroundings. An older shifter had mentioned a local pack that would be happy to have him run with them, but that didn't feel right.

He sighed and closed his eyes before he allowed the shift to take him. Spending some time in his wolf form would do him good. His human body felt tight and itchy and he needed to stretch his limbs. The shift came quickly and as naturally as breathing. His family had been one of the first the dark wizards had turned into shifters.

From what his grandfather had told him, they had been humans, but the dark wizards had tried to build a shifter army and found a spell that turned humans. There were still new families turned even now. It was illegal but that didn't stop the wizards. Some shifters were bitter toward the rest of the magical community because of it. They felt they should have done more to stop them.

Cameron's family was perfectly content, though. He felt no shame at his ability to become a wolf and he knew that despite what the other magicals said, he had magic. He might not be able to wield it or form spells the way they could, but he definitely had magic. He felt it deep in his bones.

CHAPTER NINETEEN

Philip put his arm around Cameron's shoulders and practically dragged him through the stands to where the girls waited for them. The shifter had lived with them for a couple of days now and he still clung to the growly, grumpy act. Philip saw right through it and didn't believe it for a second. Where William and Adrien took a quieter approach and let him think things through, the wizard had concluded that a more hands-on approach was required.

He guided Cameron into the seat beside Raine and sat on the other side of him.

"Who are they playing today?" Philip pulled his firebugs from his pocket. "Anyone with a good reputation?"

"The Dallas Fireflies." Sara snatched a firebug. "It's freezing today. I can see my breath. I feel as though the professors should weave a fire spell or something."

Sara looked hopefully at William who smirked and took a candy for himself. He had gained more control over his magic, but he didn't have enough confidence to try to weave a fire spell large enough to warm the entire group.

Sara sucked on the hard candy and drew warmth from it. Raine took two and handed one to Cameron. She knew that the shifter wouldn't take one for himself. He was oddly stubborn about such things. Cameron smiled and accepted it gratefully. He wished he could shift into his wolf form and gain some warmth. Huffing, he sucked on his candy and watched the field.

Adrien smiled for a change. The elf didn't often show emotion, at least away from his small group of friends. He was able to relax and allow himself to enjoy life with them. Philip proved to be a good friend even though Adrien didn't always approve of his lust for business.

Cody and Daniel bounced on the balls of their feet and tried to warm up while Matt looked through the crowd for someone. Adrien noticed the change in him when a small half-elf girl waved. There was no time to think farther as the landscape began to change around them.

The bitterly cold wind vanished to be replaced with a soft, dry warmth. Adrien turned a slow circle and tried to gain his bearings and identify where they might be. The room they were in was sterile with painfully white walls and pale silver floors. Small round lights positioned evenly along the ceiling provided bright light that hurt his eyes when he looked too closely.

Matt sniffed the air and set off toward the plain black door directly ahead. They walked through and found themselves in an art gallery. Adrien didn't know much about art, but he thought those particular paintings might have been surrealist. None of them made any sense, yet they had the crisp lines that made him think they weren't impressionist.

He paused to look at a tree sitting on a book, the trunk bent and twisted with a face that peered out from the shadows. His frown deepened. It wasn't a style of art that called to him at all. He was about to walk away when the face in the tree winked at him. Shaking his head, he hoped that the traps in there wouldn't come from the artwork. He didn't relish the idea of fighting trees with faces or clocks with arms and legs.

Matt led them through two more rooms hung with surrealist paintings and paused in a larger room. Four hallways led off it with no clear indication of where they went. Cody and Daniel had worked on tracking spells. The wizards turned to face each other with their wands held high. They whispered old words that spoke of aid and lost paths. A small fairy much like Tinkerbell formed between them.

"It was supposed to be an orb!" Cody looked at the fairy in horror. "Why is it Tinkerbell?"

"I got a little side-tracked..." Daniel chewed on his bottom lip. "Hopefully, it'll still work."

The small fairy fluttered her wings before she pointed toward the corridor on the left and flew in that direction. Matt glared at the wizards but now wasn't the time to scold them about focus and concentration. He had to trust that the little fairy would work as a tracker.

They ran after the illusion and their shoes squeaked on

the shiny silver floors. The fairy squealed in alarm before she exploded in a shower of pink and purple sparks. A group of older humans with small hats and dark purple vests converged on the team.

"What did you do to that poor fairy?"

"Why did she explode?"

"What did she ever do to you?"

"You're cruel. You shouldn't be allowed here."

The humans closed in around the players without allowing them time to answer the flurry of questions. Matt darted free, grabbed Cody's collar, and yanked him from the grasp of a gray-haired man.

"Come on. Keep moving."

The humans picked up pace after them. Adrien didn't think they were a true threat, but he didn't want to slow down to find out. Daniel almost lost his balance as he tried to take a corner too quickly. Matt helped him right himself while he urged them forward.

The group of humans suddenly stopped, and Adrien tried to see why. They had moved into a room with steel grey walls covered with masks. A shiver ran down the elf's spine as he gazed at the contorted and grotesque faces that looked back at him.

A wooden mask with red marks and sharp tusks moved. It pushed forward from the wall and a slender, steel-grey body formed beneath it. The body was elongated and the proportions were all wrong. Adrien summoned his swords reflexively and moved toward the new creature while Matt tackled another one on the other side of the room.

The wizards created fireballs and threw them at other

targets. The wooden masks caught fire and deafening, banshee screams filled the room. Adrien wanted to cover his ears and curl up until the sound dissipated.

They looked for an exit. At that point, any exit would do.

Cameron leaned forward intently and watched the events unfold before him. The team was paralyzed by the awful sound. He could see the exit they needed to take. If they could only make their way out the door nearest the blond wizard, they'd be free.

The Fireflies ran from sentient vases that had sprouted short, stubby legs. The wizards had hurled blasts of air at them which achieved nothing. Fire made no impression, so they decided the best thing they could do was run. The vases, unfortunately, moved far more quickly than they had any right to.

Raine tried not to laugh as she watched the ceramics chase the rival team through the gallery. It felt wrong to laugh but it was such an absurd thing to watch.

Matt finally saw the door. The screams made his head feel as though it would split in two, but he was the captain and had to remain in control. He dragged his three team-mates forcibly through the door. To everyone's relief, the noise subsided. Their ears rang, though, and their heads pounded with residual tension.

Daniel gulped air before he tried another tracker spell. He felt as though this was his fault and he was painfully aware that time was ticking by. Cody caught on quickly and added his magic to Daniel's. They worked together, twins in spirit if not by blood.

They focused as hard as they could and to Matt's relief,

a small green orb formed between them. It darted quickly to the right and vanished through the wall. Matt glared at the wizards who shrugged helplessly.

The orb re-appeared, having apparently realized the problem, and scooted off toward the far end of the room. They peered around the archway and saw the rival team running away from a set of vases with small, stumpy legs. The wizards tried occasionally to throw fireballs at the vases but with little effect.

"We'll have to ask Professor Powell how to deal with sentient ceramics." Matt grinned as he nodded at the rival team.

The orb moved in the opposite direction to their opponents and they hurried after it. Adrien kept his eye out for vases and any other ceramics. He didn't particularly want to fight a pottery urn. It felt like something that would damage his ego. They paused at the entrance to a room that looked as though it had become an impressionist painting. The floor rippled with something blue that Adrien thought might be the water of a babbling stream or a similar body of water. Dark smudges in the rough shape of boats floated along the walls, and a dark orange orb with orange ripples around it hovered beside the doorway.

Matt reached his foot out tentatively and touched the blue. To his dismay, it sank into it like quicksand.

"Which of you can form a raft or something?" He looked at the wizards. "I guess they don't really teach that in basic spellcraft."

Cody and Daniel had a silent conversation formed of raised eyebrows, tightened jaws, and small, jerky hand motions.

"We believe we can adapt an earth elemental spell to help us." Cody chewed his bottom lip. "Hopefully."

"Time's ticking." Matt made a hurry-up motion.

Adrien stepped beside the wizards. "We bring the earth into a central pathway." The elf envisaged a straight line between them and the doorway in his mind. "That was your thinking, yes?"

They nodded and raised their wands.

Adrien hadn't used his magic together with the wizards, but time now slipped through their fingers. He called the earth magic and pressed it against the blue faux water. The wizards' magic twined with his and he felt it strengthen. The blue shifted to a more solid and glassy appearance.

Matt poked the glassy part with his toe. It was solid.

A crash of ceramics against a wall caught their attention. The rival team raced into another room nearby with a pair of armless statues now hot on their heels.

"I don't think I'll ever feel safe in an art gallery again." Raine frowned at the statues. "And I'll never get too close to a statue."

Cameron laughed. "I'm sure you could take that statue." He grinned. "It wouldn't have a chance."

She wasn't entirely convinced but smiled anyway. She liked seeing the shifter relax and talk a little. He had scowled and given little more than short answers ever since she'd met him.

Adrien led the way and pushed more earth magic into the path as he did so to make sure his teammates weren't sucked into the paint.

The rival team pitched into the room behind them as Cody stepped off the path. A tall, lean witch stepped onto the narrow path Adrien and the wizards had formed but fell when it began to crumble as they released the magic. She fell into the thick blue paint and vanished, thrown from the game.

The rival team looked from the statues at their back to the Cardinals ahead. Matt led his team through the next room full of modern art and finally saw the golden token on a glass pedestal in the middle of a plain room. He circled it and checked for any traps. The leader of the rival team entered, dripping blue paint. He'd obviously had a narrow escape which would likely make a good story. Matt threw caution to the wind and leapt onto the gold token.

The crowd cheered and screamed in celebration. They'd done it. That was the first step on the way to the big championship.

Adrien grinned and looked at his friends in the stands who all applauded wildly. Even Cameron joined in. He'd known the shifter would come around.

CHAPTER TWENTY

Raine had finally mastered the stealth spell and volunteered to put one over Cameron. Evie stood ready to help as it was more difficult to do it for someone else. Raine almost covered Cameron but Evie stepped in and extended it over the top of his head. She squeezed Raine's hand.

"You're getting better."

Raine smiled, happy to see her hard work had paid off. Cameron remained close to her as they slipped past the seniors and darted down the stairs to the kemana. Their stealth spells didn't last long, and they needed to lose themselves in the crowd before the seniors or any professors spotted them. It was Cameron's first time there and he breathed deeply and absorbed all the scents once he'd slipped into the trading post for his Ruby Falls coins.

The stealth spells wore off as they jogged past a Willen-run stall and ducked around a corner.

"We're heading to Bubble and Fizz, right?" Sara looked at the others. "Cameron needs to see that place."

The shifter wasn't entirely impressed with the name of the place. He preferred meat and savory things over sweet, but he had begun to form bonds with them and didn't want to screw that up.

"Definitely." Evie grinned. "I think this would be a good opportunity to speak to the Ifrit, too."

William narrowed his eyes.

"Don't give me that look." Evie glared back at him. "You can huff and scowl as much as you like. The fact remains that we need to get that curse removed. You look like hell and it's only getting worse."

"What are we supposed to do against a community of Ifrit?" William looked away from her challenging gaze. "We don't stand a chance."

"Actually..." Raine smiled and drew his attention. "I read in the library that we are within our rights to demand the removal of the curse due to the offense it brings on your bloodline. They can argue that you aren't pure, but by cursing you, they have dishonored your father. That is enough to force them to remove it. They're very honor-bound, and I think you said your father is really respected."

"Yea. He's a big chief or something." William thrust his hands into his pockets. "I guess it's worth a try."

He didn't want to cling to false hope. He had adjusted to the nightmares a little. They weren't pleasant as the dark shadows under his eyes clearly revealed, but he could live with them.

Cameron gawked at the witches running the crystal

shop and the gnomes guarding the expensive jewelry. He held back a growl when he saw a pair of Kilomeas with a weapon's shop. He didn't much trust the creatures. They were too prone to aggression and breaking shifter bones.

"What's the deal with the Ifrit, then?" He put his hands in his pockets. "You're a half-blood, right?"

William tensed. "My father was an Ifrit. My mother wasn't."

"What's your heritage?" Sara looked pointedly at Cameron. "Given that you've raised the topic and all."

"Full-blooded shifters going back many generations. We were one of the first bloodlines to be turned. I'm the son of the alpha of a very respected pack." Cameron shrugged. "I haven't really looked into names, but ours carries weight in the shifter community."

He said it as though he'd said he enjoyed vanilla ice-cream. There was no arrogance to him.

"What about you?" Cameron nodded to Sara. "You don't normally see kitsune out with the rest of the magicals."

A dark-haired witch stopped and stared at Sara at the word kitsune. Sara glared in response as if daring her to try something. The witch raised her wand but her friend pushed it down and the students moved on.

"I'm from an old line, but most kitsune are." Sara turned her attention to a crystal rose that slowly changed color. "I think we should decorate our room. What do you think?"

Raine pursed her lips. "It wouldn't be fair to do much without Christie's input." She leaned against the wall of the shop. "It might be cool to put a couple of posters up."

Cameron let the blatant change in topic go. Bloodline

meant a lot to some magicals, his parents included. He had been treated differently because he was the alphas' only child.

"Old horror movie posters would be fun." Evie played absently with the hem of her shirt. "Although I prefer prints of watercolor paintings."

Raine looked at Sara. "We could put some of your art up." She grinned. "That'd really personalize it."

"We could each paint something?" Evie looked at the other girls. "I'm not much of an artist but I'd give it a try."

"Yes! I'd love to show you guys the art room. You'll love it. They have everything in there. I've hit a block with my current project, but maybe this will loosen everything up."

"We are not painting things." Adrien crossed his arms and looked at the three other guys. "If we decorate at all, I vote for useful things, like knives."

"There's no way the professors will let us put knives on the wall." William shook his head. "And we're not medieval knights or something anyway."

The elf grinned and sauntered off toward Bubble and Fizz. Cameron hadn't been allowed to add personal touches to his bedroom at the pack house, but the idea of personalizing his dorm room appealed.

"What about posters of weapons?" Cameron looked at Philip and William. "We're allowed posters, right?"

"I'd rather have music and movie posters." Philip crossed his arms. "Weapons don't seem that cool."

"Why don't we each decorate the patch of wall nearest our bed?" Cameron wouldn't give up on this plan. "Then it doesn't matter so much."

Philip didn't like the idea of the room not matching with his vision, but it wasn't worth making a huge fuss over.

"Deal." He nodded firmly. "We can look around here after Bubble and Fizz."

William tried to decide what he wanted in his space. He'd never discovered what movies or music he liked as his aunt hadn't allowed him such entertainment. He wasn't interested in art like the girls were, and he agreed with Philip about pictures of weapons.

They walked through the crowds and saw a poster shop run by a pair of young witches with luminous purple hair. A trio of landscapes caught William's eye. The first showed a barren desert with red rock formations and a dark storm on the horizon. The second was a vibrant rainforest full of animals and color, and the final was a simple beach scene with a calm sea. He dug around in his pocket to see how much money he'd managed to scrape together.

There wasn't enough there for both Bubble and Fizz and the posters. He frowned and walked away.

Cameron saw the way William looked at the posters. His parents gave him a very large weekly allowance and he didn't have anything to spend it on. The half-Ifrit left the shop and looked disheartened, and the shifter hated that. He picked up the posters and added a fourth displaying stark clifftops with a thin layer of bright pink flowers at the very top. He paid for them and added a little orange ribbon to hold them together without crushing them.

The shifter jogged to catch up with the rest of the group and handed the half-Ifrit the posters without looking at him. William felt a bloom of anger at first, but he realized Cameron had simply tried to be generous. The shifter refused to speak or look at him and simply held the posters out for him to take.

William finally conceded. "Thank you."

Cameron smiled and said nothing.

They had claimed their preferred booth in Bubble and Fizz. Cameron studied the menu with an expression of bemusement on his face. He'd assumed they were joking when they said the menu consisted of sugar, chocolate, and unhealthy comfort foods like pizza.

"Does anyone want to share a pizza with me?" He looked hopefully at his companions. "I thought the ham, pepperoni, and red pepper."

William went to speak but Sara covered his mouth. "No. He puts pineapple on his pizza." She removed her hand and he looked disapprovingly at her.

Cameron considered this. "I'm okay with pineapple."

The half-Ifrit grinned. "And I'm okay with the ham, pepperoni, and red pepper." William smirked at Sara. "I'd be happy to split one with you."

The rest of the group ordered macaroni and cheese or large ice-cream sundaes. Sara ordered extra sprinkles and cookie dough with her dessert and seemed very pleased with herself. She found she craved sugar more as her kitsune magic stirred. Her sisters were certainly in love with everything sugary, so maybe the two were connected.

"Is there a particular way to approach the Ifrit?" Evie

looked at Raine. "With this issue, I mean. They're kind of scary."

"Confidently. Weakness will make them aggressive and they'll simply push us around." Raine drew herself taller. "We are in the right and we can't leave until they give us what we want. Oh, and we need to destroy any of the little glass salamanders they like to send after people. They're spies and when we destroy them, we send a signal that we don't mess around."

William hunched his shoulders. He didn't like the new turn to the conversation. Ifrit weren't easy to get along with and Raine was right. They hated weakness. They still out-numbered their small group, though, and had more magic in their little finger than they had combined. It didn't auger well for their prospects of success.

Cameron wrinkled his nose as the scent of smoke and fire surrounded him. He hadn't met any Ifrit before, but the smell of fire made him want to run. It wasn't something you screwed with. Raine's fingertips brushed the back of his hand and he calmed a little. They were there to help William and he wouldn't back out and flee like a coward.

Raine ran the words through her head repeatedly. She wanted to be sure that she spoke perfectly so they didn't get pulled into some awful deal with the Ifrit. They turned the corner and saw the fire and the glass salamanders. Three dark red creatures scurried deeper into the neighborhood, probably to tell their masters they were approaching. She stamped on one that moved within reach.

A young Ifrit narrowed her eyes at the group but let them pass without any trouble. The farther they moved into the neighborhood, the more aware of watching eyes they became. Finally, the broad, older Ifrit they had expected to speak to stepped out of a shop and stood in the middle of the pathway. He squared his shoulders and looked at the students with disdain.

"We are here to demand that you right the wrong you have committed. You have disrespected the bloodline William carries when you cursed him. Doing so brings just wrath from the entire bloodline in question." Raine stood tall and stared fearlessly at him. "You understand the laws and the punishment will be enforced with full severity."

The Ifrit's flames hurtled skywards and licked around the edges of the buildings on either side. Raine stiffened her spine and merely raised an eyebrow. They couldn't hurt them while she conducted legal business—or so she hoped. She had read that in one of her searches, but as much as she loved books, there were times when they were wrong.

"He was cursed due to his lack of pure blood." The Ifrit took a step closer. "His bloodline is of no—"

Raine held up her hand to interrupt.

"That is of no relevance. He is still his father's son. The curse broke the old laws that have stood through the generations, and we are within our rights to call upon those gathered to demand just punishment for our friend's suffering."

Slowly, a grin spread across the Ifrit's face as respect for the bold young witch before him crept in. He waved his hand and William felt the curse snap within him. Suddenly, his head was clearer and he felt as though a weight had been lifted.

"Leave now. Your business has been concluded." The Ifrit gestured back in the direction from which they had come. "If you wish to exchange money, we will take it."

Raine turned slowly and walked with her head high and made sure to maintain a confident bearing. The others followed her lead and did the same. Sara resisted the urge to stick her tongue out at the Ifrit as she didn't think there was a law to protect kitsune.

Once they were safe and far from the Ifrit, everyone grinned.

"You were amazing."

"Who knew books could be so useful?"

"I'd rather we didn't do that again..."

"Thank you." William hugged her quickly. "I appreciate your dedication to looking after me."

The group put their stealth spells hurriedly back in place and left the kemana. Evie looked at her watch and realized that she was due in the kitchens with the pixies in only a few minutes.

The group separated and returned to their respective rooms. William stood at the end of his bed and gazed at the wall for a long time while he decided how best to put up his new posters. They gave him hope and something to focus on. He wanted to travel the world and see everything that it had to offer.

Cameron shifted into his wolf form and sprawled on his bed with a happy smile on his face. The school and everyone in it weren't so bad. He hadn't liked the Ifrit, but the kemana had the potential for a lot of fun. People there viewed him with disdain as a lowly shifter, but he found it didn't bother him anymore. He had his friends to back him up and show them there was far more to him than simply the son of the alpha.

CHAPTER TWENTY-ONE

Professor Fowler waited patiently as everyone settled themselves in their preferred seat.

"Today, you will brew a calming potion."

Evie put her hand on Raine's. That was another recipe Evie had made many times as her aunt often needed to soothe her nerves. Raine struggled with potions as she hadn't connected fully with her magic. Evie helped her through it, though.

"The recipe is on the card in front of you. You'll brew this one individually although you are welcome to talk."

Raine read through the laminated recipe twice. It was a complicated potion but she had more than enough time to work through step by step. She arranged her ingredients in front of her in the order she'd use them in.

Sara glared at her recipe card and muttered under her breath. She didn't understand why potions was so difficult. It was simply a matter of following a recipe, but she wasn't much of a cook, either.

Raine dropped the three pale-pink rose petals gently into the ice-cold water. She stirred them three times clockwise and once counter-clockwise. Evie watched and smiled as the water took on a glittery sheen. So far, it had gone well.

They followed the recipe together. Evie didn't say anything as she didn't want Raine to feel that she didn't think she could do it. Raine pursed her lips as she stirred the bubbling potion with a lavender stem. The potion was supposed to turn a bright, glittery blue, but it took on a distinctly greenish hue as she watched.

"You need to push your magic down through the lavender stem," Evie whispered.

Raine pulled her magic and tried to press it through the lavender. It resisted her at first, but she persisted until it gave and flowed into the potion. The right shade of blue appeared.

She continued diligently with the final steps and was delighted to see that it was the same color and consistency as Evie's. The professor came around to assess the attempts.

"Well done, Raine. That is beautifully done."

Happiness washed through her. She felt as though she had really made progress. Her hard work had started to pay off. Now, she was ready to ask if she could have some time in the potions lab for extra practice. There was a strong chance the professor would say no, but she really needed the additional time to use the skills she'd learned in a practical way.

Sara crossed her arms and glared at her black potion. "I followed the recipe."

"You put too much fire magic in." Evie squeezed Sara's shoulder. "It's not your fault."

Sara looked down and away. She hated struggling with her magic. The rest of her family made it look so easy and she still hadn't made any progress with hers. She huffed and left the class to go to Art Club. Painting would make her feel much better.

Evie and Raine waited to speak to Professor Fowler.

"Just the girls I wanted to talk to." She smiled and tried to push her red mane out of her eyes. "I need a little help with my greenhouse. I hoped that you two would be willing and able."

Evie's eyes lit up. She had missed gardening.

"I'd love to." Evie bit her bottom lip. "I mean. Thank you for thinking of us, Professor Fowler."

Raine wasn't sure it was a good idea. She'd managed to kill her cactus.

"Come along, then. I'll give you a tour."

Evie wasn't sure why she didn't know there was a huge greenhouse on the grounds. She realized she hadn't really wandered around much. There could be all sorts of interesting things out there she wasn't aware of.

They followed the professor along a narrow black stone path toward the greenhouse that sprawled in the sunlight. The silver dragon had landed nearby and watched them with a small smile.

"Do you have new helpers?" He took a step closer. "I still think you should raise chickens."

Professor Fowler shook her head. "I am not raising chickens for you to eat."

The dragon lay down and Raine swore that he pouted.

The woman opened a small door and led the girls inside. Evie took a deep breath and smiled at the rich herbal scent that immediately surrounded them. The air was damp and warm, a familiar sensation that made Evie feel as though she was at home. Raine didn't dare touch anything in case she accidentally harmed it.

Short, stubby green plants with red-tipped leaves sat in dark-blue ceramic pots in neat rows to their left. Evie breathed in their sweet candy-cane scent before she hurried to catch up with Professor Fowler.

"If you could water the healing herb section back here, I would very much appreciate it." The professor gestured to a large area full of green herbs in every shape and size. "And pruning the roses would also be very useful."

"Do you have somewhere to put the stems and preserve the petals?" Evie smiled. "I assume they'll be used in classes."

Raine wandered to the rose bushes and smiled at the myriad of colors on display. Professor Fowler even had some blue roses that were incredibly rare. Humans usually dyed them rather than cultivating them, but there were one or two uncommon hybrids. She would have to look at her schedule and fit her time in the greenhouse around her time with Smoke.

Evie grinned at her. "This place is amazing."

"It really is." Raine smiled. "Damn, I meant to ask if I could practice potions."

They looked around and the professor had somehow vanished. Raine made a mental note to ask her next time she saw her. It wasn't the end of the world to go without extra practice for a few days.

CHAPTER TWENTY-TWO

Raine brushed her hair and tried to understand exactly what she was feeling. It was her first Thanksgiving without her Uncle Jerry and there was a sadness to that. Yet she couldn't help but smile at the joy that radiated through her room. Christie talked at a mile a minute while Sara laughed at whatever story she shared. Evie pored over a new recipe book the pixies had given her. She would help them create the variety of desserts that would be served at the Thanksgiving feast later.

These were her new friends and they understood her in a way no one had before. She missed Uncle Jerry, but she knew he wouldn't fit into this world no matter how hard he tried. Magic surrounded her there, and that was increasingly a big part of who and what she was.

Butterflies formed in Evie's stomach as she walked to the

kitchen. The Thanksgiving feast was the highlight of the year food-wise. It was when the pixies pulled out all the stops and she was involved this year. She had always been included in the cooking back at home, but this was something different. Everyone expected a true spectacle from the pixies, and she'd help them cook for the entire school.

She walked into the kitchen and cheerful music filled the air. Tori and Mags danced around the big preparation table in the middle with huge grins on their faces. The room was filled with magic and happiness. Whatever worries Evie might have had faded the moment she stepped over that threshold.

"Today, as we have an extra set of hands, we'll serve a selection of desserts. We'll make this the biggest and best feast yet." Tori looked at Evie. "Evie here will bake three pies and those walnut pillows we liked the look of. Mags will take on the cheesecake and torte. And I will make those wonderful pumpkin and walnut squares."

Evie swallowed hard. She'd expected that she'd bake a few things but she hadn't anticipated three varieties of pie and some delicate cookie parcel things. She'd hoped Tori would take on the walnut pillows, but she also felt honored that she believed Evie could pull them off.

The pixies fluttered around and everyone got to work. The turkeys and hams were already in the oven and cranberries proliferated in various forms. Evie went to her workstation and studied the recipes she'd been given. A happy calm settled over her and she started with the sweet pie crusts.

They were deceptively difficult to master. Evie's family prided themselves on having perfected the art of a thin, crisp, and balanced crust. Their recipe had been passed down the generations and it was thrilling to use it that morning. The key was to make sure you worked quickly, were gentle with the pastry, and had cold ingredients. The moment the butter warmed, the consistency faltered, and the entire thing was a dismal failure.

Evie's magic flowed smoothly as she used it to set the whisk mixing her ingredients while she continued with the delicate pastries. Time flew by in a happy blur while she baked. Tori stopped to check on her a few times and was free with her compliments. When her desserts were placed on the big table in the middle, she was justifiably proud of them. Her latticework on the pumpkin pie was perfect and the walnut pillows had come out evenly sized with delicate, light pastry. It was her best work and she thanked the pixies for that.

"Go and enjoy the feast." Tori hugged her. "We're proud to have you in the kitchen with us."

Evie beamed and returned the hug. The others gathered around for a huge group hug and she finally managed to squeeze out of the huddle and head into the main hall. She found her friends waiting for her.

Raine looked at the hall in awe. The seniors had created the decorations and they had done an amazing job. Strings of tiny pumpkins and little turkeys hung suspended from the ceiling by invisible threads of magic. Delicate, silky leaves in all the autumnal colors coated the ceiling in a kaleidoscope of colors and shapes and gave the space a feeling of warmth and comfort.

Every table had a different centerpiece. The one on their table was a complicated arrangement of orange and gold ribbons twisted around thick pillar candles. Small ceramic pumpkins were interspersed with glass leaves that slowly changed color.

All the candles around the room lit at once and drew a startled squeak of surprise from a freshman at the next table. Raine undid the deep umber ribbon around her silver cutlery as the first course appeared on the pristine white plate before her.

Large soup bowls were filled with a creamy orange-colored soup with a delicate dash of what looked like cream. Cameron sniffed at his and wrinkled his nose.

"It's spiced carrot and pine nut." Evie smiled and picked up her spoon. "It's divine."

The shifter glanced at the others as they began eating theirs. Pine nuts didn't sound as though they should be eaten. Still, he tried a spoonful tentatively.

"What was your role in this feast, Evie?" Sara looked at her. "You did the desserts, right?"

"Not all of them. I did the pumpkin pie, sweet potato pie, and cranberry and apple pie. The walnut pillows are mine too."

"We won't be able to move after this." Philip grinned. "It sounds amazing. I can't wait to try them, Evie."

They finished their soup and the pixies gave them a few minutes to relax and talk before the next course arrived. The classic Thanksgiving meal complete with turkey and cranberry jelly appeared and Cameron looked far happier.

"I didn't know turkey could be this good." Sara cut another piece and shook her head. "I thought it was dry and chewy."

"This is amazing," Raine agreed. "We need to do something nice for the pixies to thank them for their hard work."

"Agreed." William nodded enthusiastically. "I've never had a Thanksgiving this good before."

Once the main meal was finished, they each stretched their legs a little and looked at each other. The pixies rather obviously made a small white card with "give thanks" in gold script appear in front of each person.

Philip picked up his card and went first. "Today, I am thankful for the amazing opportunities this school offers. I'm thankful for good friends, incredible food, and the potential for so much more."

Cameron and William both looked away. Neither were happy to try to give thanks. The shifter had a tumultuous past with the holiday and William had never celebrated it like this before. He wasn't sure how to express his happiness.

Raine picked up her card and smiled as she looked at her friends. The school had opened her world and given her so much to think about and enjoy.

"I am thankful for my amazing friends. For my wonderful family, even if it isn't a traditional one. I'm thankful for the gnomes and professors and all they do for us. I'm thankful to have been given a chance to explore this incredible world full of magic and have the tools at my disposal to make the world a better place."

They continued around the table, each thankful for

each other and their surroundings. William managed to speak honestly of his gratitude for the acceptance his friends showed him. He had never known happiness or family even remotely like what they had shown him.

Agent Connor was blown away by the quality and variety of food that appeared before him for the Thanksgiving feast. It was all completely beyond his very human experience. He looked at Raine a few times and was happy to see her having a great time with her friends. He'd spoken to Jerry that morning and promised to put her on the phone with him after the feast.

Xander looked drawn and pale but he had made an effort to come to the professor's table. The faculty was worried that he wouldn't be able to conduct his classes for much longer. The poison ate away at him and they hadn't found the cure yet.

The small flock of tiny turkeys that acted as their centerpiece fluttered their wings and walked around, much to Bruce's delight. He hadn't yet adjusted to the sheer amount of magic around him on a day to day basis. Mara lifted her wine glass with a sad smile.

"We should give thanks to the pixies for this beautiful feast."

Everyone lifted their wine glasses in agreement. Bruce saw that the pixies watching from the kitchen doorway were clearly delighted by the tribute. He made a mental note to approach them and thank them properly once the feast was done.

"This has been a difficult year." Mara pursed her lips. "However, there is always something to be thankful for. I am thankful for my friends who have helped guide me through difficult times and offered support during the darkness. I'm thankful for my family. Even though they can't be here today, I know they are safe and well." She squeezed Xander's hand. "And I am grateful for the magic that will bring Xander back to full health."

The professors nodded thoughtfully. They had given their all to find the cure for him, but it proved particularly difficult. The poison was something very unusual and the cure hadn't been discussed in any of the texts they could find.

Once everyone had given thanks, the pixies made the desserts appear in the middle of the table. The tiny turkeys ran, flapped their wings, and clucked at the intrusion. Bruce held his hand out at the edge of the table when one tried to walk off. He didn't want to have to chase it around the hall.

"Wow." Lucy looked upon the arrangement of pies and desserts. "They've really outdone themselves."

"Evie O'Connell helped them this year." Mara smiled. "They have taken a shine to her since she started her Baking Club."

Mara took a small slice of the sweet potato pie and one of the delicate pillow things. She bit into the confection and found the pastry light and sweet with a rich walnut filling.

"I'll have to try to get the recipe for these pillows." Annabelle took another one. "They're little slices of heaven."

The professors each took a piece of each dessert and enjoyed the wines the pixies had paired with them. Everything was perfect. The students were all happy and well behaved and no one tried to throw any food. Mara shook her head, remembering the last time someone had thrown food.

The pixies did not approve of wasting food, particularly when they put so much time and effort into it. They had removed everything, only to make it reappear on a trajectory with the students. It had taken all day to clean up. Thankfully, the older students warned the younger ones against repeating it.

Christie grinned at her friends. Thanksgiving wasn't something they celebrated in England, but she had grown to love the holiday. Everyone was so happy and full of life.

"I think we should try to take something like this to England. I know we can't have actual Thanksgiving because we don't have the history behind it and that would be weird. Although that doesn't stop some Americans from celebrating Guy Fawkes night. I think they saw the movie *V for Vendetta* and went from there. I do think you guys simply love fireworks, though." She took a breath. "Anyway, I think having a day where everyone's happy and thankful is a really good idea. I mean, it makes us focus on the happiness and the things that enable that. It can be so easy to get wrapped up in the scary and unpleasant things, but we need to stop and smell the roses sometimes."

Her friends all nodded in agreement. They knew better

than to answer yet as Christie would likely have another essay to say before they'd get a chance to really talk. She curled her toes and felt the happiness fill her completely. When she'd first come to the school, she hadn't really fit in but now, she had a group. Everything was perfect.

Agent Connor approached Raine as she left the hall.

"I promised your uncle you'd call him today."

Raine smiled. She'd hoped to speak to him.

He took her into the headmistress's office and gave her a phone before he left the room to give her some privacy. A small flicker of sadness settled in Raine's stomach, but she pushed it aside. Her uncle would have friends around him and she knew he'd be happy to hear how well everything had gone for her. She now even had a grasp on her magic thanks to all her reading and the help from the gnomes.

"Hey, Uncle Jerry. Happy Thanksgiving."

"Raine, it's so good to hear from you. Happy Thanksgiving. How're you doing?"

"I'm great. I've worked with a young horse called Smoke. I'll back him in the spring, and I think he has real potential as a jumper. I have fantastic friends here, and my magic is coming on really well. Oh, and they have the most amazing library here."

"That sounds wonderful. I'm very happy for you."

"How are things there?"

"They're good. It's quiet without you but I've helped the agency out again and that feels good. We're making a real difference out there."

"I can't wait to be an agent like you and Dad. I hope to learn more combat and defense magic so I can be a better agent."

She could feel her uncle's pride down the phone and could picture the smile on his face.

"Your dad would be so proud of you."

"Thanks. That means a lot."

CHAPTER TWENTY-THREE

Matt looked at his team, who waited expectantly for him to speak. He wasn't very good at rousing pep talks, yet for some reason, there was a call for the captains to do it. He considered asking the coach if he could skip that part in the future.

"All right. So, this is it. Today's game is the defining moment. If we win this one, we're through to the first stage of the championship."

Cody bounced on the balls of his feet. It was bitterly cold, and he wanted to get on with the game. He hoped it would be somewhere warm and dry.

Cameron had claimed the seat beside Raine in the stands. He had brought the firebugs this time and handed them to the little group while they waited for the game to start. A small group of fairies sat on the very top row and their wings glistened in the pale sunlight like fresh frost. They chattered amongst themselves and were the first to cheer when the team walked out onto the field.

Etienne walked with a determination that amused Cameron. The elf was so serious. His brother Adrien wasn't much different. "Almost can't tell them apart," he chuckled. He leaned a little closer to Raine who rubbed her hands together while she waited for the firebug to warm her. He felt a fondness stir softly within, a sense that his friends had become a secondary pack. He wouldn't tell them that, of course, but he enjoyed it. For once, he felt he really belonged.

Great trees took shape and brightly colored flowers formed a carpet beneath the thick canopy overhead. Adrien looked around quickly to establish some sense of where they were. It was obviously a forest, but the type of forest would give them some idea of what traps they would face.

A soft snort issued from their left and the team turned to see an Irish elk. The deer-like creature stood some six and a half feet tall at the shoulder, possibly taller. Its huge antlers spread far from its head and were tipped with sharp points. Adrien rolled his shoulders and summoned a bow and arrow from the ether. After the comments made at movie night, he thought it would be a good idea to train with one.

The elf had been trained in most weapons over the years. His family were proud of their warrior heritage and took their role as guardians and protectors very seriously. Adrien was no different. Once school was finished, he would return to France and take up the mantle of a guardian. The elk turned to look at them as Adrien took a slow breath and sighted on its heart. He released the arrow and the elk vanished in a soft puff of smoke.

"Wow, I thought elves were only awesome archers in the movies." Cody beamed at him. "That was so cool."

Adrien pursed his lips and his bow and arrow vanished. Matt sniffed the air for any clues as to where they should go. Something called to his instincts and he obeyed. The wizards tried to form a tracking spell, but their magic fizzled with every attempt.

"Sometimes, the Louper officials block trackers." Matt shrugged. "We'll manage."

They jogged through the forest with bright pink and white flowers underfoot and broad trees around them. The trunks were wider than Adrien's arms would stretch, and it gave him a sense of comfort. Birds broke from the trees and called out in alarm. The team slowed and tried to see what had startled them.

Raine's jaw dropped when she saw the huge oak tree move. Its trunk split into two legs and two of the wider boughs formed arms. It approached the team methodically. They'd be squashed beneath its foot—or whatever a tree walked on. She wanted to call out and warn them as they huddled together and tried to pinpoint the source of the noise.

Etienne was the first to feel the magic of the tree creature. His brother sensed the same thing. He shoved Cody and shouted at the others to move. Adrien looked back at his brother. "Help the others!"

They wouldn't stand a chance against the creature. None of them had anywhere near enough earth magic to defeat it. Their only choice was to run. Of course, they couldn't outrun something that size, but they had to at least try.

The players ducked beneath heavy branches and leapt over small streams in their quest to escape the giant tree that pursued them with casual ease. Without warning, their feet stepped into space and they fell through pitch blackness.

At first, Etienne thought they would land back on the field and that they'd fallen into some form of trap. Instead, they landed on something soft and musty. It took his eyes a moment to adjust but it appeared to be feathers and dried leaves.

Matt scrambled to his feet and Adrien stood and helped Daniel up.

"What now?" Cody looked at Matt. "Do you have any idea where to go from here?"

Daniel used his wand to form a bright white orb of light. Cody added two more and they could clearly see the dirt tunnel around them. Roots protruded from the ceilings and walls, and there was only one direction to walk in.

"It looks like we go that way," Etienne said with Adrien close behind.

They crept through the underground corridor for what felt like an hour. Raine leaned forward in her seat and searched for the rival team or upcoming traps. She was completely invested in the match and seeing the Cardinals win. Cameron smiled as he watched her rapt expression.

Etienne ran his fingertips along the dirt wall and tried to sense any magic that might provide a clue as to what to look out for. Something caught his attention when the tunnel split in two. The magic tingled and then everything went deathly quiet before he felt a vibration in the floor.

"Run!" The elf pushed Matt down the left tunnel. "We need to run."

He wasn't sure exactly what approached but knew it was full of magic and danger. They heard the sound of hooves pounding damp dirt behind them. A sweet, sparkly taste coated their tongues and the scent of horses filled their noses.

"Unicorns!" Matt pushed himself to run faster. "Don't let them get close."

The brilliant white horses with long, sharp, golden horns stampeded after them. Their numbers filled the tunnel.

Cody threw a few fireballs. One of the unicorns caught fire but it only enraged the creature and it emitted a terrifying roar.

"Why is a unicorn roaring?" Adrien shouted.

"Because they're vicious monsters and monsters roar," Matt replied.

Oddly enough, it made sense. They dove into a smaller tunnel and finally saw something positive. The gold token lay ahead in the middle of a small bowl of water. The rival team hurtled out of another tunnel with an army of blood-stained songbirds after them. Their team leader lunged forward and snatched the gold token before Matt could move.

Adrien fought to catch his breath as the cold air hit him and they stood back on the field.

Matt dragged his fingers through his hair. "We were so damn close."

"Unicorns, man? I'll have nightmares for a week now." Cody frowned. "Who does that to someone?"

They all laughed, more to push aside the frustration than out of genuine humor.

"There is another match yet." Etienne patted their captain on the back. "We'll win that one."

CHAPTER TWENTY-FOUR

Raine frowned when she saw a pair of witches buying a pack of what looked like hand-made cookies in the hallway. There had been a proliferation of cookie sales recently, and she wasn't sure why. She suspected that Philip was involved somehow, given his love for business, and the students seemed happy to pay for them.

She headed into the library where the head librarian waited for her beside a fresh batch of books.

"Do you know what's going on with all of the cookies?" She glanced over her shoulder and saw someone else making a purchase. "They seem to have popped up out of nowhere."

"I'm not sure, but I don't like it. Those aren't ordinary treats." He glared at an older Wood Elf who tried to bring some into the library. "There's magic within them but I haven't gotten my hands on one to find out what type yet."

Raine looked at the tempting pile of books and then the

hallway and sighed. If she wanted to be an FBI agent, she had to investigate the small crimes too. The delicacies could be entirely innocent, of course, but something about the expression on the students' faces when they made the purchase worried her. It didn't look at all like an innocuous sugar-hit enthusiasm.

"I'll look into it." She put her hand on top of the books. "Would you be upset if I came and read these later?"

"Of course not. But please, tell me the whole story with those cookies when you get back." He picked the books up. "And I'll be here if you need any help with the magic within them."

Raine strolled into the hallway and followed a pair of witches who held their prize as though it was the source of life itself. When she looked around in earnest, she realized that most of the students clutched the baked treats.

Something was very definitely weird. Everyone joked that Girl Scout cookies were addictive, but she began to wonder if perhaps those cookies really were. She decided to change tack when she didn't see anyone selling the cookies and went to the kitchen in search of Evie.

She knocked on the kitchen door and waited.

The head pixie with a shock of pink hair opened the door and raised an eyebrow.

"Hi, could I speak to Evie a moment please?"

The pixie looked over her shoulder and ushered her friend over.

"Hey! So, erm...this will sound really weird, but a lot of cookies are changing hands at the moment." Raine tucked her hair behind her ear. "You wouldn't know anything about that, would you?"

"Sure. Philip had this business idea to sell my hand-made cookies so we could start a group social fund." Evie shrugged. "They are easy to make and they're selling almost quicker than I can make them. We have a nice stash of money tucked away in our fund, though."

Raine sighed. "Is there magic in the cookies by any chance?"

Evie frowned. "No. They're normal cookies. Mostly chocolate chip but there are some white chocolate and macadamia too."

"Do you have any idea where Philip is?"

Evie chewed thoughtfully on her bottom lip. "I think he's probably in the movie room."

"Thanks. Happy baking."

Worry lines settled around Evie's eyes. They had made a fair amount of money from the sales, and it was weird that they were so popular. She knew that her cookies were good, but were they really that good?

"Go." Tori shooed her out of the kitchen. "You were only cleaning anyway. Find out what that little swine has done to your precious cookies."

Evie gave Tori a quick hug and rushed after Raine. "Hold up, I'm coming with you."

As they walked through the hallways, Evie began to see what had worried Raine. There was definitely something weird afoot. She didn't miss the odd expressions in the students' eyes, either, as though there was magic at play. Evie hadn't put any magic in the cookies, though. She would never take that risk.

The girls entered the movie room and found Philip

counting money while making notes in a simple black book.

"Is that all from the cookies?" Evie pointed at the money. "That's rather a lot."

"We're doing great. We've already made five hundred. I think we'll be able to buy a new TV, and there'll be plenty over for group trips."

Evie and Raine exchanged a look.

"Did you do anything to the cookies?" Evie moved to stand in front of Philip with her arms folded. "I make good cookies, but they're not that good."

Philip didn't meet her gaze.

Evie nudged his leg with her toe. "Philip. What did you do?"

He sighed and raised his eyes. "Fine. I added a little something extra to ensure that we made a nice profit."

Evie glared at him. She was hurt and absolutely livid. "You had so little faith in my baking that you felt the need to 'add a little something extra?'"

"What did you add, Philip?" Raine stepped beside Evie. "Was it magic?"

"It was only a few drops. No big deal." Philip ran his fingers through his hair. "Simply a little potion."

"A potion that does what?" Raine looked around for signs of a concoction but saw nothing. "What are the intended effects?"

"Light addiction," Philip muttered.

"What?" Evie threw her hands up in horror. "You made my cookies addictive? What is wrong with you? You turned me into a drug dealer? How am I supposed to trust you after this? Why would you do this? Money isn't everything."

"What type of light addiction?" Raine stepped closer to him and her hands balled into fists. "And is it dark magic?"

"No. It's not—at least I don't think it's dark magic." He stood up. "Look, it's simply a little Cloud potion."

Evie's jaw dropped. "Cloud potion? You do realize that long-term exposure to that can cause serious addiction and physical problems?" She restrained herself from throttling him by clasping her hands together. "You don't screw around with things like that."

"What's Cloud potion?" Raine glanced from one to the other. "It sounds illegal."

"It's not illegal. It's designed to calm people's nerves, but when added to sugar, it becomes something more." Evie sighed. "It's difficult to get hold of for that reason."

"So where did you get it, Philip?" Raine gave him her best FBI agent glare. "Because we all know you're a B-student in potions."

He looked away again and shifted his feet uncomfortably. "A business contact."

Evie put her hands firmly on his shoulders. "Tell me who." She looked at Raine. "We need to find out how to undo this, too."

"We'll have to go to Professor Fowler." Raine clenched and unclenched her fists in an attempt to curb her rising anger. "How badly has he hurt those students?"

"I didn't mean to. It was only meant to make them taste a little better so they came back for more." Philip licked his lips nervously. "I really didn't know it could hurt."

The girls stepped away and sighed. Philip seemed genuine enough.

"We'll go to Professor Fowler. She'll have the best idea how to undo this." Evie grabbed Philip's arm. "And you won't escape your punishment."

They couldn't find Professor Fowler and instead, settled for the headmistress. Philip tried to think of ways to spin everything in a positive light, but he found nothing that would help his cause. He hadn't realized that Cloud was so potentially dangerous and had simply wanted to make some money for his friends. He knew that William struggled with cash and he'd hoped to find ways to help the half-Ifrit.

The headmistress called them into her office and Evie nudged Philip forward.

"What happened?" Ms. Berens glanced sharply at each one in turn. "Is someone hurt?"

Evie poked Philip hard in the ribs. "No. I...well, I screwed up." Philip sighed softly. "I wanted to make some money to help my friends and I put a little Cloud potion into the cookies Evie kindly made for me. Everyone who's bought the cookies is now addicted. I didn't realize the dangers of using Cloud until Evie told me."

The headmistress closed her eyes and rubbed her temple. She could already feel the glares and hear the complaints from the parents. First, dark wizards had attacked the school and blew sections of it up. Now, one of the students had gotten the rest addicted to Cloud. Some days, she thought the students would be the end of her.

"We'll have to find Professor Fowler and speak to the kitchen pixies. You will help Professor Fowler brew the cure, and Evie will work with the pixies to put that into the mixture." She looked sternly at Philip. "You will personally hand out the cure cookies to every single student at this school and will do so at no charge. And from here on out, you will draw up a business plan and bring it to myself and Professor Powell for a thorough vetting. Do you understand?"

Mara called her magic and held out her hand. Philip shook her hand to seal the agreement between them. He couldn't start another business without her and Professor Powell examining it first. Of course, he already tried to think of ways around that, but he wouldn't admit that to anyone present.

They bustled out of the room in search of Professor Fowler. She had returned to her office and listened in silence while the headmistress related the entire story.

"He did what?" The potions professor looked at Philip and put her hands on her hips. "You'll scrub cauldrons every evening for the rest of the week."

Philip sighed with relief. He'd expected something far worse.

———

Evie returned to the kitchen.

"Tori, could you help me to integrate this into the cookies?" She held up a thick white syrup. "It's the cure for Cloud addiction."

Tori raised an eyebrow. "That boy put Cloud in your cookies?"

Evie nodded. She was still furious that Philip had done that.

The pixie put her arm around Evie's shoulders and led her to her workstation.

"It'll be a little difficult, but we can do it. We'll think up something suitable for that boy too."

Philip started in the west wing and made his way methodically through the school and handed out the free cookies. It hurt his soul to give them away for free and lose his business like that. The profit margins had been amazing and he wouldn't build another viable business up any time soon.

Word of the free cookies soon spread through the school and the rest of the students flocked to him, which saved him some walking. When he was finally done, he headed into the hall for dinner. A large stack of cauldrons waited for him once he had eaten, but he was starving and looking forward to a hot meal.

He sat in his usual seat and tried to ignore the glare from Raine. "Did anyone do anything fun today?" He looked at the rest of the group.

"Why did you go and make everyone addicts?" William crossed his arms. "What's so wrong with legitimate business?"

Philip wasn't sure how to explain that his grasp on

business ethics didn't quite line up with William's in a way that didn't make him seem like an ass.

"Well, I thought it was a legitimate business. Look at fast food places. It isn't that unusual for them to put extra salt on or in the food to encourage the sale of drinks." He shrugged. "I didn't realize it would cause harm. I wouldn't have done it if I'd have known."

"You mean you'd have found a different way to get them addicted?" Evie spat.

"I'm sorry, Evie, really I am. Your baking is amazing, and it would never have worked if the cookies had been inferior. I'm sorry that I hurt your feelings. That was never my intent." He looked away. "I really do appreciate all the hard work you put in too. I wanted to gather some money for all of us to use and enjoy."

He held back that he wanted to help William as he thought the half-Ifrit would be offended and perhaps set him on fire.

Their food appeared and Philip thought he'd never been so happy to see a bowl of chili in his life. To his confusion and horror, the first bite tasted like wet, moldy mud.

"Does this chili taste okay?" He looked at the others and frowned. "Mine taste like mud."

Evie smirked. "That's what you get for screwing with pixie baking." She took a big mouthful of her chili. "Everything will taste like mud for a few days."

Philip looked longingly at his food. He was starving but a bowl of mud didn't appeal at all. After a long moment in which he tried to think how he could get around the pixie magic, he took another taste. It would be a very long few days.

Raine and Evie followed Philip to the potions lab to keep him company while he scrubbed the cauldrons. Raine couldn't help but think about how many criminals had started out the way Philip did. It was so easy to begin with good intentions and a desire to make money for people. His understanding of ethics and business made him particularly susceptible to the criminal path. Raine didn't like the idea of having to arrest him later in life.

Philip looked at the large stack of cauldrons and his shoulders hunched. He knew that he had put people in danger and he wouldn't shirk his punishment, but that didn't mean he would enjoy it either.

He pulled on his pink rubber gloves and got to work.

"You know, we could watch cheesy Christmas movies in the run-up to Christmas." Evie sat on the table closest to Philip. "It would fit within our cheesy theme."

"I don't know." Raine shook her head. "There's something charming and fun about the cheesy horror movies. I think it's about how over the top they are. The monsters are also completely unbelievable."

"Those Christmas stories are completely unbelievable too." Philip put more weight behind his scrubbing. "I mean, the reporter marries the prince she met three days ago?"

"You're such a grinch." Evie laughed. "Are you one of those bah-humbug types?"

Philip snorted. "No. I'm more of a realist." He stood and stretched. "They're so contrived. At least with the horror, they're supposed to be ridiculous. The Christmas movies give people a weird false hope."

"No one really thinks a prince will show up in their stocking." Evie laughed. "I'm sure some people would like that to happen, but no one expects it."

"I still think Raine's right. The horror movies are a better fit." He scrubbed a particularly stubborn patch of green. "Any idea what was made in these last?"

"I think it was a growth potion for the roses." Evie peered at it. "Or maybe a health potion?"

Philip sighed. "Well, it's very stuck."

"Do you think he's learned his lesson?" Evie looked at Raine. "Or should I hold back the secret to getting that off?"

Raine looked at Philip who had a hopeful expression on his face.

"I don't know...he doesn't seem that repentant."

"And he did put a lot of people in danger." Evie looked at Philip who gave her his best puppy-eyes impression. "I suppose there are lots more cauldrons left yet."

CHAPTER TWENTY-FIVE

Philip looked absolutely pitiful as he bit cautiously into his omelet. Once again, it tasted like mud. It had been three days and Evie began to develop a little sympathy for his plight. Then she thought back to how dangerous his actions had been, and the sympathy faded.

The pixies had watched him closely for signs of remorse, and more importantly, any attempt to mitigate the effects of the spell. If he was caught at that, they'd sworn they'd make it last for a year.

Mara shook her head as she saw the wounded-puppy look Philip gave his friends. She had lived a long enough life to understand his personality type. He needed strong consequences to keep him on the straight and narrow. She was sure that he was loyal to his friends, but his love of money and business made it difficult to make him understand ethics.

"He looks as though he's learned his lesson." Lucy looked at Philip. "Look at him. He's miserable."

Annabelle shook her head.

"Don't let him fool you. He knows exactly how to charm people into what he wants." She sipped her orange juice. "I know I sound cruel. He is only fourteen, but he follows in his father's footsteps."

Lucy waited for Annabelle to expand.

"He is the son of George Webster." Mara pushed her empty plate aside. "The business tycoon."

"Ah." Lucy found her sympathy fading. "I see."

George Webster was a talented and single-minded businessman who had even given to many magical related charities and good causes. He had never been caught doing anything illegal, but his reputation defined him as a cutthroat. Mara hoped quietly that Philip's friends would soften his sharp edges and give him more empathy for the people around him.

The friends finished breakfast and made their way casually to the common room. The rain lashed down and Raine had spent her time with Smoke before breakfast. The young horse didn't much like the wet weather and that made him difficult to work with in the outdoor arena. He had pranced at the end of his line and kept retreating toward the stable.

"Have any of you done the history homework yet?" Sara flopped into the armchair. "I swear, it's impossible."

Raine laughed.

"It's not impossible. You merely need the right books." She tucked her legs up under her. "Have you asked the gnomes for help?"

Sara wouldn't admit that she actually hadn't been to the library at all yet.

"Can you believe how much reading we need to do for potions?" Philip sighed. "I swear, there isn't enough room in my head for all these herbs."

Evie pointed at the page he was looking at. "The key is to group them into families in your mind." She gestured to the family name below each diagram. "Once you know the family of the plant, you'll have a rough idea of the category of herb it is. Then you can go from there."

Philip wasn't convinced. The plants all looked the same to him. They were all green with leaves.

Raine opened her own book and continued to read on the history of witches and elves in South America. She had been surprised, at first, how much influence they'd had on Aztec history and culture. The more she read, the more it all made sense, though. The style of written language adopted down there matched closely with a lot of the ancient spells the old witch covens used. The head librarian had found a very old book focused on ancient witch magic and showed her some of the pictographs in there.

She found the way that everything came together absolutely fascinating. If you looked at one thing, you could find a thread to something else entirely and suddenly, it all came together into one beautiful picture. It infuriated her that they had made no progress on the druid problem. Still, she was determined that they would find the clue that would break the whole thing open.

Raine sat in the class on kemanas and underground cities

with Professor Grant and felt a little guilty at having slipped into the underground city. She tried to act interested as the professor explained things she'd seen with her own eyes but wasn't supposed to have. It wasn't in her nature to break the rules, but they hadn't done any harm. And once they solved the druid problem, they would have done something good.

The professor explained that each kemana had a large crystal at the heart of it.

"The magic within that crystal powers the kemana. There is no magic like it anywhere else in the world. In fact, the crystal in the kemana below this school helps to power the defenses and protections all around this school. We received permission from those living in the kemana to do so."

A Wood Elf raised his hand. "Is it true someone tried to steal the magic from the crystal last year?"

Annabelle smiled tightly. It was true, but they had tried to keep the details from the students. And the parents, for that matter. One of their own, the professor of magic and mechanics, had actually believed that he could become more powerful by stealing the magic from the crystal.

They had found out after the fact that he had belonged to a brotherhood of wizards who dealt specifically in dangerous magic designed to improve the power of magic users. As far as Annabelle could tell, they weren't malicious, merely poorly directed.

"Yes, that is true." She made her smile deliberately open and unperturbed. "It's also true that the person was caught and punished severely for their transgressions."

That part wasn't entirely true. The man in question hadn't been caught, exactly. He had been consumed by a darkness no one had fully identified.

"Can anyone tell me the neighborhoods and beings present within the kemana here?" Annabelle looked around the room. "Anyone?"

Only two hands went up. She was surprised to see that Philip was one of them.

"Kilomeas and Willens."

"Who here can tell me about the Willens?" The professor once again looked around the room. "Has anyone met a Willen?"

Raine kept her hand down. She wasn't sure that she wouldn't give herself away if she said something. Still, the professor pointed at her.

"Raine?"

"I've read that the Willens are large rat beings who are very loyal and related to the large rats in the New York subway." She chewed on her bottom lip as if in thought. "And I think they're supposed to be very fond of stealing things."

"You have to be careful around the Willens. They'll take anything not pinned down," a wizard in front of Raine said.

"It's horrifying how they hide things in their folds."

"Absolutely disgusting. You wouldn't want whatever they stole back."

The professor held her hand up. "What can you tell me about their preferred living situation?"

A dark-haired witch in the front row raised her hand. "They prefer places which are shabby with lots of places to hide their stolen goods. They enjoy being close to their families where they show affection and keep them safe."

Raine knew all of this and found herself bored in a class for the first time. Usually, everything was so shiny and new that she was excited. This time, they shared knowledge that she already had, and she hated that.

"What are you baking later?" she whispered to Evie.

"Brownies with walnuts." Evie doodled on her notepad. "The pixies are teaching me how to make them really rich and gooey in the middle."

Raine watched as her friend doodled a little scene with mushrooms with legs that appeared to wander around a shop. Evie added little details such as a clothes rack and a small muffin, also with legs. It made no sense at all, but she stared in fascination.

The group made it through the last of the classes for the day and Philip dragged his heels to the dining hall. Cameron had joined them in history class. He didn't take the magic-focused classes due to his inability to use magic.

"Will you guys watch the volleyball match tonight?" Sara hooked her arm with Evie's. "It's magic volleyball."

"I'm baking." Evie smiled. "I'm perfecting brownies."

"I'll watch. I've never seen magic volleyball." Raine shifted her book bag a little. "When is it?"

Raine sat in the stands with Sara and Cameron. The indoor hall looked exactly as it had in her middle school. The shiny, pale wooden floors were marked the same way and the net looked identical. Raine wondered how it was magical, or if it was at all. Sara wanted company to watch it with and Raine knew that she would twist the truth a little if need be to get what she wanted.

The teams walked out onto the court and the referee soon joined them. The moment the whistle blew, the floor began to move. It rolled from the front to the back like waves crashing against a beach. When the first team struck the ball, it changed its motion and the rippling began in the center of the court immediately below the net.

Raine wasn't sure how the team managed to keep their feet as the floor rolled and rippled. The longer the game went on, the more dramatic the motion became. Initially, it had risen by no more than three inches at the crest of each wave. Now, they competed for their fourteenth point and the floor rose by almost a foot. The team had to jump and side-step the moving timber.

"Will they play to twenty-five points?" Raine watched as a blue team player dove over a ripple in the floor and spiked the ball down on the other side. "Because those crests are really high now."

"No, eighteen. The ridges in the floor are limited to fourteen inches in height and eight inches in width." Sara pointed at the court. "Otherwise, the players wouldn't be able to move around them."

Raine really wasn't sure how they managed at the size they already were.

"Are we expected to play volleyball for fun?" She brushed her hair from her face. "In gym class, I mean."

"Yeah, I think so. I prefer dodgeball, myself." Sara grinned. "The ball fights back."

Raine had only played normal tennis in gym so far and

done a little sprinting, but nothing with magic. As she watched the volleyball game she was incredibly happy that was all she'd tried and hoped that it stayed that way.

CHAPTER TWENTY-SIX

R aine curled up in her preferred spot on the couch as Philip fussed with the DVD player. He and Sara kept glancing at one another and then at Cameron who had sat down beside Raine.

"Why do you keep looking at me?" He narrowed his eyes at Philip and Sara. "What are you hiding?"

"We're debating whether to watch *Dracula* or *Franken-stein*." Philip smiled. "I think *Dracula* won."

"What happened to *An American Werewolf in London?*" William started popping the popcorn. "I was looking forward to that."

"Well, with Cameron—" Philip started but the shifter's glare silenced him.

"You thought I'd be offended by werewolf movies." Cameron raised an eyebrow. "As it happens, I love were-wolf movies. *Ginger Snaps* is one of my favorites because it's hilarious and entertaining. It is completely aware of what it is and plays to that. The werewolves aren't too bad either, not compared to some. The werewolf in *Van Helsing* with—what's his name? Hugh what's-his-face. It's the best I can think of off the top of my head, though. Admittedly, that isn't a werewolf movie, but the point stands. *Underworld* is eye-roll-worthy but I still watch it sometimes, but only the original, not the sequels. The way werewolves are portrayed in that is a bit groan-worthy, but it is what it is. Then *Blood and Chocolate* is way too romance-centric for me, but I enjoyed the way the pack part was portrayed."

He leaned back a little and enjoyed the discomfort on Sara and Philip's faces.

"I'm completely comfortable in my skin as a shifter. And I'd really like to see *American Werewolf in London*. I haven't seen it yet." He took the bag of sweet and salted popcorn William handed him. "Thanks. Would you like some?" He offered the open bag to the half-Ifrit.

William wrinkled his nose. "No. Sugar and salt is wrong. I'll stick to M&Ms, thanks."

Cameron looked to see which type of M&Ms William ate in case he wanted to trade for some. He had the crispy variety which he wasn't so keen on.

Evie handed Raine a pack of Twizzlers before she settled down beside William. Adrien looked very pleased to see his cheesy popcorn and dug in before they'd even started the movie.

"Is everyone ready?" Philip looked around. "Hopefully this one won't be quite as ridiculous as the swamp creature one."

"The ridiculousness was the fun." Evie threw one of William's M&Ms at him. "That's why we watch old cheesy horror instead of the modern stuff."

Philip smiled. He had enjoyed the swamp creature movie in a weird way. He still hoped that the werewolf one wouldn't be quite so stiff and cartoonish.

They were five minutes into the movie before Cameron frowned. "Do British people really talk like that?"

"Yorkshiremen do." Evie bit off a piece of her Twizzler. "Some of my family are from near there. We're mostly Irish but some moved to Scotland and throughout England."

"How big is your family?" Sara stole a little of Philip's toffee popcorn. "It sounds huge."

Evie shrugged. "Yeah, I guess there are a lot of us. There are quite a few branches and we all stay in touch."

"Are there subtitles for this?" Adrien frowned at the TV. "I'm not sure if they're still speaking English."

Evie laughed but Raine had to admit she struggled with the strong accent. Philip dug out the TV remote and found the button that gave them subtitles. He wouldn't admit that he, too, had no idea what the English people had said.

"You know they'll wander onto the moors." Sara pointed. "Way too many people have told them to stay away from them."

"Was that supposed to be a wolf howl?" Raine looked at her friends. "It sounded like a sick dog maybe."

They all laughed.

"Well, we can tell this will have fantastic special effects," Evie said between her laughter.

"It sounds like an elephant or a rhino now they're closer." William chuckled. "How is that even close to a wolf?"

Cameron watched with a huge, goofy grin on his face. Raine smiled because she hadn't seen the shifter this relaxed before. She chewed on a Twizzler as the werewolf came into view.

"Is that a stuffed dog?" Adrien put more popcorn in his mouth, unable to look away. "Have any of you seen the really old werewolf movie where they threw a stuffed dog over a balcony and the viewers were supposed to believe it was a werewolf leaving?"

"You made that up." Sara looked indignantly at him.

Adrien shook his head. "No, I swear I saw it. I can't remember what the movie was called, though."

"This is way better than slime people." Sara took a sip of her coke. "Werewolves kick ass."

"Hey! We're still watching the slime people one." Evie poked her in the ribs. "It's a super cheesy classic. You'll love it."

Sara tried to steal a piece of Adrien's popcorn. "Well, I do love cheese."

The elf narrowed his eyes but allowed her a small handful.

"Did that doctor tell his secretary to tell the person on the phone that he's dead?" Raine took a deep breath to calm her laughter. "That seems a little extreme."

"Do you think it'd work to get out of potions class?" Sara chewed on her bottom lip. "They'd check, wouldn't they?"

"They'd definitely check." Evie retrieved another Twizzler. "Besides, you wouldn't be able to do Art Club or transfiguration if you were dead."

Sara sighed melodramatically. "True. But potions sucks." She gave Evie a big puppy-eyed expression. "You could do my homework for me, you really love potions."

Evie snorted. "Not a chance."

"Did they call the pub the Slaughtered Lamb?" Cameron looked at Evie. "Is that a normal pub name in England?"

"No. Not at all." Evie frowned. "They like the Crown, and royal names—the Queen Victoria is very popular."

"Ah, so the Slaughtered Lamb is something gruesome for the movie?" Cameron returned his attention to the TV. "It seems a bit on the nose."

"That's the nature of these type of movies, though, isn't it?" Philip stretched his legs in front of him. "That's why they're so cheesy and fun to watch. There's isn't a hint of subtlety in them."

"What was that?" Sara pointed at the screen. "That thing with the big teeth—was that meant to be a werewolf? It looked more like a zombie gorilla."

"I'm not entirely sure." Evie looked a little more closely at the movie. "I think so. I mean, it's part of his transformation, isn't it? You're right, they're absurd, though. I would never have thought they were werewolves if I didn't know this was a werewolf movie."

"Werewolves are really easy. How do so many people screw it up?" Raine sighed. "I mean, it's halfway between wolf and man. And yet some of them go in really weird directions with it."

"I think the real question here is, why aren't they vampires?" Philip grinned at the others. "We all know vampires are superior."

"No, the real question is, is that supposed to be a kiss?" Sara pointed once more. "They look as though they've only heard what a kiss is from a vague description on some ancient tablet."

"Werewolves are far better than vampires." Raine gave Philip a stern look before he could push the kiss topic. "Vampires are parasites."

"They far sexier, though." Sara sipped her coke. "I mean, the whole furry thing isn't all that attractive. Vampires are suave."

"Not always. The original vampires were closer to corpses, haggard and almost zombie-like." Cameron thought for a moment. "Really, they are simply zombies that drink blood instead of eating brains."

"No way." Sara's mouth fell open in mock horror. "Vampires are intelligent and rich and exotic."

Cameron laughed. "Like Raine said, they're leeches." He put his feet up on the coffee table. "They can't survive without human blood."

"Werewolves are poor monsters because they're not scary anymore." Philip sighed softly. "Back when wolves were scary, they were great, but in this day and age, wolves are no longer scary. For a monster to have bite, so to speak, they need a basis in something seriously scary. Wolves don't have that. Vampires, however, are twisted, predatory humans. They hide among us, and what's scarier than that?"

"You're missing the real superior being here." Adrien spread his arms wide. "Elves are clearly the best."

Everyone burst out laughing.

"Elves aren't scary!" William gestured at Adrien. "Grow your hair long and we'll give you a bow. Elves are about as scary as a bunny rabbit."

"Would that make you my dwarf?" The elf grinned at him. "If I'm the archer elf."

The half-Ifrit rubbed his chin. "I'm not sure I could pull off the beard," he said thoughtfully, and everyone laughed again.

"I do think it's sad that we've reached a point where the classic monsters don't scare us anymore." Cameron chewed on his bottom lip. "The modern movies really do center around other people and sometimes ghosts and such, which really are allegories or something I don't want to think about."

"You mean you're sad you can't terrify poor humans?" Adrien grinned. "Poor little shifter losing out on his fun."

Cameron laughed but made no reply.

They all turned their attention back to the movie and Raine frowned at an upper-class older man who walked into the pub.

"Please don't tell me that's Van Helsing." She sighed. "I thought he was supposed to be a badass. He looks like he should own a tweed shop or something."

"A tweed shop?" Evie laughed. "I know what you mean, though. He really doesn't look like a werewolf hunter."

"That's his cover." Philip smirked. "He can blend in anywhere."

"Clearly not." William pointed to the TV. "They're kicking him out of the pub."

"His Guinness just refilled." Sara pointed with a laugh. "Do you think we could get the pixies to give us refillable coffee?"

"No." Evie snorted. "The pixies hate the idea of us on coffee. They think the students will cause far too much trouble and make a big mess."

Sara sighed melodramatically.

"I could likely get us some coffee if you really wanted it." Philip kept his gaze on the TV. "I don't think it'd cost too much."

Sara chewed on her bottom lip. She had tried to be frugal so she could get something nice for her sister for Christmas but coffee was so tempting. The caffeine had an interesting effect on kitsunes. It energized them and made them more aware of everything. It could easily become an addiction, though, and Sara wasn't sure it was worth it.

"No, we'll survive." She smiled. "I'll take a vitality potion if I really need something."

"Are they televising darts?" William looked at Evie. "Is that a thing there?"

"Maybe." Evie shrugged. "I don't know anyone interested in darts so I'm not sure."

"I thought darts was only a pub game?" Cameron frowned. "Why would they televise it?"

"They'll put anything on TV if people will watch it." Philip was distracted by thoughts of new business opportunities. "So people must like darts."

"Do you crochet, Evie?" Sara looked at Evie. "They have some neat crochet blankets in this movie."

Evie raised her eyebrow. "No. I never had a desire to learn. Do you?"

All eyes turned to Sara. "Yeah, it's nice and soothing in the winter." She flushed a brilliant red. "I can't do anything too complicated though."

Raine couldn't picture the fiery kitsune crocheting. It was far too calm and orderly for her. Sara was always so bouncy and hated being calm or still.

"What is with this transformation?" Cameron gestured

at the TV. "Why is his hand so long? How does that possibly make any sense? Have they never seen a wolf's paw?"

"Well, it's certainly more dramatic than other ones I've seen." Raine watched the movie with her lips pursed. "They're really drawing it out."

"I'll have to put that down as one of the weaker trans-formations." Cameron folded his arms. "Although I'm not sure which I'd put at the top. Van Helsing's transformation in *Van Helsing*, the modern one with Hugh Jackman, was pretty good."

"Do you have a list somewhere for all this werewolf stuff?" Evie nudged Cameron in the ribs. "Because you seem to have everything neatly ranked."

He shrugged. "Only a mental list."

They continued watching the movie in relative peace and calm. Sara threw her hands up at the big finale. "That was it?"

"It looks like it." Evie shrugged and began to clear the trash. "It's kind of fitting."

Sara put her hands on her hips. "It was so disappoint-ing. After all that, they end it like that?" She huffed. "I want a do-over."

"I don't think they've ever fired a rifle before either." Philip gathered the discarded wrappers near him. "Because they sounded nothing like rifles, even in a confined space like that."

Sara huffed again. "So they screwed it up all around."

Raine put her arm around her friend's shoulders. "It wasn't so bad."

Sara laughed. "No, it was worse. But we're watching

slime people next time." She looked around the group. "Right?"

"I think it's time for vampires, actually." Philip smiled. "But who's for slime people?"

Raine raised her hand. She wasn't that interested in vampires. Cameron joined her but everyone else kept their hand down. It looked as though they were outvoted.

"Vampires win." Philip shrugged his backpack on. "We can discuss which one tomorrow. It's later than I thought."

Sara groaned. "Lights out in fifteen."

"I'm not running." William folded his arms.

"Poor dwarf." Adrien grinned at him but the half-Ifrit refused to rise to the bait.

CHAPTER TWENTY-SEVEN

Raine brushed her hair out of her face and tried to find the book on druids that had first referenced the symbol she wanted to research. She had missed something, she knew it. Her pages of notes hadn't provided much of anything to work with. It simply spoke about territory, old ways, and shadows. She knew that the druids in the kemana were all of the same group, so there would be no argument over territory. Druidry was of the old ways, and the shadows could mean anything.

The head librarian brought three more books for her to look through. She'd seen every book on Druidry in the library so he'd snuck one from the professor's private library once he made sure that it had nothing dangerous in it.

Raine thanked him and looked through the newest book in the hope that it would provide the missing link. It was a wet and dreary day. Rain streamed down the windows and grey consumed the sky overhead. Normally, she would have felt it was a perfect day to sit in the library, but she couldn't shake the feeling that time was running out for the druids.

Evie moved the heap of books into a towering pillar of knowledge and set one single black leather-bound book on the table.

"I told my Aunt Beth that we were researching the old druid traditions. She sent this over this morning." Evie sat down. "She's the knowledge keeper for my family. Aunt Beth knows everything there is to know about Irish magic, and the druids fall under that."

"Have you looked through it yet?" Raine opened the book carefully. "I've had no luck at all with these others."

"No, I brought it straight to you." She leaned in and lowered her voice. "Philip is trying to charm his way into the professor's library to see if we can get any better information from there."

Raine shook her head. Philip was sure he could charm anything out of anyone. She was confident that this wasn't something he'd succeed at, though. Still, she appreciated the thought and attempt. Her friends didn't have to help her with the druids.

Evie scooted her chair a little closer and they looked through the old book with tissue-thin pages.

Raine's face lit up when she saw the trio of symbols together. Finally, it looked as though they might have a lead. She read through the pages surrounding the symbols and found that they were a sign of an ancient branch of Druidry. They were the sigil of a darker path that had been pushed away from the mainstream community and denied access to the collective knowledge and magic.

"What does this mean?" Evie frowned at the pages. "Are the dark druids trying to harm the others?"

"Could you ask your Aunt Beth about them specifically?" Raine looked hopefully at Evie. "Would that be really suspicious?"

"No, I think she'd be okay." Evie retrieved her phone. "We'd best do it outside the library."

Raine picked up the book from Aunt Beth, gathered her notebooks into her arms, and followed Evie out of the library. Librarian Decker watched them closely. He really hoped they weren't up to anything dangerous. He had grown fond of Raine. The Irish witch was always polite and had given him a batch of cookies in thanks for helping her friends. He put his hands on his hips and ignored his poppy which growled at a less favorable student.

Evie talked quietly to her aunt and Raine tried not to pace. They started with the weather and seemed to talk baking before they finally got to the dark druids. She chewed on her bottom lip and waited as Evie frowned and leaned back against the wall. Raine caught snatches of her aunt's accent—a mix of thick Boston and something almost Canadian, she thought. It was an unusual accent that she didn't think she'd be able to find anywhere else.

Finally, Evie hung up and took a deep breath.

"Okay. From what Aunt Beth said, it's very likely that it's a lone dark druid who is trying to rebuild their grove. She says that the shadow sigil means they're a shadow walker and to stop them, we'll need to use light magic to block that. She says the mainstream druids should be okay. The dark druid needs them for their grove, and they'll have less magic if they're injured. We'll be able to find them in the heart of the forest. There'll be something called a nematon there? It'll be something weird with trees. She said to look out for naturally occurring archways, perfect circles formed by trees, and things like that."

"What do we do with the dark druid?" Raine shifted her weight. "I mean, how do we get the other druids safely away from them?"

Evie looked away. "Aunt Beth said that we should kill the dark druid, but we can bind them with light magic and perform a spell that will break the power their dark magic has placed over them. Then the other druids will take it from there and cleanse them and strip the magic from them if need be."

Raine nodded. She really didn't want to kill someone. "Now what?" She looked at Evie. "We need a plan of action."

"Now, we make potions and other things to aid us. Our magic and spell work aren't strong enough to go up against something like this."

"Sara will be livid." Raine laughed. "She hates potions."

Evie shrugged. "She can always stay behind if she feels that strongly."

Evie had talked Professor Fowler into letting them practice in the potions lab. She merely hid the fact that she wasn't actually practicing what they had studied in class. Everyone in their circle of friends gathered there and they all brewed useful potions for the upcoming encounter with the dark druid.

"Am I doing this right?" Sara pointed to her cauldron. "I

really don't want to screw up something that could save my life."

Evie looked at the gently bubbling white liquid and nodded. "It's perfect."

Cameron ferried ingredients and utensils back and forth. His familiar scowl had returned but he didn't complain. If he was honest, he was glad to be able to help. His lack of magic as a shifter made things like that difficult. Still, no one complained, and he did his best to help where he could.

"Remind me what exactly we're making here." Philip stirred his potion. "This is a light potion?"

Evie nodded. "Yes. Your potion will act like a big sun flare. You'll throw it hard at something and it'll explode with a huge burst of brilliant white light. That'll destroy any shadows the druid tries to form." She pointed to Sara's. "That is something to strengthen and purify our own magic. Raine is making a healing potion, and William's working on the binding agent for the ritual."

She returned to her own cauldron. " I am imbuing these crystals with pure light. We can place them in a circle around the area we're working in and they'll act like a cage to hold the druid."

Raine had considered telling one of the professors or even Agent Connor about what they planned. They needed to sneak into the Kemana and into the heart of the forest behind the druid neighborhood. She had weighed up the pros and cons. If they told someone, they had to admit they'd visited the kemana against school rules. That would mean a years' detention and no ability to go to Bubble and Fizz again.

On the other hand, if they remained quiet, she was confident they could save the druids. If they told someone, there was a good chance that person would tell them to stay out of it. What if the druids died because of that? She knew she couldn't live with the death of innocents on her hands. It was a big risk, but she had to help those people if she could.

Agent Connor had driven all around the state to gather the herbs and crystals needed for the cure for Xander's poison. Unfortunately, there was one final piece that only Mara could secure. Xander struggled to keep his eyes open as he slumped in his old armchair. The fabric was worn along the arms and the seat sagged beneath him, but he had spent too many hours in that chair to throw it out.

Lucy Fowler and Anabelle Grant both watched over him as he slept fitfully. Mara had hoped there was another way, but time was running out. She turned and walked out into the wet miserable day. It seemed fitting to have cold rain lash down when she had to face the task ahead of her.

She got into her car and ran her fingertips over the simple black brooch in her pocket. It had been a family heirloom, something she had hung onto since she was a little girl. She knew that it was the only thing that would work.

Mara drove off the school grounds and turned the radio on to keep her company during the long drive deep into the middle of nowhere. A slow acoustic song came on and the singer warbled about love and loss. A tear pricked the corner of Mara's eye. Xander could be a stubborn fool and he had certainly made some mistakes in his time, but she wasn't ready to lose him.

They had a long and tumultuous history together.

"I can't lose him." She gripped the steering wheel a little tighter. "This will work."

The final piece of the cure sounded so simple on paper and yet it would require a sacrifice. That was how these things worked. Sometimes, magic was cold and cruel in its need for balance. She sighed and calmed her nerves. There was no point in getting herself worked up over the inevitable. The brooch was merely a possession. The memories attached to it would remain with her.

She drove through the heavy rain as the landscape changed around her. The sun had set by the time she entered the Monongahela National Forest. Winter had stripped the deciduous trees of their leaves and left the slender trunks dark and bare. Mara drove deeper into the forest, trying to remember exactly which turn she needed to make. It was so easy to get lost once you left the main road, but she had no choice.

She turned off and parked her car at a pretty look-out facing the sharp points of the mountains with a creek below her. Drawing on every scrap of strength she had, Mara slid out of her car and set off between the tall trunks and across the sodden ground. Her instincts guided her as she hadn't been there in decades. She'd hoped to never step foot there again.

Everything changed subtly around her as she began her ascent up the sharp grey rocks. Magic became more prominent. It coated her slick, cold skin with a fizzing sensation.

She had entered their space now, and they would be aware of her. Mara continued to climb the rocks despite the tiredness in her limbs and the numbness that spread through her hands. She did this for Xander.

Finally, she crested the rock formation and found herself at a simple log cabin. The fire inside flickered across the wide windows that no doubt had a stunning view across the valley. She brushed herself off and tried to make herself look as presentable as possible. Mud flecked her jeans and her hair was slicked to her scalp from the rain. Still, she walked with pride and dignity as she stepped onto the veranda and knocked on the door.

Nothing happened for a few minutes. Mara raised her hand to knock again when the door swung open to reveal a young, red-haired witch with violet eyes.

"Mara Berens. We knew we would see you again."

She said nothing and maintained a neutral expression. The younger witch stepped aside, and Mara entered the cabin. The warmth spread through her and washed away the aches in her bones.

"Would you like some tea?" an older grey-haired witch asked.

"No, but thank you. I'm here for phoenix root."

A tension filled the air immediately. Mara knew they wouldn't have thought she was there for a cup of tea yet they desperately wanted to cling to the old traditions and rituals. She was too tired to pretend interest in that particular game.

"You understand the sacrifice we will require for that?" The younger witch walked forward to face her. "We will require blood, spirit, and memory."

Mara's jaw tightened. Demanding a piece of spirit was a very high price indeed. She reminded herself that this was for Xander and nodded.

She followed the younger woman deeper into the log cabin and past the large open fire and the cluster of witches gathered around a table playing cards. They didn't pay her any attention. Mara walked with her head held high. She wouldn't grovel for the root.

"And what do you plan to do with it?" The younger witch held the door open for Mara to walk through. "It is a powerful herb."

Mara didn't acknowledge her. Knowledge was a precious thing that should be held onto. It was far too easy to say something that would later prove to be your downfall when walking among witches such as those.

They stepped into a simple room with a plain white floor and dark-cream walls. Unlike the rest of the cabin with its wooden walls, the decor in that room was all ceramic. It was much easier to clean blood and other fluids from ceramic than wood.

The older witch remained outside and stood guard. Her younger counterpart slipped on a dark green robe with gold trim and pulled the hood up. Mara resisted the urge to roll her eyes. Such things were worn purely for ego and appearance. They did nothing to aid the magic.

She knelt in the middle of the room and exposed her wrist, well aware of how these things worked. The witch knelt in front of her and drew a curved silver knife from a fold in her robes. Mara didn't flinch when the woman sliced her wrist and watched droplets of her blood fall onto the white floor between them.

The spirit price came next. The witch took a small pocket watch and turned the big hand around to the number five, and the small hand to the number two. Mara gritted her teeth and said nothing. She would give up five years and two months of her life. This was for Xander. She would give a decade if it meant that he would be safe and well.

Magic passed between them and Mara held back a gasp as she felt the years ripped from her very essence. The tugging sensation became something far crueler as it increased in intensity and the final seconds were yanked free. Her heart raced and pounded against her ribs, but she maintained a calm exterior.

Finally, the witch pressed her fingertip into the small pool of Mara's blood and drew that along her lips. Mara closed her eyes as she watched old memories flicker through her mind in a blur of color. The magic found one it liked, a particularly sweet moment when she was a little girl. It slipped through her mental fingers and left a small dark spot, a gap where the memory had once been.

"So, it is done."

Mara stood and ran her fingers over her wrist. It had healed entirely thanks to the magic. The young witch handed her a root that resembled ginger and looked pointedly at the door. Her time with the coven was done. It was time to return to Xander.

The older witch held her hand out as she left the room. Mara dropped her brooch into the extended palm without looking at her. She had made the final payment.

Xander's lips pursed as he was pulled into a familiar nightmare. He was pursued through an unfamiliar forest where the shadows clawed at his legs and the trees twisted and bit into his ribs and arms. The thing was behind him and he could feel it closing in. His legs wouldn't obey his commands and the shadows drew him into their darkness. The cold silk of their magic caressed his hot skin and whispered of bliss. He knew better than to trust the shadows. Only lies hid within their dark depths.

He opened his eyes suddenly and dug his fingers into the familiar fabric of his favorite armchair. He was safely in his cottage. Annabelle gave him a weak smile and held out a sweet, flavored tea. He took it with shaking hands and drank a little. The honey and lavender taste coated his tongue and washed away the bitterness of the nightmare.

His magic was buried deep within him now. When he tried to wiggle his toes, they were slow to respond. The poison had progressed through his system and he didn't know how much longer he had. He wished Mara were there, so he could see her beautiful eyes one last time.

Mara's hands were entirely numb when she fumbled with her keys and finally managed to open the door to her car. She climbed in and turned the heater on while she shivered against the soft leather. The rain crashed down in heavy sheets now. Thunder rolled overhead with bright slashes of lightning. She swallowed hard and put the car into reverse. She needed to get back to Xander.

It was close to sunrise when she finally pulled into her

usual parking space. The rain had eased but the ground was sodden. Dorvu the dragon looked particularly pitiful as he peered out from beneath the shelter Horace had built for him. The dragon hated big storms. They didn't scare him but made him miserable. Mara felt for him, but she had bigger issues to worry about.

She hurried down the pathway to Xander's cottage. The lights were still on, but it had been a long night. She didn't know if anyone would still be awake. Numb and weary, she walked inside and removed her coat and boots. The rest of her clothes clung to her cold, wet skin, but she ignored it in favor of going see Xander.

He sat staring into space with a pale glassiness to his eyes. Lucy hurried to her.

"Did you get it?"

Mara nodded and handed her the root.

"It will take an hour to brew. Get a hot shower and some food."

Mara tore her gaze from Xander. His cheeks were hollow, and the spark had left his eyes almost entirely. He had been a fine specimen of a man who turned heads only months before. The poison had consumed him, and she still didn't know who had done it. They had narrowed the list down to three people, but they couldn't be sure exactly who the culprit was. A vicious voice in the back of her mind demanded she smite all three. They were all dangerous dark wizards.

Mara ignored the voice and returned to her own cottage for a hot shower. Professor Hodges would watch over the school for her that morning while she cared for Xander. The faculty had rallied around them during this difficult time and she very much appreciated their help and support.

Once she was dressed in fresh, clean clothes, she returned to his cottage. She perched on the arm of his chair and entwined her fingers with his. He didn't acknowledge her and she didn't think he knew that she was there. Xander was lost to some dream or buried thought. Mara hoped he wouldn't be lost there for much longer.

Lucy emerged from the kitchen amid a plume of purple smoke. She carried a small, delicate ceramic cup that seemed entirely out of place in Xander's home. Mara took the cup and pressed it to his lips. A furrow formed between his brow but he drank reflexively.

"How long?" Mara didn't meet Lucy's eyes. "And what are the chances?"

"Six hours, and sixty percent."

There had been no infallible cure for the poison. Not for the stage he had reached. He now had a sixty percent chance of survival. They'd know if it had worked within six hours.

Xander blinked and frowned at the bright sunlight streaming through the windows. He felt as though he had woken from an extended dream. Everything felt more solid and a little fuzzy at the same time. Mara's fingers squeezed his own and he looked at her with a smile. She blinked tears away and he brushed his thumb over her delicate cheekbone.

"I couldn't leave you. Not like that," he whispered.

Mara looked away. She couldn't express her profound relief to have him back with them. The color had returned to his skin and he already moved better than he had done in a month. Annabelle brought a large plate full of freshly made sandwiches and small pies. Mara realized she hadn't eaten since the previous day and took one.

The storm had receded and brought with it a fresh hope for a beautiful week ahead of them.

CHAPTER TWENTY-EIGHT

Xander Powell took a deep breath and felt his magic ignite within him. The cure for the poison had worked its way through his system and he finally felt as though he was well enough to teach. The students filtered into the room and for the first time in a long while, he wasn't irritated at their idle chatter. In fact, he enjoyed it.

Once everyone was seated, he clapped his hands together to draw their attention.

"Today, you will learn how to break through restraining spells." He looked around to make sure everyone was listening. "They are a common weapon that dark wizards like to use. Once you're restrained, you're an easy target for much more dangerous attacks and curses."

A hush fell over the room. Now, he really had their attention.

"There are a variety of different forms of restraining spells. The obvious are, of course, ropes and other similar ones. Today, we will look at those that work like quicksand and the more commonly used ropes."

The students watched him with rapt attention.

"Who will volunteer first?" He held back a smirk as that would be cruel. "Anyone?"

Evie the Irish witch raised her hand slowly. Xander nodded and gestured for her to come to the front.

"Now, the key to escape these spells is to remain calm. Much like real quicksand, they will constrict and bind you tighter if you begin to panic and struggle." He turned to Evie. "I'll keep the bindings loose. You must remain calm and push your magic through your hands and into the vines. You won't always be able to use your wand, so you'll need to be able to focus."

Evie nodded and listened to the words she would need to utter. She ran them through her head and made sure she had them memorized before the professor explained the spell to the rest of the class. She began to think she'd regret her offer to be the guinea pig. Her specialty was potions and herbs. Her spell work wasn't awful, but she lacked confidence in it.

Thick vines suddenly pinned her arms to her side and despite the knowledge of what it was, she felt panic rise in her throat. She closed her eyes and pictured herself in the warm, damp air of the greenhouse. The familiar view of the green herbs and flowers formed around her and calm descended and pushed the panic away.

Next, she dug deep inside and felt her magic. She hadn't really done much without her wand and it was unnatural and difficult for witches to do so. Elves didn't need a wand, but she didn't have any elf blood that she knew of.

Her magic fought against her when she tried to push it into her hands. It went instinctively to her wand, but she drew it back and redirected it. The vines tightened around her and began to restrict her breathing. Determined, she drove her magic into her hands and the vines exploded outwards.

The professor gave her a small smile of approval and sent her back to her seat. Raine's eyes were wide when Evie sat down. She squeezed her friend's hand. "Are you okay?"

"Yeah. It took me by surprise, though."

Raine chewed on her bottom lip. She had only begun to get her magic to flow through her wand and wasn't sure she could direct it into her hands. Still, when the professor told them to pair off, she told Evie to do the vine spell. Raine visualized a calm, happy meadow with the sun shining and focused on that when she felt the vines lash around her. She swallowed her fear and panic and fought to find her magic. She knew it was in there and that she could work with it.

The liquid fire of her power slipped through her mental fingertips and refused to obey her. It remained deep within her and the vines began to tighten. She remembered what she'd worked on with the gnomes and dipped her hand into it and dragged great ribbons out. Her magic began flowing and she felt it slip through her veins into her hands.

The visualization of disintegrating vines didn't come easily to her. Every time she tried, the vines grew a little bit tighter. She swallowed hard and bent her hand to press her fingertips against them. Enough magic seeped through to ease them a little.

She had made some progress. Raine dug deep and told herself to picture the vine explode into small pieces. She envisioned each little snippet disintegrating. Suddenly, she could breathe and the vines were gone. She opened her eyes and grinned.

Evie hugged her tightly. "I'm so proud of you. I know your magic doesn't come as easily as it does for the rest of it. But you work so hard and you've made amazing progress."

Sara found that removing the vines came easily to her. For the first time, her magic slid into her fingertips and did as she asked without any problems. She smiled and wondered if her kitsune magic had finally begun to awaken. A small flame of hope ignited.

William's fire flooded his system and the professor put his hand on the boy's shoulder. "No. You can't lean on your fire for everything."

He ground his teeth and looked inside himself for the rest of his magic. It was much harder to find and access than his fire which came so naturally. He saw how Raine had blown her vines apart and drew a deep breath. She worked hard, and he wouldn't give in. He took a leaf from her book and forced himself to really focus.

The vines were brutally constrictive and had almost cut his breathing off when William finally broke them. He gasped for air but smiled when he realized he'd succeeded with his other magic.

Xander returned to the front of the class and began to teach them about the other forms of restrictive spells. The students had worked well and that brought a genuine smile to his face. They listened to everything he said and gave their all. Agent Connor hoped that some of them were budding agents. As he looked around them, Xander thought that perhaps they were. Raine, in particular, had a determination that he was sure meant she could truly do anything she put her mind to.

He formed the next spell, this time around a cocky elf's feet. The boy's eyes went wide as he was suddenly sucked down into the wooden floor. He was up to his knees before he even remembered there was a spell to free him. He waved his hands and jumbled the words he needed. Xander held back a sigh of frustration.

Eventually, when the elf was up to his ribs in the floor, he pulled himself together and cast the spell to free himself. Xander suspected that Mara would say he had pushed them too hard, but he had been up against dark magic. He knew that coddling them would only lead to them being injured or worse, even killed should they come up against that. The school trained them to protect both themselves and the greater public.

Raine frowned as her feet were pulled down into the floor. It was such an odd sensation when the wood became a thick, viscous, mud-like substance. She looked at it and saw the way the grain swirled and slipped into the dark brown substance that wrapped around her ankles.

Calming herself, she once again looked for her magic. It came more easily this time, but her legs sank into the wood despite her calm state. She slowed her breathing and noticed the rising panic she hadn't before. Raine reminded herself that she was in the classroom and the professor wouldn't let her drown in the floor.

She focused on her father's face and drew on her determination to make him proud of her. He had been a dedicated agent who had died fighting dark witches and wizards. He had devoted his life to keep good, innocent people safe and she wouldn't be defeated by one silly restraining spell.

Her magic came sluggishly but it flowed. She drove it into the floor and focused on her father's smiling face in her mind. He had been her world, and they had taken him from her. One day, she would come up against this spell in the world, and she would be ready for it.

Raine's feet popped free and the wood was solid again. She exhaled slowly through her nose and let the rush of emotions go. She was safe, and her father would be proud of how far she had come.

Librarian Decker looked up from his book on the Oriceran influence on ancient Mayan culture to see Raine walk in. He picked up her stack of books and greeted her with a smile. His poppy blew a raspberry at her in greeting.

"Did you learn anything interesting today?" He handed her the books. "I see you had a dark magic class with Professor Powell."

"Yes. We learned about restraining spells. He had us practice the vine spell and the one which turns the floor into something like quicksand." Raine smiled. "It was very difficult to push my magic into my hands but I did it."

The head librarian smiled as pride welled up within him. He and Joe had helped her get a grasp on her magic and she had made real progress.

"Where do your legs go with a spell like that?" Raine frowned. "I mean, did my legs sink into the actual foundations of the school?"

"Yes." Librarian Decker nodded and led her toward her favorite table. "The spell turned the ground you stood on into something akin to quicksand. Had you been stuck there, someone would have found your skeleton within the school foundations."

Raine thought that through and decided it did make a lot of sense. She didn't like the idea of being stuck in the floor like that, though.

"Do you have any tips to deal with those spells?" She placed the books down. "Professor Powell said the real key was staying calm."

He nodded. "I have to defer to Professor Powell on subjects of dark magic. He is the resident expert." He rocked back onto his heels. "The magic responds to your emotional state and a calm emotional state gives it less power. If you panic, your magic and body react in a way that feeds into the spell."

Raine nodded. She'd read something about magic like that in one of her books. It was such a complicated thing, but if you looked deeply enough, emotional state could be found at the heart of a lot of it. That led her to think that perhaps there was an emotional block within her that hindered her magic.

"Could it be that my magic is more difficult because of something within my emotions?" She sat down. "I might not realize I'm doing it."

"And that may well be your kitsune friend's problem too." Librarian Decker looked around to make sure the hot-headed kitsune wasn't listening. "She has a lot of magic inside her, but she can't use it very well. There could be an emotional blockage that prevents her from really accessing it."

Raine contemplated whether it would be a good idea to mention that to Sara. The look on his face suggested that it was probably best to let her work through it on her own. Her friend was far more of a closed book than she would have people believe.

CHAPTER TWENTY-NINE

Raine stepped over the small fallen tree and looked around her. They had made it down to the Kemana without incident and seemed to have attracted little attention from the druids themselves when they skirted the first houses and slipped between the trees. The place had an eerie feel, and she sensed the presence of Druidry more strongly than in the walkways. They followed the tracker spell that Adrien had formed.

"Playing Louper does have some uses." Philip watched the tracker dart around a slender tree. "Although I still think there's validity to the argument that tracking spells are cheating within the game."

Adrien gave Philip a sharp glance but let it drop. He knew the wizard was only making conversation and didn't mean anything bad by it. Still, he could feel the shift in the magic around them and that set his teeth on edge.

Cameron walked at Raine's side and kept his ears pricked for unusual sounds. He'd chosen to accompany his friends in his large wolf form. He felt he would be better able to watch over them like that. They all had magic, but he wasn't sure if the potions would work for him. Evie had reassured him they'd work for a human, but his wolf form felt like the better choice.

Raine stretched her fingers and brushed them over the top of Cameron's head. Something about the way he walked made her think that he was nervous, and she wanted to reassure him. The soft clink of glass against glass cut through the eerie silence. They each had small bags full of potions and crystals to use against the druid.

Evie had headed up the potion production but Raine's hours spent in the library allowed them to explore options Evie hadn't thought of and they'd produced some fire crystals as well as potions.

"The druid will have earth magic, which means air and water won't be very good against them. Fire should be able to burn through the wood they'll try to use. My reading says that druids focus more on plant life and animals than true earth manipulation." She tried to see between the increasingly dense trees ahead of her. "William's fire should be particularly good against them due to the nature of Ifrit."

No one said anything. They'd been over all of that back in the potions lab and it wasn't anything new. The silence pressed against them like an invisible blanket and threatened to smother them. Still, they walked deeper into the forest with a determination to save the druids. No one else seemed to notice or care, so it was down to them.

Sara rolled a small black crystal back and forth over her knuckles while she looked around her for any sign of movement. She'd never had much interest in nature hikes and this was no exception. A small bird took flight and the branches shook and sent drops of water everywhere. The group froze and peered around for some unseen predator.

Nothing appeared, and they continued. Adrien felt the change in the magic as a darkness slipped along the ground beneath them. His mind expected the vines to come alive or perhaps another unseen trap door like they'd had in his last Louper game. He gritted his teeth and reminded himself that this wasn't sport. Lives were at stake and he cursed himself for not having his head straight. His family had prepared him for things like this his entire life.

Philip put his arm around Sara's shoulders to try to calm the skittish kitsune. He didn't feel overly confident himself but he could put on a good front and sometimes, that was all that was needed.

"Any idea how much farther?" He looked at Adrien and Raine. "Are we going in the right direction?"

"I'm not sure, and yes." Adrien pointed to the tracker. "The tracker is glowing brightly which means we're on the right track."

The small blue-white orb bobbed next to a tree and waited for the group to jump over a small stream and catch up with it. Sara huffed when her boot sank into the mud and she had to pull it out with a noisy squelch. She began to really regret allowing Raine to persuade her into this.

They continued through the forest for another half an hour before the orb swelled in size and took on a lilac hue. They were close and Adrien could feel it. The dark magic dripped from the trees and added a bitter taste to the air. They had quietly hoped the druid wasn't too dark. If he was too far along the dark path there would be no way to save him. The mainstream druids would take his life.

A shiver ran down Raine's spine and she looked around for what had caused it. Something made her instincts scream to either run or fight but everything looked as it had for the past twenty minutes. Mature trees with dark bark and bare branches surrounded them. Thick, woody vines encircled the broad trunks and a thick layer of old leaves covered the muddy ground.

Any sign of life had been left behind within the safety of the school defenses. Raine wrapped her fingers around a small fire orb. Evie and William had worked together to put some of his fire into small glass orbs that would explode on impact with something. It reacted in such a way that it would consume anything magical it touched. Evie had wanted to experiment farther with it, but William had glared at her.

Raine straightened her spine and asked herself what her dad and Uncle Jerry would do. They would assess the situation, find any potion weapons, and move in to control the suspect.

"We should separate and look for the natural archways which will show us where he is. We don't want to lose him." Raine pointed to the right. "Sara, Philip, and Adrien should go right. We'll go left and meet you on the other side of this stand of trees in ten minutes."

The group split up without a word. Cameron leaned against Raine's thigh for a moment before he took point with her not far behind him. William's fire coated his hands as he moved back to protect everyone from attacks from behind. They could feel that they were close but had seen no weird archways or anything as yet. Raine hoped they hadn't stumbled onto something else dark and sinister. They only had a limited number of potions with them.

They followed the curving line of trees on their right and looked at the tree trunks and ground for any signs of sigils, runes, or other magical markings. There was nothing. Then suddenly, they were everywhere. Cameron snorted and rubbed his nose. The magic veil they had stepped through made him want to sneeze.

Evie clutched her wand as she saw a series of naturally formed archways, each of which looked onto a perfectly circular clearing. The captives were there, and it was worse than they had expected. Ten or more druids were gagged and bound in the middle of the clearing. They were muddy with tangled hair and a look of desperation in their eyes.

The rest of the group sidled up beside Raine and Cameron.

"It looks like the dark druid plans on sacrificing them," Evie whispered.

Raine nodded and refused to let emotion cloud her judgment. She was there to save lives. Emotions could come later once they'd completed the job they were there to do. Adrien's tracker had vanished given that it was no longer needed.

"There's an altar of vines through there." Philip pointed at a second set of archways beyond the curve of the clearing. "Did your books say how long we have?"

Raine closed her eyes and tried to remember what she'd read about this. "I think we have until sunset to get them out." She looked around. "Has anyone seen the dark druid?"

The temperature in the air suddenly dropped before it

returned to normal. A shadowy figure stepped out of the shadow cast by an old oak tree. He wore a long black robe with a deep hood that covered his features.

"We need to set up the crystals to hold him within the clearing." Raine retrieved her crystals. "He'll see us in a minute, so move quickly."

They had planned how best to set the circle up while they were back at the potions lab. Each of them withdrew a handful of clear quartz crystals and jogged into their assigned positions. Cameron's hackles rose, and he ran into the clearing with his teeth bared. He acted as the distraction while the others created the trap. Once they had him confined, they could bind him and begin the cleansing ritual.

The dark druid turned to face Cameron. The shifter felt the ground move beneath his paws. He jumped sideways before the mud formed hands and tried to drag him in. He bit at the fingers and shook his head. Some tore off and he spat them out in disgust. The dark druid wasn't supposed to have that type of earth control. This had already gone beyond their expectations.

He circled the man and evaded the mud that clutched at him while he edged in closer. His purpose wasn't to harm the druid but simply to keep him occupied while his friends placed the circle.

Raine set her crystal down at her feet and felt the spark of magic within it. She moved four steps to her left and placed the next one. Cameron darted in and out and snapped at the shadowy figure to keep him focused on him. She only had two more crystals left before the trap was secure.

Cameron yelped when something hard hit him in the ribs. Pain bloomed, and he felt the familiar warmth of blood trickle through his fur. He bared his teeth and ran forward as the druid looked at Raine. He wouldn't allow anything to happen to her. She had been the first person to see him as a person instead of an abomination or the son of the alpha.

Raine gasped as she saw the shifter sink his teeth into the druid's arm. He was supposed to simply distract him, not get too close. She placed her last crystal and a circle of pure white light formed around them. The druid screamed and kicked at Cameron, who hung on with everything he had. He dug his back feet in and dragged the druid away from the captives toward William, whose fire now ran up his arms.

Pain slowed the wolf down but he was determined to make sure no harm came to his friends. The druid called a shadow which wrapped around Cameron's throat and squeezed slowly with cold tendrils that made their way to his mouth. He dragged a breath through the constriction, fighting the dizziness and odd spots before his eyes.

Suddenly, the pressure snapped and he released the druid who now screamed obscenities. Raine threw another orb at him.

"I was a state champion softball player. Best pitcher my school ever saw."

The man spread his arms wide and darkness pooled around him while he chanted. The shadow threads spread across the ground and raced toward the young students. Cameron limped away to heal his wounds while he searched for the best way to help his friends. Evie and

Philip each threw a light potion. Blinding white light exploded and filled the bubble they had formed with the light crystals. The druid screamed again, an agonized, high-pitched wail that made Raine think of banshees.

Sara had made her way quietly to the captured druids. She worked to untie them and checked that they were all okay. Once they were free, she pressed a pale-pink healing potion to the lips of an older woman who looked haggard and exhausted. Light and fire exploded all around them, but Sara tried to ignore it and focus on her task.

A younger druid was unconscious and she struggled to bring him back to awareness. They couldn't lose him. They were there to save each and every one of them. She shook him and ducked as a fireball careened over her head and landed at the feet of the druid. Finally, the young man woke with a deep frown on his face. Sara held the back of his head and helped him drink a healing potion. She had no idea what the dark druid had done to them, but she hoped they would recover quickly.

Raine moved constantly. She had no desire to provide an easy target for the dark druid's wrath. His robes were scorched and pock-marked, thanks to William's fire orbs. Evie and Philip maintained a steady bombardment of light which prevented him from using his shadow magic. Unfortunately, the fire had a limited effect against the earth magic.

It was up to Raine to control the druid's movements and prepare the necessary magic for the cleansing ritual. He had kidnapped and harmed at least ten others, but she refused to believe that he was beyond redemption. Cameron took one of the larger crystal's from her hand

and trotted off with it in his mouth. He nosed it into position at the north point of the pentagram they had formed. Raine couldn't help but smile. The shifter had come so far in such a short amount of time.

She had barely placed the silver disk at the southern point when suddenly, she couldn't move. Her feet were sucked deep into the mud. She retrieved her wand and remembered what the gnomes had taught her. Her dad's voice echoed in her mind and reminded her to remain calm. Panic didn't help anything. She found her inner serenity and called the liquid fire that was her magic. The gnomes had helped her refine the spell Professor Powell had taught them to free themselves from entrapment magic.

At first, her magic refused to budge. It remained deep inside, a blazing pool of power. She couldn't access it and panic began to rise as she sank to her knees in the mud. Once again, she focused and calmed herself. She needed to make her dad and Uncle Jerry proud. She dug deeper into her magic and pushed it outward. It began as a small trickle and then a dam broke. It flooded through and filled her wand with explosive magic that blasted the mud away and left a small crater. She scrambled out and pushed the silver disk into the ground.

Cameron ran to her and nudged her forward with his nose to guide her toward the final point of the pentagram. He jumped in front of her when a thick vine burst from the ground and snaked at her. The wolf sank his teeth deep into the woody stem and tore it apart with a series of death shakes.

Evie and Philip had used most of the light orbs and

potions, but Sara had led the other druids to safety outside the light circle. She had her arm around the waist of an older druid with long steel-grey hair. She had broken her ankle and stumbled over the uneven ground. William rushed in and formed a wall of fire when the dark druid tried to launch a series of sharp wooden darts at Sara's back. The missiles burned and left small piles of soot at the base of William's fire.

Sweat poured off the half-Ifrit's forehead, and he knew he couldn't maintain this level of magic for much longer. They needed Raine to set the final wooden disk in place. She stumbled, and Cameron broke her fall with his body. He guided her to the final position where she kneeled and hoped her friends' faith in her was well founded.

They all had better access to their magic than her, but they had nominated her to begin the cleansing ritual.

She closed her eyes and felt Cameron's head rest against her shoulder to provide support and reassurance. Her magic came more easily this time and seemed almost eager. She whispered the old words that she had practiced over and over the night before to ensure her pronunciation was perfect. Her magic rushed into the wooden disk and she coaxed the power around the pentagram into the other four items.

The druid shouted in rage as the magic began to take root and hold him in place. Her friends came to her side and recited the next verse in the spell as one. Raine stood and they each held hands and pushed their magic deeper into the pentagram. Focused on their critical task, they ignored their adversary's thrashing and cursing.

The screams of pain and anguish were almost unbearable. Raine closed her eyes against the sound and tried to ignore the smell of burning hair and flesh. They continued with the spell and shouted the words louder and louder as the magic reached a crescendo. There was no room for doubt. They tried to save lives, and the pain would fade once the hold the darkness had over him had been broken.

They weren't able to remove it entirely, but they needed to do what they could and then allow the druids to do what was necessary.

The spell finished, and silence descended around them. Raine opened her eyes to see a young man with singed hair in a crumpled heap. He curled in on himself and whispered a phrase she couldn't quite hear over and over. The light circle around them spluttered and faded. It was up to the druid elders now.

"Are any of the druids well enough to help us get him to their neighborhood?" Philip looked at Sara. "They looked like they were in pretty bad shape."

An old woman with gnarled hands and white hair tied back into a thick braid down to her waist stepped out of the wide oak tree to their left.

"You did us a great honor here today." Two more druids stepped out of the tree. "We will not forget the effort you went through to save our people."

The latter two ran to those Sara had led to safety. The group huddled together as they shivered and tried to offer comfort to one another. Raine didn't know what ordeal they had been through, but she hoped they would recover. She rested her hand on top of Cameron's head and watched as the old druid approached the young man.

She crouched down next to him and placed her hand on his cheek.

"Oh, Jordan, you had such potential." The man raised his eyes to her and tears tumbled down his cheeks. "You could have been so much."

He sobbed. "I wanted to bring honor and pride back to our grove. I didn't want to cause any harm but there was no other way."

The old woman nodded and helped him to his feet. "Thank you." She nodded to the students. "You need to return to your school now. Your professors will not be quite so understanding."

"We'll be in detention for years if we get caught out here." Sara looked at her muddy clothes. "How will we explain this?"

"We went for a hike through the woods and got lost." Philip shrugged. "We're freshmen. It's not our fault we can't feel magic properly yet."

Sara handed Raine her last healing potion and she kneeled in front of Cameron to help him drink it. The pain faded from his mind almost immediately. He'd still have bruises and small cuts when he reached the school, but thankfully, the druid hadn't been able to do too much damage.

The group turned and began the walk back with their heads high, safe in the knowledge that they'd saved lives that day.

CHAPTER THIRTY

The final day of the semester had arrived. Sara strutted proudly around their room in a hideous Christmas sweater. It had an ugly reindeer on the front, complete with mismatched colors, lights, and tinsel around the collar. Raine had never understood the love of ugly Christmas sweaters but they made Sara happy, so she wouldn't argue.

The other girls packed the last of their things while Raine sat on her bed and watched them with a smile.

"Are you excited for Christmas? I'm nervous about getting on the train. It's really convenient that it goes everywhere but it's so confusing too. Have you been down to the station? There are stairs and paths everywhere and they really need to work on their signs. London will be horribly busy too. Londoners really don't like other people and they get particularly grumpy and glare-y at this time of the year. Oh, I bet it'll be grey and rainy too instead of this pretty snow. I do love London, really, but it's very different to here." Christie popped a toffee in her mouth.

"I think it'll be a quiet Christmas but I'm looking forward to seeing everyone." Raine shifted her weight. "I don't like lying to my friends, but it's best that they don't know about this place. They're good people but the government is right. Humans aren't quite ready for the complete integration of magic into society."

"Christmas will be a lot of fun." Evie closed her bag. "The entire family will be there this year. I think there will be thirty-five of us, maybe thirty-six. I can't quite remember all my aunts and cousins. It will be spent baking, playing games, and watching cheesy Christmas movies."

Evie sighed contentedly. Her family wasn't perfect, but she loved them dearly. They were a big and often very boisterous Irish-American family. The men were drastically outnumbered by the women, so the women got what they wanted. That usually meant an abundance of baking and laughter, which suited Evie just fine.

Sara sat on her bag to squash it and close it.

"Christmas is an odd one for us. We celebrate it, but not in the same way I think you guys do." She frowned as she tugged on the zip. "We have big bonfires and yule logs. Kitsunes love fire, and there'll be lots of sugar too. My grandparents bring unusual forms of candy and we'll make delicate paper decorations to hang over the fireplaces."

"That sounds cozy." Raine stood and slung her bag onto her back. "I hope you have a wonderful time."

Sara threw her arms around Raine's neck. "Don't worry. We'll be back together in no time." She squeezed her friend. "You have my number if you want to talk over Christmas."

Evie hugged Raine and reminded her that she had her number too.

William looked out the window in dismay. He had quietly hoped he'd be able to stay in the school over Christmas but it didn't look like that would pan out. The silver dragon blew puffs of icy air in neat strips along the grass. He had worked in a methodical way for some twenty minutes or so and the half-Ifrit suspected he was spelling something out.

"Don't look so glum." Cameron walked to the edge of William's bed. "It's Christmas."

"If you had my family, you'd look glum too." William continued to stare out the window. "Christmas is particularly miserable."

"That's why you're not staying with them." Cameron grinned. "You're staying with me."

William frowned at the shifter.

"I spoke to the headmistress and my family. We're taking you in. You're honorary pack for the duration."

"Are you screwing with me?" William couldn't believe what he'd heard. "They're really okay with a half-Ifrit?"

"Yea. My pack takes in waifs and strays. No offense." Cameron gestured to William's unpacked bags. "So you'd best pack quickly. We need to get on the jitney."

Adrien smiled at the exchange. He had hated seeing William look so down for the past couple of days and wished he could have helped. Unfortunately, his family wasn't quite so open to allowing strangers in their home.

Philip put his bag on his back and gave Adrien a quick hug with a pat on the back. The elf wasn't really comfortable with people too close to him, but Philip wanted to express his caring somehow.

"Any plans for the holidays?" Philip looked at Adrien. "Do you do anything special in France?"

The elf stood. "It will be a typical Christmas." He settled his bag on his back. "You?"

"Same. Lots of cake and food. Probably some arguments over something stupid. Ugly sweaters." He shrugged. "The usual stuff."

"Will I have to wear an ugly sweater?" William looked distrustfully at Cameron. "Or something else awful?"

Cameron laughed. "Ugly Christmas sweaters are banned in our house. It's all good fun. We enjoy running and hiking through the forest. Eating lots of good food, playing games. You'll love it." He put his hand on William's shoulder. "And they'll love you."

Everyone met up at the bottom of the grand staircase. Sara made sure to hug everyone in turn despite the fact she'd already hugged the girls back in their room.

"You know we're riding the jitney with you right?" Philip raised an eyebrow. "Or did I miss something?"

Sara shrugged.

Agent Connor approached them with his hands in his pockets. "Are you ready to go?" He looked at Raine. "I can wait if you're not."

"No, I'm good." Evie and Sara hugged her one more time. "Merry Christmas everyone!"

She walked with Agent Connor into the snowy landscape. His was one of the few cars waiting on the circular driveway. Most of the remaining students would ride the jitney to the train station. They had chosen to wait an extra day to enjoy the time and freedom together.

"Are you looking forward to seeing your uncle?" The agent opened the trunk for Raine. "He's eager to see you."

"Yeah. I'm excited, although I feel bad that I haven't gotten him a gift yet. I've been so busy." She dropped her bag in the trunk. "I'll have to risk the crowds and try to find something in the city."

"I'm sure he'll be glad to have you at home with him." Agent Connor got into the car. "He won't worry about a gift."

Raine slid into the car. "I want to get something for him, though. I'll think about it." She put her seatbelt on. "It's a long car drive after all."

Mrs. Beasley had wrapped her beanie hat in gold and red tinsel and she won the ugly Christmas sweater contest hands-down. The bulk of the sweater was a blinding green. The snowman on the front had a nose of copper tinsel. Christmas carols had been knitted into the back in every conceivable color with more tinsel woven in there too.

Sara stood and compared her sweater to Mrs. Beasley's and had to admit that the bus driver had her beat. She'd win next year, though.

Mrs. Beasley handed out toffee-flavored hard candies as the students scrambled onto the small bus. The vehicle itself had been decorated with yet more tinsel and small ceramic snowmen that hung from the ceiling. She turned the Christmas songs up even louder and encouraged everyone to join her in singing along. To her delight, she had the entire bus singing *Rudolf the Red Nosed Reindeer* before too long.

Evie sucked on her hard candy and joined in the verses she recognized as she watched the snowy landscape pass her by. The mountains were beautiful in the soft winter sunlight with their snow-capped peaks. Charlottesville was in full festive attire with pale blue and white lights draped around the trees. Less subtle lights adorned many of the houses and shops.

Giant reindeer, Santas in all shapes and sizes, and snowmen lit up the front yards and climbed over the roofs of their houses. Many of them had signs telling Santa to stop there and Evie smiled at the happiness that filled the air. Everyone had a smile on their face as they hurried down the streets toward the shops in search of last-second purchases.

William still wondered if it was some cruel joke and whether Cameron would abandon him at the train station. He couldn't believe that he didn't have to spend the holiday with his awful aunt and the others and would be surrounded by nice people. They disembarked from the jitney in front of Starbucks and each student said goodbye to Mrs. Beasley.

She waved them off and began singing *Frosty the Snowman* as she climbed onto her bus. The group made their way through the throngs of people around the small tables and tried to reach the counter to order. Their train wouldn't be there for forty minutes and Sara was desperate for a peppermint latte.

"I tried convincing the...erm, cooks to make one for me, but no dice." She looked around at the humans and tried to keep all magical talk out of her conversation. "I've been dying for one since the first snow fell."

Adrien wrinkled his nose at the idea. He ordered an Americano and muttered about respecting coffee.

Once they had their drinks in hand, they used the magic portal through to the train station that was in the wall near the bathrooms. They emerged at the top of the white stairs which led into the large and complicated station.

They walked carefully down the first two flights of stairs, avoiding a family of Kilomeas who carried far more luggage than anyone else would have thought to pack. Adrien left the group with a quick farewell and turned toward the European platforms. Slowly, they split up and set off to their respective American platforms until only Cameron and William walked together.

"I'm not taking it back." Cameron elbowed William gently in the ribs. "You're really staying with us for Christmas."

The half-Ifrit allowed himself to grin and accept it. For the first time in his life, he looked forward to Christmas.

The students had all left and the school felt quiet and empty. Mara retired to her cottage and settled into a comfortable chair with her latest book. It told the story of an elf spy who raced through Europe and stopped ridiculous bad guys. She enjoyed the escapism.

Xander knocked on her door and greeted her with a warm smile. He finally looked like himself again. The usual shine had returned to his eyes and there was a bounce in his step. He took Mara's hands gently.

"Would you do me the honor of joining me for lunch on Christmas day?"

She tried to maintain a nonchalant expression but couldn't. Seeing Xander's health decline and thinking she would lose him had made her realize how much she still cared about him.

"I would love to."

He smiled a brilliant smile that lit his eyes and spread throughout his entire being.

"I look forward to it."

It had been a long and exhausting drive but Raine perked up the moment they turned onto her road. The car had barely stopped moving when she leaped out and ran into her Uncle Jerry's arms. The school had been fantastic fun and she loved her new friends, but there really was no place like home.

The End

The story is far from over. Don't miss when Adrien and Raine's future collide in ORPHAN WITCH.

FREE BOOKS!

 WARNING:
The Troll is now in charge.

And he's giving away free books
if you sign-up!

Join the only newsletter hosted by a Troll! Get sneak peeks,
exclusive giveaways, behind the scenes content, and more.
PLUS you'll be notified of special **one day only fan
pricing** on new releases.

CLICK HERE

or visit: https://marthacarr.com/read-free-stories/

DARK IS HER NATURE

For Hire: Teachers for special school in Virginia countryside.

Must be able to handle teenagers with special abilities.

Cannot be afraid to discipline werewolves, wizards, elves and other assorted hormonal teens.

Apply at the School of Necessary Magic.

AVAILABLE ON AMAZON RETAILERS

Vulnerability is not my usual go to. I started out needing more than my share of grit as a young woman to pursue a dream of being an author without a thumbs up from the family. Was more of a, *what the hell are you thinking.*

Over time, as a single mother and a writer, it became an ingrained habit. I got used to walking things alone and became more comfortable reporting about what had happened, after I've had a chance to absorb the shock or breathe a sigh of relief at the success. I was too scared to be able to mix in someone's gasp or expectation of what should happen.

When the Offspring, Louie was small, failure seemed like a distinct possibility and definitely not an option. It took every ounce of optimism I could scrape together to believe I could raise this kid alone and do it successfully. It was such a big task that I could only do it one day at a time with breaks to worry about the future. I got really good at getting things done and only asking for help when I wasn't able to do something. Turns out, I'm pretty capable and that's the good news and the bad news.

It has taken me years to learn that just because I can do something doesn't mean I should, or that I can't ask for help. It's in community that we thrive and all of my independence was cutting out some of the fun in life. Plus, the more I've asked for help, the more I've realized I didn't actually know how to do it better. My way was not bad, maybe even good, but there were other ways to get something done and sometimes that way was better.

What a relief. I didn't know it till I cut it out (and that's an ongoing lesson for me), but I was wearing myself out. Being able to ask for help *and* accept it drew me into a world of people where a constant state of vulnerability and humility is required. The payoff has been collaborating with Anderle, or venturing into dating with a positive attitude (that last part is the key element along with a willingness to hang with it – I keep telling myself if it was a job hunt, you don't get to quit just because no one hired you yet), or welcoming neighbors over for dinner, or working out with 30-something's – huffing and puffing alongside them. In other words, a good life.

It means I'm anxious more than I used to be because what if I look stupid or fall short, but I go anyway. Tomorrow, I'm headed over to work out with a neighbor I've never met, wearing a large knee brace on that one leg that's missing muscle from one of the cancer bouts. I can pretty much guarantee it won't be pretty, but I'll be there. Next week will be new author pictures that I can use on dating sites too, and there's the Peabrain Adventures coming out that were my big idea with just my name on the cover. All scary to me – doing it anyway – but this time, not alone. There's a crowd of people cheering me on that I can give back to as well, including all of you. Bravery in the face of adversity is sometimes necessary, but I'm finding out that awkward as a daily condition is okay too. More adventures to follow.

AUTHOR NOTES - MICHAEL ANDERLE

NOVEMBER 23, 2018

THANK YOU for not only reading this story but these *Author Notes* as well .

(I think I've been good with always opening with "thank you." If not, I need to edit the other *Author Notes*!)

RANDOM (*sometimes*) THOUGHTS?

Welcome to our new School of Necessary Magic series! I hope you are enjoying Raine and how she was introduced to this school, and why.

On the subject of schools, my personal feeling is school can suck.

Sometimes it sucks more, and sometimes it sucks less. Well, I've heard it can be a whole LOT of fun, and I believe those who have had that fun, but I've not personally encountered the situation. My youngest, Joseph, seems to be enjoying his time at the University of Texas – Arlington so I suppose it is true.

However, I believe the purpose of school is to teach and train. If you need to learn something as dramatic as how to wield magic, it might get you to be a bit more focused on your training.

Martha and I have worked together to bring you a new story in the School of Necessary Magic that will intrigue you with the government slant and our new protagonist.

May she provide you much joy as you read Raine and all of her stories (hopefully) deep into the night!

HOW TO MARKET FOR BOOKS YOU LOVE

We are able to support our efforts with you reading our books, and we appreciate you doing this!

If you enjoyed this or ANY book by any author, especially Indie-published, we always appreciate if you make the time to review a book, since it lets other readers who might be on the fence to take a chance on it as well.

AROUND THE WORLD IN 80 DAYS

One of the interesting (at least to me) aspects of my life is the ability to work from anywhere and at any time. In the future, I hope to re-read my own *Author Notes* and remember my life as a diary entry.

Right now, I'm sitting at the kitchen table in La Puente, CA. (I guess it is more accurate to say "dining room table." It's a smaller house, and we have JUST a tiny amount of space to put in a two-person kitchen nook sometime. *That* would be the kitchen table.)

It's 8:35 PM on Friday night after Thanksgiving and I went to Pasadena, CA (first time) to the Apple store to see about the 2018 MacBook Pro. I'm damned undecided STILL on whether to pony up the money to upgrade my 2015 MacBook Pro or to hold on for another year. Unfortunately, I don't think Apple is going to upgrade the design of the laptops until at least 2020.

My luck, the keyboards (which is what makes me hesitate) will be made of glass, and I'll be wishing for the scissor-tablet keys they have now. I'm not fond of the shallow key-travel because my fingers hurt after typing hard on the new laptop's keyboard.

This old dog doesn't want to learn new typing habits. I want to pound the keys as hard as I want without pain or consequence. (*Editor's note: Preach it, brother! Me too! And I'll be right next to you in rehab from carpal-tunnel.*)

I guess I have to toe the line if I want that Mac goodness.

…and I do.

I wonder if they are making typing difficult to push a new generation strictly to voice? I can't see how that would work since we would all hear whatever we are trying to do on our laptops or tablets and that would be pretty confusing.

FAN PRICING

If you would like to find out what LMBPN is doing and the books we will be publishing, just sign up at http://lmbpn.com/email/. When you sign up, we notify you of books coming out for the week, any new posts of interest in the books and pop culture arena, and the fan pricing on Saturday.

Ad Aeternitatem,
Michael Anderle

OTHER SERIES IN THE ORICERAN
UNIVERSE:

SCHOOL OF NECESSARY MAGIC
THE DANIEL CODEX SERIES
I FEAR NO EVIL
THE UNBELIEVABLE MR. BROWNSTONE
THE LEIRA CHRONICLES
REWRITING JUSTICE
THE KACY CHRONICLES
MIDWEST MAGIC CHRONICLES
SOUL STONE MAGE
THE FAIRHAVEN CHRONICLES

OTHER BOOKS BY JUDITH BERENS

OTHER BOOKS BY MARTHA CARR

CONNECT WITH THE AUTHORS

Martha Carr Social

Website: http://www.marthacarr.com

Facebook:
https://www.facebook.com/groups/MarthaCarrFans/

Michael Anderle Social

Website: http://kurtherianbooks.com/

Email List: http://kurtherianbooks.com/email-list/

Facebook Here:
https://www.facebook.com/TheKurtherianGambitBooks/